The Kite

LAURENTIAN LIBRARY 20

The Kite

W. O. MITCHELL

Macmillan of Canada
A Division of Gage Publishing Limited
Toronto, Canada.

First published by Macmillan of Canada 1962

First published in the Laurentian Library 1974

Reprinted 1978, 1981

ISBN 0-7715-9603-0

Originally published in 1962 by The Macmillan Company of
Canada under ISBN 0-7705-1176-7

Macmillan of Canada
A Division of Gage Publishing

Printed and bound in Canada

FOR MAGGIE

Chapter 1

He unlaced his shoes, slipped them off and slid his feet into the paper slippers, tipped back the seat; sleeping through it was the best way to get it over with. Even though it was the most pain-less way of travelling, he had felt nervousness return to the pit of his stomach when he fastened the safety belt, tightening even more now as he looked through the black window to the blow-torching engines. The Gravol pills were supposed to help but they couldn't fool a shrewd and seasoned ulcer that knew too many people were using airlines to kill off their wives or hus-bands or mothers-in-law to cash in on flight insurance. Actually it was only the landings and take-offs that bothered him; on this non-stop flight there could be only one of each for him to sweat through. Eight hours was a small price to pay for crossing four-fifths of a continent and time was the important thing; he simply could not afford the three days that the train would have taken.

As a matter of fact, he couldn't afford this assignment; it would cost him five weeks at least; three weeks doing his leg work in the foothills, two more weeks when he had returned to Montreal. He would be lucky to get by without one re-write which would mean another week – six of them. Six times five hundred made three thousand – take away the one thousand Earl would pay. He'd be out two thousand. He had thought himself through with this medium for ever; now he was returning to it at a loss of two thousand dollars!

Money hadn't really counted in his decision; part of it had been Earl's persuasion; part of it had been challenge; a great deal of it had been dissatisfaction with the fleeting nature of most of his work, the panel show, the bits he broke off every week for his column. Not that there was anything so durable about a magazine article; it was read; it was used to wrap the garbage, to start the incinerator fire, or to be rolled into cylinders and soaked with chemicals for a yule log that would give pretty flames; not much more lasting really than the television image that flashed upon the passive eye and the idle ear. How had the supply of time become so breathlessly small? The world's contemplative time was almost non-existent; he himself had used up thirty-nine years of David Lang time, done not one persisting thing.

'You're talking your life away, David,' Earl Whitton had said to him in the Arts and Letters Club barely a week before. 'Talk – talk – talk.'

'It's not just talk,' David had protested. 'The talk has to be written. It's good journalism.'

'On the run,' the editor said. 'Every week – every day . . .'

'And what's so leisurely about this article you want me to do for you? No Flauberts on your *Mayfair* staff that I've noticed. You want me for a quick assignment . . .'

'There's a difference.'

'Not much.'

'I'm not asking you to play guessing games . . .'

'At five hundred a game.'

'I can pay you a thousand and expenses.'

'For over a month.'

'Three weeks.'

'Oh – you want it done on the run – like television.'

'No I don't. I'd just like to see if you have some curiosity left – enthusiasm . . .'

'I have,' he assured the editor.

'You haven't even asked what the piece is about.'

'No point in asking – as soon as you told me it would take me into the foothills for three weeks. I can't drop out of *Pick a Name* that easily. When I do it's for *World Focus* and that takes me to a damn sight more curious places than the foothills.'

'I thought you'd welcome a chance to get back . . .'

'Return to the scene of my boyhood – grass roots – don't, Earl.'

'You could use it.'

'What makes you think that?'

'I just do.'

'Mainly because you want me to do a piece for you. You've got all kinds of writers – why fool around with me?'

'Kind of story it is – and I thought it was something you'd *want* to do.'

'One of your city series – or your street series – the river of my boyhood series. You should talk about the fleeting nature of television – you fellows run fast and hungry – you've digested every major city in Canada – drunk every named river on the continent – chewed up every possible personality in politics, finance, arts, show business . . .'

'It isn't a city – river – street – but it is a profile.'

'Some Alberta oil magnate – started out as a poor and honest pipe-fitter fifteen years ago – spudded in a well to establish a new field sopping with more oil than Saudi Arabia – now he has a hundred refineries – four pipelines – a fleet of tankers – apartments in London, Paris, New York, but he is still happiest amid the simple comforts of his foothills ranch where he raises palomino parade horses, has a palomino wife and can stand tepid to his navel while he telephones from his tiled swimming pool. . . .'

'This is just a man – named Sherry.'

'What about him?'

'He's one hundred and eleven years old.'

'Oh,' David said, 'I see.'

'I thought of you.'

'Oldest man in Canada.'

'As near as we can check – the world.'

'Is he bedridden?'

'He voted in the last Federal election.'

'How'd you run across him?' David asked.

'He checked us up on the "Looking Backward" piece about the Red River Rebellion and a year ago he corrected some errors in Ken's article on buffalo – something wrong with our jumping pound . . .'

'Then he must have all his faculties. . . .'

'We have a pretty thick folder on him – Canadian Press generally has something on him every year – when he manages another birthday. He lives with some woman who looks after him. He's older than Canada.'

'If he's a hundred and eleven he would be. Where is he – exactly?'

'Town named Shelby – do you know it?'

'I've been through it,' David said. 'Between Calgary and the Montana border. Can't you send Ken?'

'I could. But I thought I'd speak to you first. It's a natural for a digest reprint. I don't think you'd be out much – if you did it for us. I thought you might want to.'

'Let me think it over,' David said.

He and Earl had stepped out of the Arts and Letters Club and into a grey and sepia day, quite unlovely and quite depressing with the buildings' flat faces grimed, the snow under foot forced to slush by melting chemicals. They parted on the corner and David walked on to his hotel, passing people with shoulders hunched against the chill wind off the lake. Light snow falling made the day opaque; it possessed the cold suet pudding quality peculiar to a Toronto March. The Manchester of North America, David told himself, and rejoiced that he lived in Montreal most of the time.

As he rounded the corner onto Jarvis Street, a woman walked slowly past him, a book under her arm. 'Liberry books,' his taxi driver had told him the day before, 'they're carryin' a liberry book then they're a hooker.' How decorous that a Toronto prostitute should use a library book as the badge of her profession, a most fitting façade of righteousness. He wondered what title she might most likely carry: one of the positive-thinking-make-your-life-bountiful-books, or something solidly classic like the *Collected Works of Tennyson,* perhaps less lyric – Nicholson's *Principles of Political Economy.*

He turned off down a side street and the wind's cold fingers managed the front of his overcoat. This was March's final and stubborn week, the time of year he most welcomed a *Focus* assignment that would take him to warmth and sunshine and garish colours, wherever people sang on streets and in bazaars. But *Focus* was already over its budget for the year and Andy wasn't dishing out travel expense money if he could help it.

He was walking now past high buildings each crowded against each, their narrow brick stairs identical, all of them long dead as residences. Windows were curtainless, many of them blank with drawn blinds. Some made half-hearted business announcements: SWEET-HEART CORSETS FITTED, SWEDISH BATHS AND HIGH COLONIC IRRIGATION, TOURIST ROOMS. One displayed a phrenologist's drawing of a head, the areas mapped out and divided by seams. Just one was softened by curtains pulled aside to show a pot of hyacinths on the sill.

He tried to recall whether he had ever seen crocuses in the foothills the last week of March. Certainly early in April. April had been an exciting month there, brilliant with sunshine, warmed by the Chinook winds breathing down from the mountains. In April there was always the song of meadow larks; what a sure and pure song it was! And what a positive achievement – one hundred and eleven years of life! He could tell Ralph to get someone to take over the panel for three Fridays – no – not if he left on a Friday night after the show – missed the next week and the next and got back the following Friday in time for that one. Only two missed and he could do his column just as well out West.

He'd clear it with Ralph for the second Friday in April, then phone Earl. He would!

'Pillow, sir?'
   'Thanks.'
When the stewardess had moved on he settled back again.

How long since he'd taken an article assignment? Two – three years. Too long. Suddenly he was filled with a sense of impotency, the same old pre-trapeze feeling – no life-net. He knew he was not yet over the disappointment of last year when he'd gathered the column material together, hoping for a hard-book publisher, only to be turned down – everywhere. Too shallow and too swift; what he had written running, people would not stay long enough to read in a book – not in their homes, only on a bus, with their morning coffee, giving him just fragments of their time. He wrote always against time. He wrote and he wrote again and he wrote again.

But at least he wasn't anonymous; look at all the shy talent that hid behind print, the unlabelled *mots justes* and puns, the nameless reviews. What humble and self-effacing writers to have dissolved themselves in the one trim style so well that it seemed the material must have written itself. Perhaps one faceless person with infinite energy, encyclopedic knowledge, legion talents, did write it all, telling clerics about religion and doctors about new medicines and surgical techniques, artists about art. Here must be the man who got bingo with the digest magazine story: *I Slept With a Grizzly Bear for the FBI and Found God.*

Why hadn't he managed the time for a novel? A play? He had not tried even an hour adaptation for *Curtain Time* – something of Chekhov – maybe a Conrad novello. Then there was that lovely thing of Galsworthy's – about the two young men on summer vacation – *The Apple Tree* – the singing and the gold . . .

It was just breaking daylight when he awoke with a crick that ran from his neck and down through one shoulder-blade. He looked through the window and out over an exquisitely pure panorama of cloud. Judging by the morning light he guessed that they must be somewhere over the Saskatchewan prairies; eighteen thousand feet below, the Saskatchewan River would be winding its ancient way. Cloud was quite unsatisfying, this celestial neighbourhood too rare and lonely, proper province only for the eagle and the hawk. The prairies must have approached this emptiness when Mr. Sherry was a young man.

He hoped that the old boy would have some sparkle, that he would talk easily, that there would be a few good anecdotes. Those would come when he had urged the man into remembering what the country was like ninety years ago. Unless he found a senile and bedridden skeleton. One hundred and eleven! But Earl had assured him that Mr. Sherry had all his faculties, wrote letters to the editor, voted in elections. He could just turn out to be a natural and suggest his own theme.

Longevity – obviously – a living record of the limits of human life – the Old Parr of the foothills – the one unbroken thread of flesh and spirit unravelling vulnerably from the year eighteen forty-nine. The California gold rush – twelve years old when Abraham Lincoln became president of the United States, sixteen when the president had been assassinated in Ford's Theatre. With a thrill he felt the old snowballing feeling that had often visited him in the past when he worked on an article.

The stewardess had emerged from the door at the end of the aisle; she leaned over the first seat, then straightened up to continue with waking her sleeping passengers. David saw the light wink up the order to fasten safety belts. The motors had changed their sound, more sibilant and less labouring.

After he'd driven the hundred miles from Calgary to Shelby, he would with luck be having his first interview this afternoon with Mr. Sherry, questioning him about the Red River Rebellion, the Saskatchewan uprising, the Klondike, the Boer War . . . He was aware of a slight stir of trepidation as he felt or thought he felt the plane tilting to come into the airport.

Even as he stepped out of the plane and into the early foothills morning he could feel the elation growing within himself. There was a benign Chinook; an extra dimension of light and height had been added to the day. It was like having a balloon blown up inside himself, he decided, as he put his bags in the Drive-Yourself car waiting for him in the airport parking lot.

He took Highway Two, following the distant jumble of Rockies against the morning sky, relaxing to the hypnotic hum of tires as he drove south towards Shelby and Mr. Sherry. Thirty miles on his way he pulled into a filling station just on the other side of the town of High River. As he stretched his legs he looked up and saw the kites in the sky.

There were five of them dancing high. He let his eyes travel down and against the prevailing west wind, till he came to their masters in an open field right beside the filling station. For the first time in many years he remembered another kite.

Chapter 2

The first eight years of David Lang's life had been spent in a foothills town perhaps a hundred miles removed from Shelby, the home of John Felix Sherry; the next nine he had lived in the city to which his mother had moved at the death of his father. There, with the money from the sale of his father's shop and what was left of the insurance, she had started a boarding-house. She had managed to send him on through two years of University before she had died. David had put in a year and a half on an Alberta daily, done correspondence work during the four years of the war, returning to newspaper work in Toronto in 1945. He had done his first magazine article for Earl Whitton and *Mayfair* magazine, followed by others over the next two years. Finally he had joined the *Mayfair* staff as an assignments editor, staying with them until he went freelancing on the strength of a sale to *Saturday Evening Post*. There had been three uncertain years until he had found himself in tele-vision work with CBC and then with a three-times-weekly news-paper column: 'Lang Syne'.

His memory of the father who had died when David was

eight was quite dim, though for years he'd had the recurring dream in which he discovered that his father had not died after all, but had simply been away, returning to him, vaguely apologetic for an absence which was somehow a little shameful. Shameful perhaps because he had failed to let David know that he had not really been dead all this time. As well, in these dreams his father seemed a little frightened of David's mother. He also looked a great deal like Lon.

Lon Burke was Mrs. Lang's star boarder, whose daughter was married to a deputy minister in the provincial government. A cheque to cover Lon's board, with enough over for his tobacco and sundries, was mailed regularly and directly to David's mother on the third of each month; the deputy minister had not once been out a day or a dollar. Soft-spoken and unobtrusive, Lon would have been a prize guest even in his daughter's home with his grandchildren.

He had a heart condition, David had been told both by his mother and by Lon himself, who had explained that he must carry his pills with him at all times. 'Nitro-glycerine, boy. That's the stuff they make explosives out of, you know.' He had showed them to David, tiny and white and not dangerous-looking at all.

One spring evening Lon had made him the kite. Hunched over the kitchen table, David beside him with chin in his hands, watching every move.

'Can't be out a hair, boy,' Lon told him as he balanced the cross-stick on the blade of a knife. 'Got to balance even just like a teeter-totter with two boys the same weight to the ounce on each end.'

When Lon had found the precise centre he marked it with a pencil, bound it to the upright stick and began to outline the diamond with string.

'They got whistlin' kites, these China natives – hang a bamboo flute on her and she sings with the wind – anchor the kite string to their house roof and keep her flyin' night and day.'

'Why?'

'Hangin' up there – hootin' like that – they figure it keeps the evil spurts off. There's some natives that worships kites,' he explained. 'Somewheres around Australia or New Zealand – around there – they sing hymns to their kites whilst they're climbin' up.'

He spread the paper out on the table, placed the finished stick and string skeleton on it. He let David mix up the flour and water paste in a cup. Once a general had won a whole war because of a kite, he told the boy, using it to lay string across a river for the seed of the bridge that had won him a decisive battle. 'There's fightin' kites too.'

'How do they fight?'

'With their string stiffened – glue an' ground glass. Swoop 'em over to another kite so's their string's alongside the other kite's string an' then jerk back an' forth till she saws right through – oh, there's lots of things to do with a kite besides flyin' 'em – you can send up messages – just a piece of paper split to a little hole and the wind spins her round an' round so she travels right up till she gets to the kite,' he said. 'You can cut the paper now. Leave a good inch around her,' he cautioned. 'Lots of edge to fold over an' paste – don't want her comin' apart in a strong wind.'

When they had finished pasting the paper over the frame, Lon lifted it down from the table and stood it on its end. 'Tall as you are, boy.'

It was, for the cross-stick came just to his nose. 'Gee, it didn't take long to build. . . .'

'Not finished yet. Has to have a tail.'

As they twisted paper and half-hitched it into the tail string, Lon explained its function. 'Can't have the tail too long or too short. If she's too long . . .'

'Won't fly.'

'Oh – she'll fly all right – but sort of dead an' sluggish. She won't dive an' dash an' do acrobatics – you want her to dance, don't you?'

'Oh yes – yes – I want her to dance!'

'All right then– mustn't have the tail too long – nor too short either.'

'What's that do?'

'Only go up twenty – fifty feet an' she goes wild – right out of control – she'll dive, maybe get her balance an' go too far the other side – head straight for the ground – whang her nose right into the dirt – snap her back. Tail's important – we'll make her so's we know she's too long an' draggy an' when we get her out to fly we'll keep breakin' off a piece at a time till we have her just right.'

David could hardly support school the next day. He ran almost the whole way home, burst through the front door, raced up the stairs and down the hall to Lon's room.

'Lon – Lon – let's go, Lon!'

'Hold on, boy.'

'Aren't we going to fly her?'

'Sure we are.'

'Now!'

'No – not today.'

'You got the string, didn't you? You said you'd got the . . .'

'I got a mile of string . . .'

'Then why aren't we going to . . .'

'We can't fly her in the city, boy – they aren't for flyin' in cities. We got to ride out to the limits where there's space – kite needs elbow-room where she won't get tangled up in telephone wires – power lines . . . free of buildings.'

'Oh.' His disappointment was acute as actual physical hurt.

'We got to wait till Saturday,' Lon said.

'Oh, Lon!'

'Still gets dark early – we wouldn't have time to get to the city limits – fly her any length of time – get home before dark.'

'It doesn't get dark all that early – doesn't take all that time to ride the street car to the city limits . . .'

'We can't make it today, David.'

'What about tomorrow?'

'That's a school day.'

'We got early closing tomorrow,' David said. 'School lets out at three instead of four.'

'Does it?'

'Sure. Our class hasn't had anybody late all month – no lates, that means we get out an hour early and three o'clock would give us time, wouldn't it?'

'Sure it would. You come straight home tomorrow – we'll take the Norwood street car and we'll fly her tomorrow.'

'Lon.'

'Yes?'

'Could I – would it be all right if I kept her in my room?'

'In there on your bed now – and the string too.'

But they had not flown the kite the next day, for at noon Norman Laycock had slid into his seat seven minutes late, to ruin the class record for the month. Miss Kalman seemed to feel just as bad about it as the class, for she told them to put away their books while she read to them in the hour they were not free in early closing. David made plans for Norman Laycock, hardly listening to the whining of *Black Beauty* through three chapters.

Lon had tried to cheer him up. 'Don't you worry, boy. Tomorrow's Saturday an' we'll catch that Norwood street car right after breakfast. We'll be out there – she'll be tugging at her string.'

Even before David had opened his eyes the next morning he heard the rain on the roof, the first real one of spring. It filled him with infinite sadness when it had not let up by noon. He spent the rest of the day in his room with the kite, at first trying to hold it by the upright stick to make it swoop in pretended flight, but it was too big and awkward for that. He laid it across the bed and looked at it.

But Sunday morning he and Lon walked to the street-car stop through a washed and sunlit day. Lon let him go ahead while he put in their tickets. They sat in the smoking section across the back so that David could let the kite stick out into the aisle before himself.

The car rolled through a city hushed with Sabbath peace and David wondered briefly if it was all right to fly a kite on Sunday, though it was all right to go swimming. Perhaps it was all right to fly a kite because you weren't running around yelling and trying to hit runs or score goals against the other side.

13

Kite-flying would be a lot like taking a drive on Sunday or going on a picnic. Indeed, he felt quite picnickish, for his mother had made them a lunch which Lon held on his lap, and Lon had promised that they could buy Orange Crush at a confectionery near the car barns.

But he felt a return of his doubt as they passed a church corner and he saw people trickling down the street toward the opened church doors. Ordinarily he would be in a suit and headed for Sunday School now. As the street car crossed the city it made hardly any stops; there was no clanging of the bell, almost as though it went through its silent run with only half a mind, the proper way for a street car on a Canadian Sunday.

They were passing implement sheds and lumber yards, an oil refinery, a greenhouse, mostly buildings where people did not live. David saw the sign: Black Cat Confectionery.

'There it is, Lon! That's the one!'

When Lon did not answer, David looked over to him, saw that the old man's face was mask tense and white. 'Lon – Lon!'

The street car had stopped at a little shed, just a roof on posts with the back filled in; ahead the tracks made a figure eight almost. 'Lon!'

With a slow fist Lon was striking himself on the side of his chest. 'What's wrong, Lon?'

Still the old man did not answer and still the fist kept up its deliberate and gentle thumping. The explosion pills! David pushed the kite aside, fumbled up under the old man's suit coat and into the lower vest pocket.

'All out – end of the line.' The conductor was looking back towards them.

As he unscrewed the cap of the bottle, pills tipped out over the street-car floor. David held one up to Lon's mouth. The old man took it with his lips and slumped back against the seat.

'What's the matter?' David looked up to the conductor. 'He sick?'

'His heart,' David said. 'He's got a heart condition.'

'Maybe he'd be better lying down.' The conductor put an

arm round Lon's shoulders and eased him out on the seat. He loosened Lon's tie, unbuttoned the collar. 'Maybe we ought to call an ambulance.' He looked down at Lon uncertainly. 'He had 'em before?'

'Yes,' David said.

'I don't know,' the conductor said.

Lon was not gasping so much now; the colour had begun to return to his face. '. . . if I just lie here,' he whispered. 'We'll ride back with you.'

'I think you ought to have an ambulance take you.'

Lon moved his head slightly. 'It's eased up. The boy gave me a pill. We'll ride back with you and by then I can make it to the house.'

They had ridden the street car back across the city to the corner of their block. Using David for support, still clutching his side and making several stops, Lon made it to the house and to bed. The doctor had called soon after. For the next few days the other boarders tip-toed about the house, talked in low voices. David had gone up to visit Lon several times, but the old man lay with his eyes closed most of the time, speaking only with great effort. Then David's mother had suggested that he not visit Lon for a few days, until the old man was feeling a little better.

David's concern for his friend was great, but his concern for his kite was greater. He had left it behind on the street car. Throughout the week he wondered what he could do about it, going down to the corner several times but not daring to board the street car, for he had no ticket and it didn't seem right to get on a street car without the fare – not so bad as ringing a fire alarm when there was no fire – but bad enough. He had to wait till the Saturday after Lon's seizure, when his mother gave him ten cents for the Hi-Art and *Tom Mix*.

He had assumed that it would be the same conductor; the man was leaning away from him with his head down as David waited by the ticket box; when he straightened up David saw that it wasn't the right conductor at all. For a moment he considered not handing out his ten cents, but the conductor had thrown forward the handle and the street car was grinding inexorably forward.

David rode all the way out to the end of the line, then had to use the nickel change for another ticket to come back. When he gave it to the wrong conductor, he spoke of the kite.

'What?'

'Was there a kite? I left my kite on here last week – back in the smoking section.'

The conductor shook his head. 'Not on my car.'

'Last Sunday. I had to leave it behind.'

'Just a minute, son.' The car had stopped. David waited till the conductor had torn off a transfer for the new passenger. 'I haven't seen any kite,' the conductor said. 'Hasn't been any kite turned in that I know of.'

David walked back to his seat, balancing himself to the lurch of the car. He got off at his corner, but instead of going home he walked aimlessly for several blocks, watched without interest some men working on a storm sewer, then wandered on till he had come to a house excavation. He climbed the high mound of dirt there without any feeling of accomplishment, then climbed down. He went over and sat between two stacks of ship lap. He stayed there till darkness had fallen.

He had never before been abroad after nightfall, yet as he walked towards home, the late guilt he felt could not overcome his sense of irreparable loss, mortal loss too great for tears. It would never soar for him; he would never feel the live tug of its string in his hand; it would never dip and lash its serpentine tail. He heard the bark of a dog up his own street, the settling-down cheep of birds in branches above his head. He went up the front steps to face his mother's disapproval at his lateness, almost welcoming it as though her punishment would be a sort of antidote for his disappointment at the loss of the kite.

She met him at the foot of the stairs – crying. The tears were not his fault. While he had been fruitlessly searching for his kite, Lon had died.

Almost a week after the funeral he had visited Lon's room, quite bare of Lon – without even the apple box half filled with sawdust for spitting into. The pipes and their rack were missing; the room was quite unhaunted. David felt that in some way a person's room should hold a trace of them; something should linger. Deserted houses were generally stilled with nostalgia for those who had once lived there; there was usually a mason jar in the kitchen part – an old lady's shoe with a limp top – a rusted spoon – something. But in Lon's room – nothing. It didn't even smell of him; the open window had inhaled the net curtains into the room with its fresh and impersonal bouquet. Sunshine glinted from the tubed and bulbed brass bed boxed with a khaki army blanket; his mother would not put the quilt on till the new boarder had moved in.

David went to the varnished oak dresser, over the barren linoleum his mother had polished to such a high patina that it looked as though bare soles would kiss and stick to it. For a moment he stared at the wall above the dresser – buttercups – they ought to be more careful about patterns on wall-paper so the edges weren't skidded that way.

He opened the top dresser drawer, the one that was divided in two, but inside he saw fresh newspaper. He closed it again and opened the other half. It was not lined with new paper. He pulled it out farther, almost till it would come free and drop in his hand. He saw the druggist's bottle with the prescription pasted on its flat side. It was Lon's empty explosive pill bottle, so something had been left behind after all, a particularly important part of Lon, the life-restoring pill bottle. And it wasn't empty, for the bottom was still covered; impulsively he put it into his pocket and carried it to his own room.

It seemed terribly important to him that he place it in his left-hand dresser drawer, far back in the corner, precisely as it had stood in Lon's drawer. He had counted the pills in his Lon bottle; nineteen Lon-explosion-pills. Away from home whenever he thought of them they comforted, and when he was in the quiet and enclosing secrecy of his room, holding the bottle with its smooth and instant fit into his palm, it soothed and reminded him of when he used to suck his thumb, though he hadn't done that for years.

17

But the satisfaction had not lasted and as it weakened there was a return of his sadness over the loss of the kite; it was as he imagined it must be when a kite sinks to earth in a dying wind. Almost three weeks after Lon's death he came home from school, unscrewed the bottle top and tipped the pills into the palm of his hand. He touched one with the tip of his tongue, imagined he could feel it drawing up the moisture of saliva into its floury dryness. It was such a tiny pill that he hardly knew he had swallowed it, and at first there was a thrill of fear, for he had not intended to at all. But this was followed by disappointment, for nothing had happened; he was David Lang, eight years old, standing in his bedroom with the Lon-explosion-pill bottle in his hand, and he had just been cheated. He had imagined that when Lon took one of the pills he felt a nudging thump deep inside himself — a half-heard, half-felt gastric explosion like a fire-cracker going off under a tin can, not a lambasting fire-cracker but one of the weaker ones that went off with a flat whap.

He walked towards his door, on his way to the garbage can with the dud pills, but half way across the room he felt the pervading body tickle begin. It tingled into pins and needles, his pulse fluttering at his throat, his blood turgid at his temples and ringing in his ears. The room had begun to shimmer and he was about to do one of three things: become airborne, burst out of his skin, or deflate into a boneless heap on the floor. He could feel an urgent and steadily surging beat within himself. They were truly explosion pills, capable of causing not just the one detonation he had imagined but many small ones evenly spaced and coming close upon one another.

He made it to the bed, leaned against it for a moment, then let himself slide down and lie across it. He closed his eyes, washed in a warm flood, floating quite weightlessly, tossed like a wood chip on waves.

It took an hour to drift from him like a dandelion's grey parachute on a summer breeze, leaving him subdued and gently trembling within his elbows and knees. No one at supper seemed to notice anything different about him, though Miss

Monkman at dessert did say something in his direction about the cat having got his tongue, but she of course was always saying that.

There was a new boarder in Lon's place across the table from David, a short plump man who smiled a great deal and complimented Mrs. Lang extravagantly on her cooking. He sold encyclopedias.

Until he had taken all nineteen of the pills, David would come straight home from school to solemnly eat one. Each time he did it exactly as he had the first time. Then the pills were gone. Lon was gone. The kite was gone.

Also, in three months, the boarder who had replaced Lon was gone. He left, owing David's mother the rent for two months – not actually, for there was a demonstrator set of Berkley's *Masters and Scholars Encyclopedia*, which Mrs. Lang took down to Stein's Book Exchange. But they would give her only seven dollars for it, so she brought it home and put it in David's room for him. It was wonderful to graze through its glossy plates, discovering that Victor Emmanuel, with Garibaldi the founder of modern Italy, was a bluff and hearty man, who hunted chamois through the Alps with only bread and cheese in his pocket, that he had a great weakness for feminine society and kept several mistresses. David could flip back a few pages in the same volume to read about the bedchamber plot under Queen Victoria, in which Lady Flora Hastings, accused of immoral conduct, was subjected to the indignity of a medical examination and died several months later of an enlarged liver. Like Eliza over her ice cakes he went from dreams and eclipses to hopscotch, Horace, the horse and horticulture – infantry, insanity, Irish moss, iron and Isabella of Bavaria – orang-utan, Palestine, Palmerston, Papacy and parasitic diseases – yachting, yellow fever, Yukon Territory – Zeus, zinc, Zoroaster, Zurich, and zymotic diseases. In a way it was a sort of legacy from Lon, not a kite but something almost as wonderful.

He was not hungry when he drove into Shelby and parked the car, nor was he any longer enthusiastic about his mission; he was simply tired and cramped after his all-night flight and the hundred miles he had driven from Calgary. As he got out of the car before the hotel he saw the spiralled white and red sign of the barber shop next door. After he had registered he'd relax in the barber chair for a soothing shave. On his way to the hotel with his bags he read the sign in the window sprawling with geraniums:

Mr. Merton N. Spicer

YOUR TONSORIAL REQUIREMENTS

LOOKED AFTER

David's father, before he had died of cirrhosis of the liver, had been a barber.

Chapter 3

It was a one-chair barber shop, Mr. Spicer in a high-collared white coat, seated in the lone chair with one leg over a knee. He lowered the book he was reading as David entered, got up and took a position of readiness behind the chair. David hung his jacket and top coat on the clothes tree, then went over and sat down. 'Shave, please.'

The barber's breath whistled politely as he fastened the sheet about David's neck. He lowered the chair back. The discreet sibilance withdrew; David heard the rush of water, then came the hot smother of a steaming towel.

'Spring,' Mr. Spicer said, 'looks like early spring.'

David grunted agreement under the muffling towel. Over by the instrument shelf the brush began clucking in the shaving-mug. 'Nice change if it is. Last four – five years it's been late – late spring. Nice to see an early spring again.' The footsteps came back to the chair; David felt the air cool against his face as the barber lifted the towel. 'Ah – you look sort of familiar – not from around here, are you?'

'No,' David said, 'I'm not.'

The barber looked down on him. 'Seems to me I should know you though – isn't often I'm wrong when it comes to a face. Generally remember a face. Sticks with me – swear I'd seen your face before – perhaps just on the street – passing on the street in the city. You're from Calgary.'

'No.' This was an old experience with David, though the first time he could recall submitting to it flat on his back with a strange face tipped over him; in a moment it would light up with recognition. Their relationship would shift gears; an extra pleasantness would be required of him, the surprised enthusiasm of old acquaintances meeting.

'It is familiar – oh!'

Now he had been matched up with the image that appeared on the national television network each week; a generous deference would come or perhaps the expectant look that dared him to sparkle – to be different from ordinary people. In a way it was as though he were being requested to die – as himself.

'. . . knew you looked familiar,' the barber was saying, '. . . *Pick a Name* . . . you're David Lang on *Pick a Name*!'

There was nothing he could do but agree. He had often wondered why it embarrassed him as much as it did; politicians, he supposed, must glory in it. It was some comfort to know that it could be much worse: if he were a hockey hero – a prime minister – a freak wrestling personality – a golden goddess of song.

'My favourite TV programme – never miss it – watch *Pick a Name* regularly and I'm not one for TV – *Pick a Name* and *World Focus*. You know, I'll bet I've seen you every time you been on *World Focus* – one you did in Egypt – that interview with Nasser in Egypt – the Kenya one – that was a good one where you interviewed all those different Canadians – Canadians living in London and Paris. Well, say – imagine – you walk right into my shop – right here in my shop and . . .' He stopped abruptly with mug and shaving-brush held high, 'Don't tell me that's why you're out here. *World Focus*?'

'No.'

'Oh – just passing through.'

'I'm staying for a while.'

'In Shelby. That's nice. Stopping in Shelby.'

'I'm not on *World Focus*' David explained. 'I'm – ah – I'm here to do an article.'

'On Shelby?'

'No. One of your Shelby people.'

'Ollie Pringle!'

'Mr. Sherry.'

'Daddy Sherry! About time somebody did an article on him – long due you might say – hundred and eleven – you know he's a hundred and eleven years old.'

'I understand he is.'

The barber began to work the lather into David's face. 'Wouldn't be surprised if he was the oldest man in the world – oldest human alive – today. That little fellow – fellow down in South America – he died – died a few years back, didn't he?'

'I believe so.'

'I don't suppose they had any real proof how old he was – documental proof – Brazil or Chile or Peru – now what kind of records would they have there? Not much, I'd say – not real proof – dependable records – not the kind of records you'd get for Daddy. He's got Bible proof and he's got vital statistical proof. How long do you figure you'll be here, Mr. Lang?'

'Three weeks, perhaps.'

'I see. Little to the right there – certainly a red-letter day for us – for all Shelby district – even better than if you were doing him on *World Focus*. Printed word lasts. History – man like Daddy Sherry – way I see it – he's history – he has historical importance. All our old-timers dying off makes him even more historically important because they're the living pages of our history. Canadian history. Pages – fluttering away – unrecorded – lots of them unread. Well . . .' He straightened up to wipe the razor on the paper square, to be replaced on David's chest. '. . . glad to know that somebody's going to record Daddy before it's too late.' He bent over again, took David's nose between thumb and forefinger, lifted to shave the upper lip. 'I read a great deal. Read a lot of history – right here in the shop.

You may have noticed as you came in. I get these books regularly from different book clubs I belong to and I find – in my reading – my favourite reading is history. Not history percy – this fictionalized history that makes historical personages come alive – way they act it out before your eyes you might say – speak to you out of their own mouths.' He left David suddenly and when he spoke again his voice came from near the instrument shelf. 'Just take this book here – book I was reading when you came in. "In Felice Gagnon's lovely body flowed warm Basque blood," ' he read from the dust jacket, ' "spiced with a fiery Spanish strain – she charmed crowned heads of Europe, held kingdoms in her graceful hands, but her spirit was completely pagan." Fabulous best seller set back in the time of Louis Quinze,' he explained as he walked back to David. He tilted the chin up and began on the neck.

'Not too close, please,' David said.

'I won't,' the barber promised. 'Touchy area – the neck – going to find ingrown hairs – be the neck every time. Nine times out of ten. Never shave a man close on the neck. Something I never do. There's where experience tells – the neck. The neck and moles – always mark a mole – clear it of lather before I touch a razor to a man's face. Learn quite a lesson from history. Morals. Moral lesson. Time of King Charles – Louis Quinze – Louis Quatorze – Henry Eight – Revolution – French Revolution – American – those olden people had awful morals. I suppose you've got it all set up. You've been in touch with Belva Louise . . .'

'Belva Louise?'

'Tinsley – Miss Tinsley – she looks after Daddy – she's looked after him for ten-twelve years . . .'

'No, I haven't,' David admitted. 'I just drove down from Calgary.'

'Oh.'

'I thought I might drop in on him after lunch,' David felt compelled to explain. 'His lunch.'

'Chancy.'

'Chancy?'

'If he's under the weather – waste of time. Wouldn't do you much good to call on him on a bad day. Isn't that he has this seminal decay but he does have his good days and he has his bad days. You might hit him – might be a bad day today.'

'Oh.'

'Daddy can be clear as a bell one minute and the next thing he's way back in the Fenian Raids or the Red River Rebellion or marching with General Middleton in eighty-five. Too bad if you were to hit him on a bad day.'

'I guess I'll just have to take that chance,' David said. 'Do you think this might be a bad day?'

'This is Saturday and he hasn't been in the shop yet. Generally comes in here at eleven o'clock on a Saturday morning. Set your clock by him. Nice weather like this – he comes down town with young Keith Maclean – Bluebird Café first and they have their ice-cream cone and Daddy gets a Senate House cigar. Then Keith goes with him down the block to the Cascade – Cascade Beer Parlour. The boy doesn't go in but he waits for Daddy in the lobby of the Cascade Hotel while Daddy has his glass of beer. Next call – my shop – comes in here and I give him a shave. Then home again. That's the way Daddy generally spends his Saturday mornings – as a rule. Has done as long as I've known him – except in winter. Wintertime he holes up at home – hibernates like a grizzly. But as soon as the sky is blue and the run-off starts – down town every Saturday morning. Law nature.'

'But you think this might be one of his bad days . . .'

'Only reason I can figure he hasn't been in the shop. Also – I heard he's pekid lately.' Mr. Spicer wiped the traces of lather from David's face, stepped over to the instrument shelf, returned to rub in lime pungent ointment. His dextrous barber's fingers gently massaging, he fanned with a swinging towel. 'You know where his house is?'

'Not yet.'

'You can't miss it. Straight down from the Cascade Hotel two blocks – first block that's the Cameo Theatre – second has the Elliott Implement Company building and you turn west there – that's right – three blocks – go three blocks west till you come up against the river – then north – that's right again – and the first house is Daddy's – peak roof – brown shingles – has a new-looking foundation under it . . .'

'No powder, thanks.'

'All right. They put in that new foundation in the spring of fifty-four – flood year – you might get Miss Tinsley to tell you about the spring of fifty-four. She'll be a great help to you with your story – oh – and another person – that'd be Doctor Richardson . . .'

'About the spring of fifty-four?'

'No – but he's Daddy's doctor – close friend too – friend and doctor. Pretty active in this Honour Daddy Sherry Day. You may have heard about that?'

'No, I haven't.'

'How long did you say you thought you'd be here?'

'Two – perhaps three weeks.'

'That's too bad. Daddy's birthday – his hundred and eleventh birthday is May 17th, which means you'll be leaving a couple of weeks short of it – community birthday party. They're having an organizational meeting tonight in the Community Centre – representatives – delegates – heads of all different Shelby organizations – Rotary – Activarians – Knights of the Loyal Order of Homesteaders – Eastern Star – Rebekahs – Willing Workers' Home Makers – UFWA – purpose of the meeting is to form a Daddy Sherry Birthday Committee.'

'I see.'

'I imagine Donald Finlay will head it up. That's another fellow you ought to get in touch with. Reverend Mr. Finlay.'

'Mr. Sherry's minister.'

'Well – nobody's Daddy's minister really – he isn't much for going to church – he doesn't go to Donald Finlay but Donald goes to him. Great goose hunter.'

'Mr. Sherry?'

'Reverend Mr. Finlay. Him and Doctor Richardson hunt to-gether. Matter of fact – year Daddy was a hundred – eleven

26

from – ah – sixty – forty-nine – fall of forty-nine they all went on a hunt together. Just imagine that – a man a hundred years old and he goes on a goose hunt. Ollie Pringle went on that hunt too. You'd see his place the top of the block – as you came into town . . .'

'I don't know if I . . .'

'Licensed Embalmer and Funeral Director – big, square, white two-storey building. Ollie lives over it – lives on the second floor. He'll be at the meeting tonight for the Chamber of Commerce.'

'Will he . . .'

'He has a green thumb. If you'd been looking as you came in you'd seen his greenhouse on the South Side. Ollie has a great green thumb – especially for begonias. Begonias are his specialty. From the end of June on, his place is just a blaze of colour with begonias. He even raises orchids in that greenhouse. Somebody really ought to do an article about Ollie Pringle. How long will you be?'

'Pardon?'

'In Shelby – how long – oh yes – you said three weeks. Where are you staying?'

'The hotel.'

'Cascade – have to be. Only hotel we've got. They're only in it for the beer licence – only have rooms so they can hold onto their beer licence. Three weeks.' The barber shook his head doubtfully. 'Pretty long stretch to spend in the Cascade. I was you I'd get into a boarding-house. Wouldn't hurt to try Mrs. Baines.'

'It's a short time for that,' David said. 'I'll stick with the hotel.'

'Suit yourself. April – we're into April so there can't be any really cold weather left – yet the sun isn't high enough yet to hit that flat tar roof. You aren't likely to freeze or roast.' He had helped David on with his jacket and his top coat, walked with him to the open doorway. 'Well – good luck with your article, Mr. Lang.'

'Thank you.'

'You know – quite a few years back – I figured out Daddy's secret.'

'Did you . . .'

'Secret of his long life. Quite simple.'

'Oh?'

'Remember in the papers – eight or nine years ago – Egypt – Sahara – they dug down in the sands of the Sahara and they found this seed in this Pharaoh's tomb? Over-two-thousand-year-old corn? Laid asleep there for thousands of years – till they found it and they let it germinate and away it went. Makes a fellow think, certainly made me think. That corn made it through those thousands of years because it was buried in the dry hot sands of the Sahara . . .'

'Yes?'

'Same as Daddy Sherry – spent over ninety of his years either on the prairies or in these foothills – dry – pure air for ninety years – kind of preserved him.'

'You may be right,' David said.

'I think I am. Now I think of it – Mrs. Baines is full up but I did hear Mrs. Clifford was interested in taking boarders . . .'

'I'd better stick with the hotel.'

'That means you're stuck with the Bluebird Café for your meals – they're no culinary delight – I were you I'd consider Mrs. Clifford – if she *is* going to take in boarders.'

'I may,' David said, rather than prolong the solicitude for his comfort and gastric health. 'Right now I'm on my way with your excellent directions – to Mr. Sherry's.'

The cottage was a squat, brown-shingled box with a pyramidal roof so wide-eaved that it looked as though a too large bonnet had slipped down over the house's eyes. Under the eaves, round the front and two sides, ran an open porch. An empty wicker rocker waited to the left of the front door. David twisted the key of the spring doorbell and its tight, quick jangle within touched off the quiet thrill of nervousness he always experienced before an interview; it was the same tension that lifted in him just before he went on the air.

He could hear the low persistence of a vacuum cleaner inside the house. He twisted the bell again and looked up to a fan of violet and ruby glass. If only the old man were half as garrulous as Mr. Spicer! And just why had they put a new foundation under the house in nineteen fifty-four?

He had somehow imagined a small and bird-like woman administering to Mr. Sherry's needs, cooking his meals, tidying his house – a mother wren feeding her young. The woman standing in the opened door was not tall, but she was broad and she was solid. Her tweed skirt outlined large shanks and generous hips; her feet were encased in men's black brogues – large, as were her wrists and ankles and cheek bones.

'Yes?'

'Miss Tinsley.'

'Yes.'

'I'm David Lang. I've come to Shelby for *Mayfair* magazine . . .'

'I'm sorry – we have all we can read.'

'No – in an editorial capacity . . .'

'. . . and I'm right in the middle of spring cleaning.'

'I don't want to interrupt that.'

'You won't be . . .'

'I'd like to do an article for *Mayfair*,' David said quickly, 'they've sent me here to do one on . . .'

'That's a new approach. You do look a little old to be working your way through University, but really – Mr. Sherry has more reading matter than anyone else in the district – he buys the adventure ones and the Westerns and the Space ones and those men – only ones with the full-page photographs off the rack in the Bluebird Café . . .'

'But the reason I'm calling . . .'

'. . . and everyone's wonderful about sending him their magazines when they're through with them. Right now – in there . . .' she turned back towards the interior of the house '. . . there are four copies of this month's *Mayfair* magazine.' In profile, her bosom demanded David's attention; it strained impatiently at the neck margin of her dress in two milk-pale swellings tangential to each other. She had all the blowsing charm of a cabbage rose which has reached and just passed the climax of its bloom. 'So there's no use wasting my time or your time.'

'Miss Tinsley,' he said firmly, 'I am not selling subscriptions to *Mayfair* magazine. I'm an assignment writer for them. I hope to do a profile article and this is my first call to interview Mr. Sherry . . .'

'Oh – oh – what did you say your name was?'

'David Lang.'

'I don't recall reading any of your articles.'

'It's been some years since I've done any. I have a regular newspaper column and I'm moderator on a television . . .'

'We haven't a set and I can't be bothered to go out to watch it. The few times I've seen it – why – it's been as bad as Mr. Sherry's pulp magazines – or his comic books. Shouldn't we have had some sort of warning . . .'

'I just flew out from Toronto – on quite short notice – ordinarily you would have.' He could feel his face warm with his annoyance. 'Whether or not you're sure I'm doing a piece on Mr. Sherry – is there any reason for my not having a short visit with him?' When she didn't answer him immediately, he said, 'I assure you I am a writer – I want to do an article on your Mr. Sherry – I am not selling subscript . . .'

'. . . or a set of encyclopedias . . .'

'No.'

'. . . mining stocks – oil stocks – pay-as-you-live-mausoleum – tinted photographs . . .'

'Miss Tinsley – within forty-eight hours you shall get a letter from Earl Whitton, managing editor of *Mayfair* – I'll see that you do – I'll wire him . . .'

'No,' she said. 'Come in.' She stepped aside. 'He's in his bedroom,' she explained as she skirted the vacuum cleaner in the middle of the rug. 'I'm afraid you've called on one of his bad days. He hasn't left his bed today or yesterday or the day before.' She stopped at the open doorway on the left wall of the room. 'He has his good days and he has his bad days.'

'Yes,' David said, still not quite recovered from the surprise of her sudden capitulation. 'Mr. Spicer was telling me.'

'Do you know Mr. Spicer?'

'I just dropped into his shop when I got into town.'

'Daddy!' The loudness of her voice as she called into the bedroom startled David. 'Someone to see you!' She turned back to him. 'There's a chair by his bed. Pull it up as close as you can. He isn't deaf ordinarily − Doctor Richardson says his hearing isn't impaired at all − it's just that on his bad days you have to speak louder to get his attention. And then half the time you don't. Excuse me.' She left the room to David and to Mr. Sherry. The vacuum cleaner started up again.

His white hair electric, the old man was propped with pillows in sitting position against the high dark mahogany head-board of the bed. Gnarled hands lay before him, palms upwards, at the edge of the log-cabin quilt which seemed quite flat, as though nobody were under it to raise it − rather as though Mr. Sherry speared directly from the floor beneath, through the bed and straight up. Under the dandelion-down hair, the eyes were closed.

David pulled the chair over close to the bed. He sat down. Where the stalk neck lifted out of the collarless nightgown he could see the twin bones at the top of the chest like two knuckles there.

'Mr. Sherry,' he tried.

The closed lids in their deep sockets were very nearly transparent; chin and nose were salient above and below the enfolding crease of the mouth combed with innumerable fine wrinkles; the thin lips themselves were blue as though stained by grapes.

'Mr. Sherry!' Although he had spoken not nearly so loudly as Miss Tinsley, David saw the eyelids lift with turtle slowness. The head was turning towards him, with the reluctance of tropism. Dilute blue eyes stared at him. They did this − quite sightlessly − for several seconds. They closed again.

And now the silence of the bedroom had borrowed a harsh edge, at first an almost imperceptible and placeless sound; it strengthened and lost its ventriloquial quality – a phlegmy wheezing from deep in the old man's core. It was quite alarming and David was on the point of calling Miss Tinsley when he realized that the sound had died away again.

'I'm David Lang,' he said, 'Mr. Sherry,' and he felt like a fool.

'Yeh-yeh-yeh-yeh-yeh . . .' Autumn wind through dead leaves might have whispered so: breathy affirmation of nothing, over and over again as the tongue fluttered mindlessly in exhaled breath. David knew now that his visit was quite hopeless.

'Puhtatuhs an' Irish twist.' Though the eyes were still closed, the words came out clear and firm and sexless.

David leaned forward on his chair. 'What was that, Mr. Sherry?'

'. . . buttermilk an' pigweed greens – keep reg'lar – stay outa draughts.' The eyes flew open. They saw now. 'The secret.'

'What secret?'

'One you came for.'

'I came for? I don't understand what you . . .'

'You ain't from town – first thing – what's the secret? Ain't any secret but that – an' – hundred an' eleven – crock a day – cu-rocka day – buttermilk.'

'Oh – the secret of your long life – buttermilk?'

'Eighteen sixty-eight,' Mr. Sherry said.

'You attribute your long life to buttermilk?'

'Pigweed greens – aaaah-yah-yah-yah-yuh – an' Will an' the bobcat . . .'

'Will and the . . .'

'Eat puhtatuhs – lots of 'em,' Mr. Sherry advised.

'What about Will and the bobcat?' David asked as he sensed an anecdote.

'Will who?'

'You said Will and the bobcat.'

'Boiled – mashed – fried – scalloped – baked,' Mr. Sherry replied.

'Yes?' prompted David.

'Keep reg'lar,' Mr. Sherry cautioned him. 'Hundred an'

32

eleven – Egypt in my bones – grey hair all over my gizzard –
cold – cold – cold – "Let 'em drink tea," he says – that was a
poor war,' he said sadly, 'a poor – poor war.'

'Which one?' David asked him.

But the butterfly attention had lifted from the blossom of the
poor war. 'Tinder dry – tinder – tinder dry.'

'Mr. Sherry.'

'Lantern – who let her take that lantern – the barn fulla hay
an' a lighted lantern – somebody must of seen the light from it
– Mary Jane – Mary Jane! Didn't anybody know where Mary
Jane was at! Didn't anybody care where Mary Jane was at!
I'm not blamin' her – she done it but I'm not blamin' her for
it because she didn't know any better! Mary Jane was all right.
Nothing wrong with Mary Jane.' He closed his eyes: when he
spoke again it was to croon. 'Mary Jane was aaaaaaaall right.'

'I'm sure she was,' David said. 'But, Mr. Sherry – I was
wondering – just when did you come here – the West – you
weren't born out here, were . . .'

'Built her – built her.'

'Did you . . .'

'I built Pile-o-Bones too only they double-crossed me an'
named her Regina . . .'

'Yes – in Saskatchewan – but I was thinking of Alberta –
the foothills . . .'

'Who stubbed his toe on that old jawbone!'

'I'm sure I don't know.'

'Me. It was me. Hollered Moose Jaw an' that's where they
set her down – city of Moose Jaw . . .'

'But you are in Alberta now – when did you come to the
province – the foothill country . . .'

'First there was the Blackfoot.' Mr. Sherry laid careful stress
on each word as though he were telling a story to a backward
child. 'An' then there was – ah – there was – then there was the
fur fellahs – the wolfers – stuh-rike you paralysed! Plumb paralysed! Water'n – alcohol – an' they saved aaaaalla their tuhbaccah spit – an' red pepper – fire-water aaaaall right – throwed her
aaaall together with maybe a dollop turpentine if it was handy –

33

one mouthful for a buffalo hide. Oooohhhhh – I seen 'em take their mouthful – hold it in their gob like a mother robin to her nest with a worm for the young ones, an' run back down an' squirt it into their squaw's mouth an' come back agin an' get another hide's worth . . . Aaaaaaah!' It was a groan of pain. 'Their bellies – their poor nitchie bellies!' He closed his eyes.

David waited until he realized that the old man had drifted off to sleep. This was as good a time as any for him to leave. He doubted that Mr. Sherry had experienced a worse bad day than this one in the past two decades. Carefully he rose and just as cautiously made his way to the door. Damn Earl Whitton anyway!

'I say she was built!' Daddy's voice behind him had achieved a quavering yet declamatory strength. 'The Dominion of Canada was built on them three things!'

David stepped through the bedroom door.

'Tuhbaccah spit! Buffalo pelts! Hudson's Bay rum!'

Miss Tinsley was not in the living-room. David walked quickly to the front door.

'Long live Queeeeeeeeeeeen Vic-torrrrrrrrrrrri-yah!'

Chapter 4

It was not an illusion; the floor did slope towards the bed; and again – when he carried the typewriter to the table against the wall – it tilted upwards. Now that his eyes were accustomed to the dimness, he saw that the floor sagged from all its outer edges to form a shallow valley in which the bed nestled. Also, the room was quite fermented. He had noticed the smell earlier when he had first taken his things up, but he had spent only a few moments there before going to the barber shop for his shave. It was a pervasive bouquet and all the more annoying because it was so unaccountable.

He sat before the typewriter fully intending to rough out some sort of framework for Daddy Sherry, but impotence had settled over him. He went to the door and turned on the overhead light; even in mid-afternoon the sun could not get at the one inadequate window. Not only was it a north one, but it faced the brick wall of an adjacent building.

Mr. Spicer had been quite right about the Cascade Hotel's lack of charm! And when he had gone to the Bluebird Café after leaving the Sherry house, a slovenly waitress had told him he was too late for the lunch menu and too early for the supper one. His ham and eggs and fried potatoes must have been the worst meal concocted since man's invention of the peptic ulcer. After leaving the restaurant he had stopped in at the drug store to buy a bottle of Amphogel. His heartburn seemed slightly less acid now.

He stared at the blank sheet in the typewriter, tried to summon up the excitement he'd felt on the plane. It refused him. He tapped out a few words of description on Daddy – his housekeeper – his cottage, then ground to a halt with barely half a page of very lumpy notes. He could sit here for hours and not one usable thing was going to float to the surface. He remembered that he had clearly asked Earl in the Arts and Letters Club if the old man had all his faculties; he could not recall whether Earl had definitely said yes, but the point was that the editor hadn't bothered to *know* before giving him the assignment. You simply could not get anything coherent out of a man like Daddy Sherry – skipping all over two centuries!

The explosion seemed to come from directly underneath him; though it was muffled, he had felt it nudge the soles of his feet. Then for the first time he heard the surf of male voices below. No wonder the room smelled yeasty; the thumping detonation had been the bunging of a keg; he was established over a beer parlour. He looked at his watch: four-fifteen. This would be their slack time of day; how hellishly and vicariously convivial his three weeks were going to be! If he knew his small-town beer parlours, the one below would reach its alcoholic crescendo around ten in the evening – just about the time he would return to the room after interviews, anxious to refine his notes while they were still fresh.

That was one positive thing he could accomplish: get his room changed.

But at the desk he found that there was no vacancy. Nor was there likely to be one for a week; a regional cattlemen's convention was starting on Monday, followed by a short-course seed fair. He turned away from the desk, hardly able to accept that the rooms of the Cascade Hotel could be in such incredible demand. He stood hesitant in the narrow lobby, under the eyes of five leathery old gentlemen in five leathery old arm-chairs. They stared mildly. Now that he was down here, he decided, he might as well phone the doctor Mr. Spicer had mentioned. It was not that he wanted to interview the man so much as that he must have an informed appraisal of Daddy Sherry's mental clarity. If the doctor said too much fog, that would settle it; he'd check out, drive to Calgary for a room that wasn't over a beer parlour and take the morning flight back to Toronto.

But Doctor Richardson was not expected back for at least an hour. David left his name and a request for the doctor to phone the Cascade number. When he went out of the hotel he was not sure where he was going — simply not back to the sagging and hop-scented room.

His walk took him past the Cameo Theatre again, the Elliott Implement Company, but instead of turning up Daddy Sherry's block he crossed the street and stepped over a rail barricade, fence-high. Through the thin stand of leafless trees he had caught a glimpse of water; a river bank would be as good a place as any to sit and gather his thoughts; he wanted words of just the right indignation when he stripped a yard off Earl on long distance.

The ground had risen under him; he went up and over a rough road that seemed to follow the river. This was evidently some sort of flood-control breakwater throwing a wide protective arm round the town. Down-stream he recognized the pyramid roof of the Sherry house, its tip barely reaching the level of the breakwater. A foolhardy building site, actually. He remembered Mr. Spicer's earlier reference to the flood spring of fifty-four. Between the river and the back of the cottage there could be only a thin slice of land. The river turned sharply just above the cottage and he wondered if it were nature's whim or whether the breakwater had shoved it over from its natural course.

He sat down by a slant diving-board where the river-bank sheared steeply; above him the stream rushed down a series of shallow falls, to spread itself in a wide and quiet pool.

He lit a cigarette and leaned his back against a rock. The high sky was unsullied; across the river he thought he could make out a mist of green on the trees there. Though it should have been restful, the river's hoarse murmur was disturbing; it created a subtle tension that pulled and swirled under the surface of his consciousness.

There came a plocking sound to his right; he looked downstream to a boy and a dog perhaps fifty yards away. The boy seemed busy with a bush in front of himself. He sat back and David realized that he had just rested tilted rod against a branch.

David got up and picked his way over the rocks. The dog was a massive Chesapeake, both child and dog the faded blond known as dead grass.

'Rushing the season, aren't you?'

They turned their heads deliberately towards David; blue eyes and topaz eyes measured him. Loose thunder rolled deep in the dog's chest. 'Quiet, Chief!' The growling stopped.

'Any fish stirring this early in the year?' David asked.

The boy lifted his arm and pointed to the water before himself.

David stepped to the edge and looked over. As the breeze riffling the river's surface died and his eyes adjusted, he saw them. They held undulating low over the stream's pebbled floor; now and again a silver side heliographed from the patient ranks, faintly violet-finned. Now David was remembering them from his own foothills boyhood and anew he marvelled at their tan camouflage, so perfect they seemed transparent. He stepped back. 'Grayling.'

'They're not really grayling,' the boy said seriously.

'Aren't they,' said David, who knew perfectly well that the name was a foothills misnomer.

'Rockies. Rocky Mountain whitefish. They got a snout just like an ordinary lake whitefish. I've never caught real grayling – never seen one.'

'Like a rainbow trout only with a big sail fin,' David told him. 'They fight?'

38

'About like a rainbow. They keep it up in the net after you've landed them.'

'Oh.'

'Silver and violet and razzberry like a rainbow,' David explained further. 'Their dorsal fin is light blue with polka dots that are navy blue.'

'Where'd you catch them?'

'Northern Saskatchewan – Alaska. They're only in waters that flow into the Arctic Ocean now. There used to be lots of them in these Eastern slopes streams . . .'

'I know,' the boy said. 'I heard about them. They can't stand civilization very well.'

Ever since he had growled, the dog had been sitting bolt alert, his fawn ears lifted in the umbrella fashion of Chesapeake interest, his eyes fixed on the water's surface. Now he barked sharply.

'Hey!' David pointed to the tip of the rod which had trembled to life.

'Mmm-hmh. Let him eat.'

Of course. That was the way with Rockies: a tiny hook for their small mouths and plenty of time to nibble. He should have remembered. 'What are you using?'

'Worms.'

'The frost is hardly out of the ground – where would you find . . .'

'It isn't out at all,' the boy said, 'but I got a place where I can get them.' He looked up at David rather shrewdly. 'Get them all winter if I want. I can't tell you.' He leaned forward and stealthily lifted the rod handle. He gave it a quick pull and a following lift. He was fast to the fish.

It rather surprised David – the way he played it. He had expected him to hook the fish in and up on to the bank, much as he himself had done years ago with a boy's brutal and pragmatic directness. Instead, he played it with sensitive and elastic skill, giving and gaining, keeping the bow of his rod always away from the water.

'Where's your net?' David asked as he looked about the bank.

'Don't need one.'

As it always was with whitefish, the fight was a fierce but short one and the boy was soon holding it, as it floated spent and belly-up close to the bank.

'He'll go three pounds! You lift him up and you'll tear the hook loose from his mouth,' David warned.

'Fetch!'

The blonde Chesapeake stepped gingerly into water up to his belly. Just behind the gills, tenderly, he took the fish in his jaws. He backed up out of the stream, turned and carried the flopping fish well up on the bank. There he lowered his head and laid it down. As it flipped and began to slither down the slope, he put out a broad paw and held it down.

'Well!' David said with admiration.

'He always retrieves my fish,' said the boy, busy disengaging the hook.

'You're quite a dog trainer.'

'Nope.' He hit the fish's head against a rock, dropped it into the open creel. 'I didn't train him. Friend of mine.' He began to bait his hook with a piece of worm. 'Same one figured out where to get worms any month of the year. Right in the middle of January even. It was his idea and he says there's no sense going yapping all over town so everybody can get worms and crowd us out of the best fishing-places.'

With a slow wide cast he lobbed his grayling rig far out into the pool, laid the rod up against the bush and sat down beside David again. 'I can't have a shot-gun for another year yet – I'm just eleven. It's the only retrieving he gets – besides sticks.' He laid his arm over the dog's shoulders.

'Doesn't your father hunt?'

'My father's dead.'

'Oh.'

'He died when I was only four. My friend – the one I told you about the worms – he doesn't hunt. He used to but he doesn't now.' The boy turned to David. 'He's shot everything there is to shoot on this continent.'

'Has he . . .'

'Real grayling here when he came first. And buffalo. He's shot lots of buffalo. You know how old he is?'

'He'd have to be pretty old to shoot buffalo.' This must be the boy — the one the barber had mentioned in the shop, who accompanied Daddy Sherry on his Saturday odysseys.

'He's old. He's the oldest man in the world. You know how old he is?'

'I think I do,' David said, 'You must be Keith.'

'That's right. Keith Maclean. You know Daddy?'

'I met him this afternoon. One of his bad days.'

'Mmmmmmh. If it suits him.'

'What do you mean?'

'Oh — I guess sometimes he has a bad day all right,' the boy admitted, 'but most of the time it *suits* him to have a bad day. So he has a bad day.'

'Do you think so?'

'He doesn't have them very often with me. He has them all the time around my grandmother.'

'Does he . . .'

'That's the way he gets away from people. Ones he doesn't like. He doesn't like my grandmother. He'll do it whenever he's losing an argument or he doesn't want to do something against his will. You know how it is on a part cloudy day.'

'How?'

'When the clouds slip over the sun and they — and their shadows sort of melt across underneath them?'

'Yes.'

'Way I see it — if a person could just step inside of Daddy's hide for a few minutes then that's how it would be inside of there — with the clouds sliding over and it goes kind of darker — and then the sun comes from behind the cloud and she's bright again. But that isn't having a *bad* day — is it?'

'No,' David agreed, 'I wouldn't say it was.'

'Where do you come from?'

'Montreal!'

'What did you call on Daddy for?'

'I intended doing a magazine article about him.'

'Is that hard work?'

'Most writers think so. Your rod tip's been jiggling for quite some time.'

The boy leaned forward and jerked the fishing-pole; the fish stayed with him for a moment before the line went slack. 'I better check my bait.'

The hook had been cleaned; he baited it and set it out again.

'I mentioned he didn't like my grandmother so much. That started when he came and stayed at our house for a week. I was eight. It was when Miss Tinsley had to go to Tiger Lily and help her sister have a baby. You interested in how come Daddy isn't fussy about my grandmother?'

'Yes – yes, I am.' David resisted an impulse to take the pencil and pad from his jacket pocket.

'Well – he came over with his shawl and his gold-headed cane and his night-shirt and a box of cigars. He brought these mountain sheep feet too and he got me to nail them up in our spare room so's he could hang up his gun. Daddy says you can't travel without your gun. My grandmother didn't know anything about the gun. She doesn't intend to be bossy but she is. Her and Daddy had their first argument the next morning – at breakfast. It was the porridge . . .'

Chapter 5

'What did you say, Mr. Sherry?' Mrs. Clifford turned toward the kitchen table where Daddy Sherry hunched over his bowl of porridge. She had not heard him clearly, for it was hard to predict when his mumbling warm-up would break into true speech, and often a person wasn't ready when it did happen finally.

'No salt in this mush!'

'Yes, there is,' she assured him.

'Salt-salt-salt-salt-salt . . .'

'You want the salt, Daddy?' Opposite the old man, Keith reached for the salt-shaker.

'No, Keith – I put over a teaspoon of salt in it when I made it.'

'Not so's you'd notice it,' Daddy said.

'I'm sorry it doesn't suit your taste.' She said it stiffly in a tone which indicated that she was sorry actually that Daddy had been rude enough to accuse her of not putting salt in the porridge when she *had* put salt in the porridge.

'No use bein' sorry now,' Daddy said ungraciously. 'Nothin'' that can do — 'twon't put salt into the mush now. Nothin' flatter'n mush without salt in her.' He reached for the salt-shaker but she stayed his hand.

'Too much salt isn't good for you. High blood pressure . . .'

'Ain't any reason for not puttin' *some* salt in it.'

'There *is* salt in it.'

'Now there is — now there ain't. Now she's sorry there ain't any an' now she's glad because she's got high blood press . . .'

'I haven't high blood pressure . . .'

'Then why didn't you put salt in the . . .'

'*You* have high blood pressure . . .'

'I got anything — I got *low* blood pressure.'

'Mr. Sherry!' She punched it out with such feeling that her voice broke. Keith and Daddy looked up and saw the thin line of her compressed mouth. With the force of annoyance controlled only through great effort, she spaced her words very evenly. 'Would — you — mind — eating — your — *salted* — porridge!'

The two of them bent obediently over their porridge bowls.

That evening, because of Little League practice, Keith came home late for supper. His mother had already eaten and gone into the front room to correct papers. His grandmother took his plate from the oven, returned to the stove and came back again with a cup for Daddy, who had just finished his custard dessert. 'Mr. Sherry.'

'Eh?'

'Your drink.'

Daddy shoved away his custard dish and reached for the sugar bowl.

'It already has sugar.'

'Aaaaah . . .' Elbows on the oilcloth, he bent his head down to the cup and took a long and very noisy, siphoning slurp. 'What the hell kind of sweet swill is this!'

'Mr. Sherry — what's the matt . . .'

'Cocoa.'

'Cocuh! Coffee — I want my coffee!'

'Coffee isn't good for . . .'

'Who in hell cares if it's good for you! I never et ner drank ner fought ner screwed nothin' because it was good for . . .'

'You'll watch your language in my house if you know what's good for you!' Her face had flamed right into the dark roots of her hair; Keith could not remember ever having seen her so angry. 'What's more – you'll do what's good for you – and that's that!"

Keith had a chance later in the evening to talk with his mother about it. Since his grandmother had quite likely mentioned it to her already, it wasn't as though he were *telling* on her.

'I thought coffee was just bad for kids,' he said to her.

'And old people,' she explained. 'Coffee is a stimulant – a person Mr. Sherry's age – Mother thinks he shouldn't be drinking it.' She pushed aside the foolscap sheets before her on the card table, leaned back. 'I think she's right.'

'It isn't good for him?'

'It doesn't do any of us any good.'

'You drink it – she drinks it – she drinks a lot of tea.'

'But we're not Daddy's age . . .'

'Maybe Daddy misses his cup of coffee.'

'He might – but it's better for him.'

'Gee,' Keith said, 'he's lived to be a hundred and seven – hasn't done him much harm up till now – has it?'

'Well . . .' his mother said slowly, 'it may seem a little harsh to you, but Mother isn't . . .'

'She is bossy, though.'

'Keith! That's no way to talk! You shouldn't . . .' She stopped as though at a loss just how to finish telling him what he shouldn't. 'She isn't . . .' He saw a look of indecision on her face. 'You know as well as I do that Daddy likes to do pretty well as he pleases – if he had his own way he'd drink a gallon a day – at least. He's self-indulgent and – and – do you think it would be right for him to drink a gallon of coffee a day?'

'No.'

'All right then.'

'Just a few cups.'

'Now, Son,' she put her arm round his waist and pulled him over against her, 'let's not make it any harder for Grandma than it is. She knows what she's doing. She had a long talk with Miss Tinsley. I wouldn't be surprised if this coffee business wasn't Doctor Richardson's orders – by way of Miss Tinsley.'

'Oh.'

'It really isn't any pleasure for your grandmother to insist on people's doing what's good for them.'

Thinking it over later, Keith was not too sure his mother had sounded convinced in that statement.

Daddy was up in the spare room when Keith came home from school the next day. The old man got him to take the rifle down from the cradling crook of the mountain sheep feet above the bed. He sent Keith downstairs for an old duster. He had just torn it into strips and wrapped one of them round the cleaning brush anointed with sewing-machine oil Keith had found for him, when the bedroom door opened. Engrossed in the gun cleaning, neither of them noticed it.

'Mr. Sherry – just what are you doing?'

The old man mumbled angrily.

'What are you doing with that gun!'

'Aaaaaaaahhhhh . . .' Daddy said to the breach of the rifle.

'You shouldn't be handling a gun – in the house – with that boy . . .'

'My gun,' Daddy said axiomatically.

'I didn't say it wasn't. I said what are you . . .'

'Cleanin' her – just cleanin' her.'

'Not in my house. There aren't going to be any gun-cleaning accidents in my house.'

'Accidents – accidents . . .' Daddy wheezed his long and breathy laugh. 'Only accidents outa this rifle – I *meant* 'em to be accidents. Why – I had this gun over eighty-five years.'

She held out her hand. 'You'd better let me have it.'

'Huh!'

'Give me the gun.'

Daddy slowly raised his head; for the first time since she had entered the room, he looked at her. Keith could hear the old man's breath singing through his nose; just outside the window a pigeon in the eaves took up its hiccup lament. Daddy's hand was trembling on the stock of the gun. Daddy said, 'No.'

'What did you say?' She knew quite well what he had said; it was not intended as a question at all.

'I said no. Ain't your gun. My gun. You can't have it.'

'I only – I don't want it . . .'

'You said give it to you.'

'Of course I did.'

'But you don't want it.'

'Not permanently – I don't want to keep it. I know it's your gun. I simply don't want anyone fooling around with a gun in my house.'

'Ain't loaded.'

'That isn't the point.'

'Just oilin' her up.'

'I think that can wait until you're back in your own house.' She had not lowered the outstretched and demanding hand.

'No, it can't,' Daddy said stubbornly. 'Got to keep her clean. Somethin' can't wait. Clean your gun right away. I don't want the barr'l all fouled an' leaded up.'

'You haven't used it for years so how could it . . .'

'Take care of your gun an' your gun'll take care of you. Why – I've killed – I don't know how many elk an' antelope – moose an' deer an' buffalo I knocked over with this here . . .'

'I'm sure you have. That's all I intend you to kill with it.'

'Hah!'

'People are always accidentally killed with unloaded guns.'

'No, they aren't,' Daddy said reasonably enough, 'lots of 'em are killed with loaded guns.'

'I'll take good care of it.'

'Why – I know this here gun like I know my own right arm.' Daddy looked up to her again. 'Why don't you ask for my right arm?'

'Because your right arm isn't likely to discharge accidentally – all right, Mr. Sherry – the gun – please . . .'

'Aaaah . . .' Daddy said.

47

'Mr. Sherry.'

'Ooooooh . . .' Daddy went on in more detail.

'It won't do you any good, Mr. Sherry – I want that gun.'

'Now?'

'Now.'

Daddy's breath released in a long sigh. 'Ain't fair.'

'It's safer.'

Daddy sighed again and Keith was suddenly saddened with the hollow and helpless sadness he had known the twenty-fourth of May sports day when Tiger Lily had beaten Shelby in the bottom of the ninth.

'I'll put it away for you,' his grandmother was saying and Keith knew that she knew that she had won.

'Where?'

'You can have it when Miss Tinsley comes back and you're in your own home.'

'Thanks,' said Daddy bitterly.

At supper she was quite friendly and solicitous towards the old man; Keith recognized the warmth as the charitable softening of victor toward vanquished. In the evening when he played cribbage with Daddy on the kitchen table he played deliberately badly so that Daddy won almost every game. The old man remained subdued.

At their last game his grandmother said, 'When you've finished this – bed, Keith.' She set a steaming cup before him.

'All right,' Keith said. He lifted the cup of cocoa to his mouth, the marshmallow within bobbing against his nose.

'Well past nine o'clock,' Mrs. Clifford observed.

'Is it,' Daddy said.

'We all need our sleep,' she said heartily. 'Young,' and then with more emphasis, 'and old.'

'Sure – sure,' Daddy said indifferently. 'You dangle off upstairs if you're tired.'

'I didn't mean myself.' She turned back to the stove.

'I'll just set here,' Daddy said.

'Half-past nine,' she reminded as she poured him a cup.

'What of it.'

'Miss Tinsley said you were to be in bed and asleep by . . .'

'I never go to bed before midnight – an' then only if I feel like it.'

'You know that's not right, Mr. Sherry. Miss Tinsley said . . .'

'Miss Tinsley said – Miss Tinsley said . . .' Daddy mimicked her. 'Miss Tinsley is a goddam liar!'

'Mr. Sherry!'

'Sure she is. She lies all the time.'

'She does not! You stop that! Shame on you talking about Miss Tinsley like that . . .'

'An' that ain't all she does . . .'

'That's enough!' Keith's grandmother set Daddy's cup on the table so hard it sloshed into the saucer.

'. . . smokes my Senate House cigars . . . they cost . . .'

'Not another word!'

'How come they keep disappearing if she doesn't . . .'

'She's just trying to keep you from ruining your health by over-indulging . . .'

'All right,' Daddy almost whimpered. 'Take advantage of a old man. Make him do what *you* want – take away his coffee – hide his rifle . . .'

'Now, Mr. Sherry . . .'

'Packin' him off to bed when he's still wide awake – don't give a whoop for his feelin's. Go on an' be selfish an' . . .'

'That doesn't sound like you, Mr. Sherry – you know it.'

'Doesn't, eh?'

'No, it doesn't.' Keith felt that his grandmother was not so much annoyed as she was disappointed. 'You're not a very good whiner. There's your drink. Nice and hot.'

Daddy slurped. He put his head back and emitted a scream of anguish, as though he had scalded the roof of his mouth right through, Keith thought. 'What the hell did you do to this cocuh!'

Even though Daddy had sworn, Keith's grandmother smiled gently. 'It's not cocoa, Mr. Sherry. Coffee.'

'Coffee! You know I ain't sposed to drink coffee! Doctor Richardson's orders! Bad for me!'

'I felt that – in moderation – now and again – it might be all right for you to have a cup . . .'

'Coffee – cocuh – coffee – cocuh – make up your mind,

woman! On agin – off agin! You got me all set for cocuh then stick to cocuh! Make her one thing or the other!' He lifted the cup in both hands, drank, set it down. 'I like cocuh.'

When Keith had come home from Sunday School the next day and had changed his clothes, he helped a shawled Daddy through the back yard to the garage. Daddy sighed as he lowered himself to sitting position against the wall.

'South side's warmest,' he said as Keith sat down beside him.

They sat in silence until Daddy said, 'Sure – sure – I used to be a kid – long time ago – long, long time ago.'

'Mmm-hmh,' Keith said.

'It was all right.'

'What was?'

'Bein' a kid. That was one end of her. Now I guess I got holt of the other end.'

'Bein' old,' Keith said.

'Yeh-yeh-yeh-yeh – older'n hell. That's what I managed to be – old.'

Keith picked up a sliver of split shingle, drew with it idly in the dust at his feet.

'Wasn't what I started out to be though – just old. Know what I started out to be?'

'What?'

'Acerobat. When I was the age of you – seen a circus – then I was gonna be an acerobat.'

'Clown one?'

'Nope. Flyin'. In tights.'

'Oh.'

'Swingin' – loopin' the loop acerobat.' Daddy spit and the dust grabbed it and balled it. 'Too late,' he said sadly. 'Too late. Hundred an' seven like I am. Brittle – bones is brittle now. Don't ever hear of any acerobats a hundred an' seven years old.'

'No.' Keith could accept that. 'I guess you don't.'

'You be one,' Daddy said fiercely .'Be a good one.'

'I don't know,' Keith said.

'Don't you like acerobatics?'

'Sure – sure I do, but I figure I'd like to do it just in my spare time.'

50

'Flyin' acerobatics.'

'Uh-huh. Gruff Bailey and I had a lot of fun out of it this spring.'

'Where — where?'

'Bailey's barn — the loft — we put up a trapeze there — hung on ropes from the joist — we made the bar out of a broomstick.'

'Yeh-yeh-yeh-yeh!'

'You got to get up on the south end where the hay's piled high an' then you swing out over . . .'

'Let's go over there!'

'Huh!' Not till now had Keith noticed the excitement on the old man's face. 'Hold on, Daddy, we couldn't . . .'

'Sure — sure!' The old man was already struggling to get his feet under himself; as he grabbed Keith's arm for support he caught a painful pinch of under-arm flesh.

'But, Daddy — to get up to the loft — it's a ladder — just a ladder straight up and through a hole . . .'

'I can climb a ladder.'

'Not this one you can't! Gruff and I have trouble because when you get your elbows through the hole your feet can't reach and they swing and you have to give a hump to get yourself . . .'

'Swing — swing — swing,' Daddy sang, 'swing out an' loop the loop — summersault through thin air — no — double — triple summersault . . .'

'Daddy — Daddy!' Keith could taste the panic in his throat.

'Don't squeal.'

'I'm not squealing!' Keith squealed.

'Can you do a double summersault?'

'We practised all summer and I can't even do a single summersault. You can't . . .'

'All I want to do is try her — just grab holt of her — just take a nice gentle swing out over . . .'

'You'll kill yourself!'

'. . . the soft hay — then back an' out agin — couple times — just to get the feel of her — an' then . . .'

'You can't!'

'Sure I can.'

'You'd get hurt – bad – I – I won't take you – you don't even know where Bailey's barn is!'

'Oh.' It was quite gentle, but Daddy's pale eyes were not. 'So that's how it is.'

'I don't know what you . . .'

'You know well enough. That's the side you're on.'

'I'm not on any side!'

'Yes, you are. Ain't on *my* side. On *her* side.'

'No, I'm not, Daddy.'

'Might of known you'd be on her side – helpin' her. All right – aaaaalll right – I thought you was my friend.'

'I am your friend, Daddy!'

'. . . now I know. Not any more you aren't.'

'Sure,' Keith said, 'sure I am!'

'Prove it.'

'Prove it?'

'Let's go to Bailey's barn.'

'We can't . . .'

'See – see – that'd prove it – but oh no – you won't . . .'

'There's lots of ways to prove you're somebody's friend without lettin' them kill theirselves on a trapeze.'

'Maybe there is,' Daddy agreed.

'Sure there is – sure there is.'

'Mmm-hmh.' Daddy took a pinch of lip between thumb and forefinger, 'I guess there is at that.' His gaze was a considering one, neither friendly nor unfriendly – a monkey faulting strange fruit. Suddenly he cracked it out. 'Where'd she hide my rifle?'

The breath-taking shift in tactics caught Keith open-mouthed. 'Why – I – I'm not sure . . .'

'You know where she hid it,' Daddy accused him. 'Don't you?'

'Well – I – I know where she'd *likely* . . .'

'See – see – won't even tell me where it's hid – my own personal property – my own personal gun . . .'

'But if she doesn't figure it's safe for you to have . . .'

'Her side,' Daddy said with bitter sadness. 'I give you an easier way to prove you ain't on her side and . . .'

52

'But Daddy, it isn't fair for you to . . .'

'In the cellar?' Daddy waited. 'In the attic?' He waited again. 'Back porch? Front? Behind the pianah? Under her bed? Your ma's? Sink – kitchen stove – laundry basket – dumb waiter – clothes chute – vegetable bin – china cabinet – bookcase – preserve shelf . . .'

Long before the old man had exhausted possible hiding-places, Keith's resolve not to tell him had strengthened; he recognized Daddy's cold-blooded calculation, realized how shallow the denial of friendship had been. When Daddy refused his arm back to the house, it did not sadden the boy. He tried to bring the old man out of his sulk.

'What'll we do for fun, Daddy?'

'Nothin'.'

'Game checkers, Daddy? Cribbage? Parchesi?'

'Nope.'

'There's a bunch of magpies down behind the Co-Op elevator – we could take the bee-bee gun – go down there an' touch off some magpies . . .' He waited for Daddy to say he'd be delighted to touch off some magpies. 'Get a nickel a pair for their feet.'

The old man shook his head impatiently.

'Snare some gophers. That'd be fun,' he said with false enthusiasm. 'Snare some gophers. I got some copper snare wire . . .'

'Nope!'

'Why not, Daddy? We could have a lot of fun . . .'

'I don't wanta shoot magpies with no bee-bee gun. Ner snare gophers . . .'

'What do you want to do?'

'Go up on that trapeze.'

'We can't, Daddy.'

'Yeah – yeah,' Daddy agreed. 'I know – she won't let us.'

'Anything else, Daddy – anything else you'd like to . . .'

'Yep,' Daddy said.

'What?'

'I'd like to get that old rifle mine wherever she's hid it an' go out an' shoot some buffalo.'

'Oh,' Keith said. Like China, Daddy dissolved his conquerors.

'But she won't let me have my rifle,' Daddy was saying un-emotionally. 'And you won't help me by telling where she's got it hid . . .'

'And there aren't any buffalo,' Keith said reasonably.

'You been out after buffalo lately?'

'No – I . . .'

'Then don't talk foolish. You don't go *lookin'* for buffalo – ain't likely you'll *see* buffalo.'

'They're all gone now, Daddy.'

'That's a poor excuse. Fall comin' on . . .' Daddy's voice went under his breath, continuing as a breathy gum mumble. 'Fall comin' on – bet she ain't got a crumb of pemmican laid up against winter!'

'How could she?'

'Not a crumb,' Daddy said with disgust. 'Has she?'

'Has she what?'

'Pemmican. She ain't got any.'

'Of course she hasn't,' Keith said. 'Nobody can make pemmican any more because there isn't any . . .'

'Like I thought. Just like I thought.'

'But, Daddy, without buffalo meat you can't have pemmican . . .'

'That's right. You're real right, boy. So what does she do? Takes the gun. Keeps the gun. Hides the gun. She think she's gonna shoot some buffalo?'

'No,'

'Dog in the manger,' Daddy said. 'Ain't gonna shoot none herself an' she won't let anybody else shoot 'em – that can – not a sliver of meat for pemmican an' fall on top of us an' a long hard winter comin' on – we'll all starve to death.' He fell silent and Keith was at a loss for anything to say. 'Hope she does.'

'Does what?'

'Starve to death. Serve her right.'

'Oh.'

'Berries.'

'Huh!'

'She ain't even got her berries, has she?'

'What berries?'

'Saskatoons. Saskatoon berries for to pound up with the dried meat for the pemmican.'

'Oh.' It was best just to let him drift.

'No meat. No berries. We got a long hard gant winter ahead of us, boy.'

'Yes,' Keith agreed. 'I guess we have.'

'Unless . . .' Daddy leaned across the table and took Keith's arm, 'unless you tell me where she's hid my gun. All the signs point to a hard winter. Early. You'll starve too, boy. Not a berry picked . . . yet . . .'

'Daddy!'

'Eh?'

'That's what we better do – we got to have berries . . .'

'Yeah – yeh!'

'Like you said – can't have pemmican without berries – we can go picking berries.'

Keith heard him suck in his breath. The old man was looking at him in a strangely familiar way. Then Keith remembered the game of checkers in which he'd beaten Daddy before Daddy had even one checker crowned.

'All right,' Daddy said rather unenthusiastically.

'They'll be hanging thick and purple all along Haggerty's coulee . . .'

'I guess they will.'

'We'll tell Grandma . . .'

'Don't tell her nothin'!'

'We got to. She'll let us. She'll be pleased to have us pick a bunch of saskatoons – for – for – for pemmican!'

And Mrs. Clifford had been.

'A wonderful idea,' she said. 'I can bake some pies . . .'

'Pies! Pemmican!' Daddy said.

'What!'

'Daddy's real worried,' Keith hurried to explain. 'We haven't got any pemmican for winter – he said we didn't have any buffalo meat . . .'

'Buffalo meat!'

'. . . or – or saskatoons to pound up for pemmican.'

Keith wished that his grandmother caught onto things more quickly. 'He wants his gun back so we can – so he – so I suggested maybe he and I could go getting some saskatoons instead of going buffalo . . .'

'I see,' she said.

'I'm – I'm doing my best, Grandma.'

'All right, Keith.'

'Well – is berry-picking all right? Can we . . .'

'Of course it is. You can take the enamel pail under the sink – there's a lard pail . . .'

'We figured Haggerty's coulee . . .'

'Oh no – it's too far for . . .'

'Haggerty's is best for saskatoons,' Daddy said. 'They'll be thick there . . .'

'I'm afraid it's too far – the banks are high and steep.'

'I am going berry-picking in Haggerty's coulee,' Daddy announced.

'Mrs. Kelly was telling me they're thick behind the power house and that's only three blocks . . .'

'Naah – Haggerty's coulee . . .'

'And the choke-cherries are hanging in clusters there,' explained the grandmother.

'Don't want choke-cherries – saskatoons . . .'

'She said the pin-cherries . . .'

'Pin-cherries is no good for pemmican.'

'Pin-cherry jelly is lovely – choke-cherry jelly . . .'

'Aaaaall pit an' no flesh – got to have Haggerty's coulee saskatoons.'

'Mr. Sherry, if you're going berry-picking at all it will be close to home and not along seventy-foot cut banks out at Haggerty's coulee!'

Daddy shrugged, and Keith had the feeling that the old man hadn't at any time given a whoop whether he picked his berries along Haggerty's coulee, or not.

Daddy had been right. There were very few saskatoons in the brush behind the power house. The choke-cherry crop was staggering. Keith had just to run a hand down a cluster and a cup full of the black fruit would drop into the pail. He had never admitted to other boys that he delighted in picking berries – the mesmerizing and vibrant stillness of an enclosing stand of high bushes with a late August sun streaming through dusty leaves tapping in a light breeze – encouraged the magic release of imagination. It was not too hard to believe that one was picking a harvest of berries for the winter's supply of pemmican – to take back to a Red River fort where bright-sashed Métis had just returned from a wild prairie buffalo hunt – where the flashing-eyed Louis Riel, the rebel leader, plotted with the villainous Dumont to take the country and hand it over to the United States. . . .

He realized that it had been some time since he had heard the rattle of berries on the other side of the thick and tangled choke-cherry bushes. He had not heard the crackle of underbrush or the sigh of branches as Daddy pulled them down.

'Daddy.'

There was only the peremptory knock of a woodpecker high in a near-by tree. A crow fled cawing.

'Daddy – hey, Daddy!'

He started to go through the bushes but they resisted him. He ran round the end of the clump of choke-cherries. Daddy's red lard pail lay empty on the ground.

'He's not down there, Mother – I looked all through there. I covered every inch of it!'

'Oh, Keith. Grandma only let you go because she thought you'd keep an eye on him!'

'He was stubborn about going to Haggerty's coulee,' Keith's grandmother said.

'No – I went straight to the rise round the power house and you can see clear to Haggerty's from there and I couldn't see him. It's all open and I didn't see him headed for Haggerty's!'

'Then he's down town,' the grandmother said – 'or perhaps he came home and slipped up to his room.'

'No,' said Keith's mother. 'I would have heard him if he had.

Perhaps his own house. Keith — you go over there. I'll phone down town — the barber shop — the Bluebird Café — '

'Sometimes he drops in Seeley's Blacksmith shop,' Keith said — 'or to the express office — the Cascade Beer . . .'

'I'll try them all,' his mother said. 'You get over to his house.'

But Daddy's house was empty. On his way back Keith thought of Bailey's barn. He found his mother and grandmother truly disturbed when he got home, for none of the down-town people his mother had phoned had seen Daddy. It was pretty evident that the old man had not gone to the business section.

'Bailey's barn,' Keith blurted.

'What about it?' his mother asked him.

Keith explained about the trapeze — Daddy's interest in flying acrobatics.

'Oh, no!' his mother exclaimed. 'He was only — he didn't really mean it — it was just a way to get you to — he wouldn't!'

'He only half meant it, I think,' Keith said.

'Half's enough,' his mother said.

'Mother — keep on the phone — any other places you can think of — try Len's Harness and — and — the beer parlour again — '

Keith and his mother hurried breathlessly the four blocks and as they turned into Bailey's back yard Keith said, 'He didn't know where it was, Mother — I wouldn't tell him.'

'I'm afraid that wouldn't stop him long,' his mother said. 'He'd simply get directions from the first person he met!'

They stepped into the barn's dusk, hospitable with the ammonia tinct of manure and the sweet musk of hay. They went past the fat rump of Gruff Bailey's pinto.

'The end,' Keith said, 'where the box stall is!'

At the bottom of the ladder nailed to the stall front, Keith stooped. He turned back to his mother and held out the cane he had picked up there. They heard Daddy then, his quavering voice ethereal above their heads, hollowed by the hayloft.

"Daddy — Daddy!" Keith's mother called as she went up the ladder.

'Lay-dees an' gentlemen! You are about to witness for thee first time on thee earth – thee death-defyin' reeverse triple summersault thu-rugh thin air . . .'

He was already at the south end, high on the hay piled almost to the peak of the barn roof, dusty light limning him against the window there. He held the broomstick trapeze bar in both hands before himself.

'Please, Daddy – please!' Keith's mother pleaded, as with knees high she plunged over the loose hay towards him. 'Get down from there – no – no – stay right there till we get – ' She pitched forward, suddenly snatched from below to her hips in hay.

'. . . without the aid or pertection of safety nets – by thee world's most ay-gile an' sooplè an' gu-raceful . . .'

'Get to him – oh, get to him, Keith – grab him!'

She struggled to free herself from the embrace of hay and rotten boards.

'. . . swingin' acerobat of them aaaaaallll! The guy wires is twangin' – Alfredo dela Monterey dela Sherry now stan's a hunderd an' fifty foot up! . . .'

With his mother's beseeching cries behind him Keith scrambled on hands and knees at the slippery side of the hay mound; he'd had dreams like this when he fled a horrible unknown, terror-stricken, on rubber legs moving with swooning slowness while the horror closed in on him.

'. . . ay-bout to take death fearlessly by thee face – ay-bout to risk life an' limb.' High above his head, Daddy lifted the broomstick bar up and back. He dropped his voice and said conversationally, Are yuh quite ready, Mr. Sherry – y'are – aaaaall right then – beeegin your swing an' let her rip!'

He took off, drawing up his legs under himself that they might clear the hay.

Even as he swung, Keith's mother called out, 'Grab him, son! His legs – his knees – grab! . . .'

But Keith, who had just achieved the top of the mound, had not time even to put out his arms. The Sherry arc brought bony knees and the full weight of Daddy's swinging body precisely to his bread basket. Gasping for breath, Keith went over backwards, rolling to the loft floor where he lay spread-eagled, unable to move, to breathe, numb with pain and nausea. He was still on his back when he vomited, throwing his lunch and every single choke-cherry he'd eaten while picking berries, straight up for almost eight feet. As he got up he was only dimly aware of his mother, her arm round Daddy's waist, sleighing down the side of the hay. He was not at all interested in the rescue of Alfredo dela Monterey dela Sherry.

Not until they had got home did the nausea leave him; and even then his solar plexus was still tender to touch. Daddy was quite expansive when Mrs. Clifford met them at the door.

'Figure you're so smart.'

Keith's mother explained to his grandmother what had happened in Bailey's loft.

'Figured you beat me out,' Daddy said.

'No,' Keith's grandmother said in a chastened tone. 'No – I don't – at all. . . .'

'Can't watch me twenty-four hours a day,' Daddy said with relish.

'I know we can't.'

'I'll still be with you another five whole days.'

Keith saw his grandmother look helplessly over to his mother. 'I'm afraid you will, Daddy,' his mother said.

'Certain things is goin' to get changed around here,' he said meaningfully.

Keith's grandmother cleared her throat. 'What things?'

'Coffee – whenever I feel like it – understand?'

His grandmother said nothing.

'An' I go to bed when I feel like it – not a minute before. Maybe – if it suits me – stay up aaaaallll night.'

For a moment Keith thought his grandmother was going to fight back, but his mother slowly shook her head.

'. . . or else – ' Daddy said menacingly, 'you know what I'll do to you? I'll go up on that trapeze – first chance I get – an' I'll break every goddam glass bone in my body.' His cold blue eyes were steady on her face. 'Also — I get my rifle back.'

'No!' It was stung from her. 'As long as you . . .'

'Just a moment, Mother.' Keith's mother turned to Daddy. 'Let's be reasonable, Daddy — everything but the gun.'

'Aaaah . . . I'll think it over,' Daddy said. 'I'll think it over.'

Chapter 6

By the time the boy had told David why Daddy Sherry did not like his grandmother, the April afternoon had lost most of its shallow warmth. A small flight of mallards whispered low over the trees, bowed their wings and tipping crazily, splashed to a landing just down-stream.

'I got to go.' He hesitated, with the full creel in his hand. 'You been wondering where a person could get worms this early?'

'Yes,' David admitted, 'I have.'

'Well – you being from out of town maybe it would be all right if I told you – in case you wanted to fish some while you're here.'

'I just might.'

'Simple once you know,' he explained. 'Mr. Pringle – the earth under his greenhouse tables never gets a chance to freeze so it's just crawling with worms. They're good in a garden but I guess they're not so good in a greenhouse, so Mr. Pringle doesn't mind.'

'If I do any fishing I'll certainly call on Mr. Pringle,' David promised.

'Pretty smart of Daddy to figure that out, wasn't it?'

David agreed that it was.

'He said there wasn't anything to it – undertakers and worms generally go together. If you're talking to him . . .'

'Mr. Pringle?'

'No – Daddy – don't say anything about how you found out.'

'I won't.'

So his first day had not been a loss after all. Far from it! He could hardly believe now that he had been on the point of phoning Earl an hour ago that he had made up his mind to take the morning flight back to Toronto. He *must* be getting soft to have let one abominable meal and an unsatisfactory hotel room discourage him so!

Even the two veal cutlets that the Bluebird Café chef had breaded in janitor's sweeping compound did not dampen his enthusiasm. There was a message for him at the hotel desk. Dr. Richardson had phoned, would be by to see him at seven-thirty.

'When he calls, send him up,' David said as he turned toward the stairs.

He had finished a nostalgic piece for his column on grayling fishing, had just started on Sherry notes when there came a knock at the door. A prematurely white-haired man in his late fifties, Dr. Richardson explained that he had called a half hour early because there was a Daddy Sherry Anniversary meeting scheduled for eight at the Community Centre. This way he and David could have an hour to chat about Daddy and then, if David liked, they could go together to the meeting. He did not feel it too soon after dinner for a drink. Judging by the ruddy complexion and the spare brown hand that accepted a glass of Scotch and water, David decided that the doctor must spend a lot of time outdoors. He guessed too that he was a successful general practitioner, for he had the relaxed assurance that belongs to a man happy in his profession and certain of respect in his community. In a very few minutes David sensed warmth and sensitive understanding in the doctor; he was probably at his best with child – maternity – and elderly lady patients. Also he was quite direct.

'You've wondered,' he said, 'if I've an explanation for Mr. Sherry's great age.'

'I have,' David admitted.

'Well . . .' the doctor pursed his lips, 'though I've given it quite a bit of thought, I don't know whether I can help you very much. In the life of a human being there are two things to – to consider.'

'Yes?'

'Ageing – in anyone – is a – a – continuum that starts at conception and ends at death. Daddy Sherry's life – the length of it – must have been determined by the germ plasm from which he started. You could say he started out with an original energy charge – an unusually strong one – which has been gradually weakening ever since May seventeenth 1849 – or rather nine months before that when fertilization took place.' The doctor lifted his drink – lowered it. 'What an egg!'

'I agree,' David said heartily, 'but you said *two* things.'

'Environmental influence to which he's been exposed. Obviously there's been a great deal of luck in his achieving a hundred and eleven – he's side-stepped cholera – typhoid – smallpox before vaccination was common.'

'He's been luckier than every other one of the millions of humans born in 1849,' David observed.

'In the beginning or since? Where was the deciding luck? Was it the original inborn strength – largely – or has it been determined by the unique environment of his lifetime?'

'Same old conundrum – what makes the buttonhole – the hole or the cloth round the hole. Answer has to be – both – doesn't it?'

'Whatever it is – it's important to all of us – no matter how good an inheritance we have – how lucky our environment may have been, we can all be sure of one thing – if we don't die early we're all destined to grow old and ultimately die.'

'No argument with you there,' David said.

'Trick is – to put it off as long as possible.'

'Not for everybody, is it?' David said.

'Pretty nearly.'

'I'm not anxious to attain extreme age. Helpless – chronically ill . . .'

The doctor shook his head. 'Doesn't have to be that way. It is for a lot of people – too many – but physiological ageing in later life is normal – just as normal as growth and development earlier – it's not necessarily a time of discomfort and pain *because* of old age.'

'Old age shouldn't be blamed?' David was surprised. 'I thought there were certain failures . . .'

'Oh yes – decrease in rate of metabolism – ability to store and use glucose – alkali reserve of the blood. The colloids age and there's progressive dehydration – weakening of digestive secretions.'

'You *expect* these in old age.'

'Along with loss in height and weight,' the doctor explained. 'Osteoporosis of bone – cartilaginous atrophy. But the important thing – to come back – it's – well – the tempo.'

'Mr. Sherry's tempo?'

'Slow – and consistent – everywhere.'

'Everywhere?'

'In some persons the process of senescence of some organs begins astonishingly early – the eyes may show signs of early ageing but the circulatory system may be spared. The calendar doesn't mean a damn. I've examined forty-year-old men with eighty-year-old hearts. People haven't one age at all – actually it should be stated like a woman's bust-waist-hip measurements – thirty-sixty-twenty.'

'Quite a woman.'

'No – I mean it as a man's respiratory-circulatory-alimentary age. He has an endocrine age – a locomotor age – nervous. Longevity depends on which one reaches the finish line first.'

'Which one generally does?' David asked him.

'Heart – I guess. Atrophy of the heart normally begins between the ages of sixty to sixty-five years. It's the final arbiter of life.'

'How's Mr. Sherry's?'

'Has a tendency for premature beats – not important. I look

at him now and compare him to what I remember thirty years ago – I know his heart's perhaps fifty grams smaller – the extremely aged have very small hearts. I suppose his heart has increased supercardial fat – more rigidity – less accurate closing of the valves. It has lost some of its ability to consume oxygen. He doesn't have a hundred-and-eleven-year-old heart.'

'Eighty?' David suggested.

'Closer to seventy.'

'Where is he in other departments? What about his hearing – his sight?'

'Well,' the doctor said, 'he does have parosmia.'

'What's that?'

'It's a form of senile atrophy and generally it's distressing. The olfactory nerve ends have been injured through infections earlier in life – the patient interprets in terms of smell – it can be taste too – anosmia – '

'But with Mr. Sherry it's smell.'

'Yes.'

'Just how does it distress him?'

'It doesn't – most cases it does – patient is harried by an unpleasant odour – smell of burning feathers – decay. I once had a man who complained of smelling horse urine. You can't get them to accept that it's subjective – especially if they wear false teeth. I did think I'd convinced this patient, only to have him ask me a week later to recommend a denture cleaner without ammonia in it.'

'But you say with Mr. Sherry the – the illusion isn't unpleasant.'

'He's quite delighted with it – say it's sometimes stronger than other times – it comes and goes – smell of wolf willow. And you know it is a lovely scent – if you're familiar with the foothills . . .'

'I am.'

'Late July – early August – the air along a creek bank is perfumed with it . . .'

'Honey,' David said.

'Mmm-hmh.'

'What about his sight?'

'His eyes aren't *young* eyes. He has complained of floating spots before them – I've examined them and there are stringy opacities there.'

'What causes that?'

'Senile disintegration of the fibrous networks of the vitreous – lost its gel characteristics – oh, forgive me – doctors, lawyers, sociologists – we have a weakness for our trade terms. He has spots before his eyes – but he sees perfectly well.'

'And his hearing?'

'Oh – contracted perception for high tones – and a slightly diminished acuity for all tones – but not a great deal. That's why he speaks loudly – he hears his own voice less clearly than you or I would.'

'Then his senses aren't really impaired at all . . .'

'No. He complains that his legs feel stiff and heavy – that's common in old age.'

'Is it?'

'Yes – tendon reflexes diminished slightly. He has sensations of cold too – but it's not an objective sensory change. Altogether he's in pretty fine shape. I think you'll agree after you've met him.'

'I have,' David said, 'I called on him this afternoon but I didn't make out too well. It was one of his bad days.'

'Oh – yes – '

'Didn't strike me that he was particularly clear – mentally – would you say that he – that his mind was – well – sound?'

'I think so. Yes. He shows some functional signs of his age – no more than I'd expect.'

'He kept drifting back on me . . .'

'Mary Jane and that bloody lantern?'

'Yes,' David said, 'and a shocking recipe for fur-trade firewater.'

'One mouthful per beaver pelt . . .'

'Buffalo.'

'He does have periods when he's – less in touch,' the doctor agreed. 'He hasn't dropped a crumb of the past though the immediate present may give him trouble. He forgets where he's put things – sometimes has difficulty remembering a name or a face. I have patients in their sixties just about the same as he is in that regard. He doesn't show any signs of the usual senile psychoses or neuroses. I suspect he steps at will into the past – might even be a form of adjustment for him. His personality may have lost some of its elasticity. I'd say that most of his life he's been an exceptionally well integrated personality – a sound man then and for the most part a pretty sound man now.'

'Except for his bad days.'

'Even on his bad days – he has a sort of logic. There's irrelevancy and incoherence but no ideas of persecution – isn't depressed or agitated – no feelings of sinfulness or guilt. I don't suppose he's felt guilty or deeply regretted anything in his hundred and eleven years of life. He's more irritable on these days – may have a temper tantrum – more obstinate – but my guess is that he's always been a man of strong emotions – staggering determination – never suffered fools gladly. He sleeps soundly and regularly – doesn't wander – he's fascinated with his bodily functions – excretory organs – state of his digestion. He attributes his long life to buttermilk, pigweed greens and potatoes.'

'I believe he mentioned them this afternoon.'

'You know, it's remarkable how naturally old people drift to the things that make for their continued life and health.'

'You mean he's right about his buttermilk and pigweed greens?'

'Oh – I don't know about that – but he gets gentle exercise – keeps his bowels open – enjoys the stimulant of a glass of whiskey now and then.'

'Keeps out of draughts.'

'That's right.'

'And you consider him quite sound.'

'Yes,' the doctor said without any hesitation. 'Expediency is behind a lot of his bad days – much of his eccentric behaviour – well – perhaps it's simply because he's Daddy Sherry.'

'Would you say his judgment was unimpaired?'

'I've had doubts on a few occasions. Ten or twelve years ago when he was in his late nineties – perhaps ninety-eight – there was a woman.'

'Was there!'

'The housekeeper before Miss Tinsley – a pretty hard and nasty – ah – package. She was shrewd – she didn't have to be to know that Daddy was a wealthy man . . .'

'Is he?'

'Oh, yes. He's owned land and he's lived long enough to see its value rocket.'

'Oil?'

'And urban development. This woman – I forget her name but Donald Finlay can tell you – it's hard to say whether she proposed or Daddy did.'

'He seriously contemplated marriage at ninety-eight!'

The doctor nodded. 'She did. And he did eventually. Donald Finlay was supposed to marry them. He bailed Daddy out in an eleventh-hour rescue. I was on holidays.' He looked at his watch. 'Donald Finlay's your man. Talk to him about that.'

'I will,' David promised.

'We have time just to make that meeting,' the doctor said.

David had anticipated a light and informal gathering of a few, so that he was not prepared for a spacious hall half filled with people. Quite obviously the attendance had exceeded expectation, for when he and the doctor arrived several men were busy unstacking, unfolding and setting out extra chairs. There must be more than delegates from local groups, for no community the size of Shelby would likely boast a hundred and fifty clubs and organizations.

He was surprised at the number of young people – in their teens – till he realized that they would have come from school and church and recreational groups. He sat in an aisle seat with Doctor Richardson, wondering at the undertone of seriousness the gathering possessed: little chatter, no laughter, subdued with wake-sad earnestness. The meeting was opened by the Reverend Finlay who spoke briefly of their purpose in gathering: to elect the heads of committees for the Daddy Sherry Anniversary

Celebration. It had been decided, he explained, that there should be a general council of representational delegates from all the town and municipality groups and organizations. If this was agreeable to the meeting, those representatives sent by their groups could consider themselves automatically members of that council. It was agreeable to the meeting.

Mr. Finlay went on to explain that such a council would be unwieldy, that the actual work would be done by the special committee heads and their groups. Six such committee heads were to be elected tonight: for the Programme Committee, the Gift Committee, the Finance Committee, the Publicity Committee, the Catering Committee and the Correspondence Committee.

Several Indians in unpressed blue serge suits and sharp-toed riding boots, poppy-bright kerchiefs at their necks, had come smoothly down the aisle and seated themselves before David. The cigarish smell of buckskin and camp-fire smoke that drifted back to him reminded him of a ceremony he had once covered on an Eastern reserve, when Mohawk chiefs had inducted a jowled Minister of Finance into their tribe. He could hear again the drums and the wolf-wild soprano of the chiefs' dance punctuated by the violent sneezes of the Cabinet Minister, a former Bay Street broker who had not known before the ritual that he had a plus eight allergy to the eagle down of his new head-dress.

For this civilized community Daddy Sherry must almost have the set-apart magic of a tribal shaman; in him reposed the extra spiritual power of the witches of old. No wonder they were traditionally old, David thought, for their age was just more proof of their special power over the immutable laws of death.

As nominations went on, people one by one rose here and there throughout the hall to address the meeting in the stilted clichés that dissolved tender individualities publicly exposed. They encased an old man's birthday party plans in stiff ceremony, raising right arms in unison to signify their approval of Title Jack Dalgliesh for the head of the Finance Committee, Mr. Spicer for the Gift Committee, Florence Allerdyce as High Priestess of the Catering Committee. These people, David thought, had ceased to be their empirical selves; they were transcendent as symbols in a physics formula and E was an autumn stalk of a man lying on a mahogany bed in a brown shingled cottage blocks away. Yet he could not have been more in the centre of the ritual if he had been up on the stage.

David had the feeling that he was in touch with something old and elemental; all shared a synthesizing insight such as drops over a congregation at the taking of communion or holy sacrament; all made their obeisance to the eternal ancestors of a mythological past when man was ageless; they planned a party for Methuselah.

He had assumed that the meeting would take an hour, yet it was well past eleven when he and Doctor Richardson left the community centre. The doctor drove him to the hotel.

'Will you come up for another drink?' David invited him.

The doctor considered barely a moment. 'Yes. I'll just leave word with Central to call me at the desk. I have a pending maternity case at the hospital,' he explained, 'which would have got me up some time between two and four anyway.'

In David's room he accepted his glass. 'I feel as though I'm taking this under false pretences.'

'Oh – no – you've been a great help,' David assured him.

'Not really – a few physiological facts – vague senescent generalities . . .'

'One of the traps I have to set.'

'Daddy Sherry won't be trapped that way,' the doctor said with conviction. 'Do you hunt at all?'

'No.'

'But you did spend your boyhood in the foothills.'

'Just my very young years. You do.'

'Oh, yes.'

'It seems to me that Mr. Spicer – this morning when I first came into town he said something about a goose hunt when Mr. Sherry was a hundred years old.'

'That's what I had in mind,' the doctor said, 'when I asked you if you hunted. I'm thinking of that goose hunt eleven years ago – ah – early October – unusually early because we don't get the Northern geese down here that soon as a rule. Donald Finlay spotted them.' The doctor fell silent for a moment. He sipped at his drink. 'It's difficult to know just how to tell it because it's one of those things in which the significance of the event eludes – the event. Daddy wasn't the only important individual involved – actually . . .'

Chapter 7

The year that Harry Richardson had first heard of Old Croaker was nineteen twenty-nine, the tenth anniversary of his practice in Shelby and of his marriage. His practice was a most successful one.

The migratory bird season had been open for almost a month the morning he came out of the Post Office and saw a very excited Hickory Bob Smith in conversation with Donald Finlay on the corner. As Harry came down the steps Hickory was holding his right arm straight out from his shoulder.

'To there, Reverend – with his neck straight up his head would fit right inside of my arm-pit!'

'Old Croaker,' Donald Finlay said.

'I was headed into Jensen's field,' the carpenter was explaining, 'and I wasn't even thinkin' about geese – I was figgerin' on getting some ducks comin' off from feedin' an' maybe settin' down in that slough there in the centre. I wasn't even thinkin' about geese – let alone him! Mornin', Doc.'

'Hickory – Donald,' Harry greeted them.

'Hickory's just had quite an experience,' Donald explained to the doctor. 'Old Croaker.'

'Old Croaker?'

'This goose,' Hickory said. 'When I was a kid we used to call him Old Bull Frog Croaker? I seen him this morning – like I was tellin' the Reverend – in that south field of Holgar Jensen's – barley – the one got hailed middle August? I been to Milton so's he could yank my tooth and he slipped me in at six-thirty this mornin' and I come out of there – didn't take him five minutes an' I was all froze up – couldn't even hold a cigarette between my lips an' I knew I wasn't gonna get much done that way till the frost was out so I jumped in the truck and took the gun? Remember she was snowing kind of half-hearted earlier?'

The minister and the doctor remembered.

'Kind of weather you can get the ducks comin' in low – can't see – sometimes I've had a real slaughter morning like that . . . I couldn't see more'n ten-fifteen foot ahead of myself whilst I walked into the field – these big soft flakes – early wet ones – whole field was dizzy with them an' I was almost in the middle the field headed for where I thought the slough was – gun broke open over my arm – when I heard this croak – right ahead of me – croak like a spring bull frog? I didn't realize at first and I kep' right on goin' – automatic – and then the snow let up for a moment and I saw him? Oh God, he was clear! Bolt upright doing look-out on the edge of the whole feeding flock of 'em! I could see the white quarter-moon check piece and he had his round eye right on me! I could of told if he'd blinked, he was that close to me – he didn't! Just stared at me an' stared at me! That long black neck of his was as thick around as my forearm! Know what I was thinkin'? Hell, a man could pillow his head an' his girl's head there – both of 'em an' there'd still be grey goose back to spare! Man, what a gander! He could just taken me an' flown away – if he wanted to!'

'How close were you?' asked the minister.

'Wasn't twenty foot if I was that.'

'You didn't shoot him?' Doctor Richardson said with disbelief.

'He just lifted up outa there an' I just stood with my gun over my arm!' The carpenter's face carried a grimace of sadness

74

– almost as though he were about to cry. 'It was Old Croaker all right an' I'll never get another chance like that at him – long as I live – long as he lives.'

'Just a minute,' Harry said. 'You trying to say this is a special and individual goose – out of all the thousands upon thousands of geese . . .'

'I sure do!'

'Now, Hickory,' said Harry, as well aware as anyone in Shelby of the carpenter's weakness for exaggeration, 'it's impossible to know one goose out of hundreds of thousands . . .'

'But he's right, Harry,' the minister interrupted him. 'There is such a goose . . .'

'How could a person possibly distinguish him from all the others,' protested Harry.

'He hasn't the usual two-note call,' the minister said, 'just a deep unfinished croak – as though he'd begun to call and was interrupted in mid-call . . .'

'Yeah – yeah – that's it,' Hickory said.

'It's unmistakable. Like an ill-mannered grunt.'

'Why should it be?' asked Harry.

'Most people figger he must of got shot up years ago,' Hickory said, 'shot-gun pellet – bee-bee or maybe special goose load stuck in his squawk box – '

'Or beside it,' Donald Finlay said, 'so that he's lost the high second note of his call.'

'An' he's old!' Hickory said. 'My God, he's old! Look – I'm fifty-two – my dad took me on my first goose hunt when I was fourteen an' that was when I first seen Old Croaker. You take fourteen from fifty-two – thirty-eight years ago – if he was only two then he'd be forty now.'

'How would you measure that against human age?' the minister asked the doctor.

'Oh, I don't know – but it is old for a goose. Extremely old.'

Hickory Bob Smith had been right about not getting another chance at Old Croaker, for two years later he had died with a liver like a granite curling-rock. In the twenty years that followed that morning by the Post Office steps Harry Richardson had never seen the goose, feeding on stubble, over the barrel of his Greener, or even in flight. But out on the western edge of the Central flyway others had, and over the years he had become an internationally known grey honker. In one season he had flown over and drawn the fire of the president of the Canadian National Railways commuting between pit and private pullman in the Hanna district of Northern Alberta; of the Boston Bruins' right wing and highest scoring player of the NHL for that year, hunting near the Red Deer River in Central Alberta; of the creator of a magnificent and world renowned California cemetery, crouched in a pit precisely the depth, width, and length of those which had made him a multimillionaire; and in the Shaved Hills district next to the Montana border Old Croaker had been the cause of a coronary ending the career of an overweight Wagnerian tenor on a hunting holiday from the Metropolitan Opera Company.

Adding the twenty years that had elapsed since he had first heard of the goose, Doctor Richardson computed Old Croaker to be almost sixty. Knowing of the existence of such a champion goose deepened the passion with which he looked forward to each new season. He approached the fall of Daddy Sherry's hundredth year with a heightened anticipation, for it had been the driest year since the end of the dust bowl period. On such years the migratory flights were drawn by the magnet of more plentiful water farther west along the flank of the Rockies. If he were going to see Old Croaker the doctor knew it would be in such a year.

Harry had made a call on Daddy Sherry two weeks after the season for migratory birds had opened. He found the old man shawled and in his rocker by the window of his bedroom. Daddy said little until Doctor Richardson had finished examining him, then he mumbled something which the doctor did not catch.

'What's that, Daddy?'

'Frost – frost – frost.'

'What do you mean – frost?'

'Frost in my veins an' in my art'ries – frost. Cold all the time.'

Doctor Richardson did not, as he had often before, try to

explain to Daddy that the sensation was functional.

'Frost – frost,' the old man keened. 'My eyeballs an' knackers must be sparklin' with it.'

'It's really nothing serious . . .'

'Hell it ain't! My blood's thin – thinner'n Government rye – thin – thin – sneak her back 'round.'

'Sneak what back around?'

'Clock.'

'Oh.'

'Whilst the old fellah wasn't lookin'.' He lifted his eyes conspiratorily to the doctor. 'You know what old fellah I mean?'

'I think so.'

'Only old fellah I can call old an' get away with it.' His shoulders convulsed under the knitted shawl as he wheezed up the faint tissue of a laugh. 'Death.'

'Well – you've cracked a hundred – he must hold you in some respect.'

'Turn her back – turn her back.'

'We'd all like to do that, Daddy – sooner or later.'

'Ooooh – aitch of a ways back.'

The doctor broke the embrace of the stethoscope at his neck, dropped it in his bag. 'When you were young.'

'Yeh. Thirty years.'

'Seventy – that's not exactly young.'

'When you get to a hundred – the seventies is young.' Daddy sighed. 'They come – they come!'

'You'll be out and around – down for a cigar and a beer in the Cascade,' Doctor Richardson tried to cheer him up.

'Nope. She's fall – I'll set here like a froze stook in a field – right till spring break-up. Used to be I'd look for her.'

'Look for who?'

'Fall. Now I look the other way. Not fussy about fall at all. Winter's hard work for me.'

'I know it is.'

'An' fall too. Fall just gives me time to square off for my fight with winter. One more year to set out – watch 'em, watch 'em . . .'

'Watch what?'

'Ain't slep' eight nights in a row – callin' – callin' . . .'

'Who or what?'

'Armies of 'em,' Daddy said impatiently, ' – wave after wave.'

'You been having bad dreams, Daddy?'

'I ain't dreamp in fifty years . . .'

'But if you're seeing things . . .'

''Course I'm seein' 'em. You'd see 'em too only it ain't quite time for 'em.' He hawked in his throat, leaned forward and spit into the paper shopping bag by the side of the rocker.

'Four o'clock.'

'Four o'clock.'

'On the dot.'

'Every day?' the doctor primed him.

'Top right-hand square there – just below the corner.' Daddy lifted an arm and pointed toward the window with a crooked finger. 'I generally see 'em there first . . .'

'The spots before your eyes . . .'

'. . . then they work their way kitty-cornered through the next square an' the next an' the next – right out below that bottom left-hand corner.'

The doctor cleared his throat thoughtfully. 'You – if I stayed I suppose I'd see them too.'

'Silly – sort of silly if you did.'

'Why?'

'See 'em better the other side – shoot 'em better too.'

The doctor decided that the best course was to humour him. 'Like me to shoot them for you?'

'I was thirty years younger I'd shoot 'em myself.'

'Just – ah – just what are they?'

Intense concentration seized Daddy's face. He lifted his head; his mouth opened in a round well. 'Grrr-aw-eeeeeh! Grr-aww-aw-eeeeeh!'

'Daddy – Daddy – you all right?'

'Grr-aw-eeeh!'

The doctor jumped quickly to Daddy's side.

'Stan' clear – I'm captain fer tonight . . .'

Doctor Richardson began to slap the old man smartly between the shoulder blades.

'. . . hate the stubble prickin' into my wishbone so I'm comin' in on your summer fallah – got five-foot wing spread an' muscles whang leather – they're peelin' off an' tippin' down behin' me . . .'

The doctor stopped slapping Daddy's back.

'. . . leadin' my grey army in to feed. Leave me be – I'm all right.'

'I see that.'

'Asked me what I seen through my windah – I told you – geese – geese.'

'I realize that now.'

'Grey Canada Honkers – lines of 'em unravellin' from the horizon like the old lady's ball yarn – dawn when I wake up to make sure I'm still alive – then agin from five o'clock on for the evenin' flight. You got any yet?'

'No – not yet.'

'Thirty years sucked from my marrah – I'd be outa this rocker an' pitted in – waitin' for 'em – watchin' for 'em – pluck thirty years outa my bronchial toobs, Doc.'

'Wish I could, Daddy.'

'Then I could paste 'em right in the beak with double ought shot.'

'You could,' the doctor agreed.

'Give anythin' for one more goose hunt – just one more goose hunt!'

Doctor Richardson carried away with him a quite persistent image of turtle eyes closed as though in silent prayer, the lips moving soundlessly, juniper root hands on mop handle arms, clenched desperately. And in the following days, the more he thought of it the more convinced he became that the old man's wish might be granted. The pit was the thing – big enough to hold Daddy and his rocker – insulate him with wool and eiderdown – hang him with hot-water bottles – perhaps heat large rocks and drop them into the bottom of the pit just before Daddy and rocker were lowered away. It would have to be dug large enough to contain three men actually, and the trick then would be to camouflage it from the cynical eyes of low-flying geese. Finally he confided in Donald Finlay.

'. . . whisk him from a heated car and into a heated pit.'

'Take a large one to swallow him,' the minister said doubtfully.

'We could dig it.'

'What about his heart – the excitement . . .'

'I'm not worried about the excitement – that's what keeps the man going. He *is* excitement – the only way I've been able to explain him to myself.'

'The life force sparkles more through him,' the minister suggested. 'Draws its breath a little more deeply and with more – more . . .'

'Excitement,' Harry Richardson insisted. 'Like a damn good hail storm – a blizzard . . .'

'But if he took a chill – the dampness . . .'

'I've thought of that,' Harry assured him. 'It's a chance however well heated the pit is – but it's a calculated chance really and a successful hunt could mean so much to him. It would warm him through the winter.' He noted the distant look on Donald's spare face. 'Just a minute – you haven't geese spotted already, have you?'

'I've had my eye on some the past four days. I don't know where they're feeding but they're sitting on McConky's Lake.'

'Whites?'

'The aristocracy. Greys.'

'I see.'

'They're flying out south but quite a distance – I've lost them twice – both of us ought to spot – one south-east and one south-west four miles apart. There's Mission Band at three but I think I can get away decently by four.'

It was the doctor who caught the geese in his glasses as they landed almost five miles south-east of McConky's Lake, but when he checked them again at dawn the field was empty. Nor did they land there the next evening. They had abandoned him.

'I've never seen them so flighty,' he complained to the minister. 'Ever since opening day, I've pitted in four times and never a goose. What we need is a cold snap to settle them down to a regular feeding place.'

'I have a hunch,' Donald said. 'I'll check it tonight.'

At noon the next day he phoned just as Doctor Richardson was leaving the hospital. 'I want to see you after lunch, Harry.'

'What is it?'

'Not on the phone. I'll drop in to your office.'

It was the geese, of course, and the minister with automatic goose-hunting caution was taking no chance of being overheard on the telephone.

'How many were feeding in that flock you spotted on the stubble?' he asked in Harry's office after lunch.

'Thirty – perhaps fifty.'

'That explains it then – why they left – they've joined up with the main flock. . . .'

'Where – how many?'

'Thorborn's west field – five bands anyway – a hundred and fifty.'

'We should get five chances at them as they come in – if they come in,' Harry added pessimistically.

'I think they will,' the minister said with simple faith.

'Unless somebody frightens them – drives into the fields after them – unless they change their minds and go . . .'

'Nobody has – we can go out this evening and watch to see that they don't – but it's hardly necessary actually.'

'Everything's necessary with geese.'

'Nobody's likely to spot them – you can square the field and you can't see a feather of them after they're down – it's a saucer – Jim Thorborn didn't even know they were in there. Of course – he doesn't hunt. There is just one thing, though.'

'What's that?' the doctor asked.

'The reason I think they'll be back – they've just changed their diet – they're feeding on short green feed about two inches high – not a wisp of cover.'

'I see.'

'That huge pit we'll have to dig for Daddy – hard to hide it in that field. Be a lot of spoil to pile round the edges – not like a one-man pit – wearing dark clothes and covering with screen and sprigs of grass . . .'

'Mm-hmh – that is difficult . . .'

'More than difficult,' the minister said, 'it's impossible.'

'Ought to be some way . . .'

'Keep an eye on them until they move to stubble and grain . . .'

The doctor shook his head. 'Somebody will spot them before that – I don't care how well hidden they are. Green,' he said thoughtfully – 'green – if we could cover Daddy and his pit with green . . .'

'Won't work. Green cloth . . .'

'I wasn't thinking of green *cloth* – that Athenians' Book Club tea in the Centre last Saturday . . .'

'What about it?'

'Beautiful job of decorating – '

'Yes – I know . . .'

'Just an idea,' the doctor said, 'just an idea.'

Perhaps he had pushed the patients through a little fast that afternoon, to finish by five so that he could make his visit to Ollie Pringle, Licensed Embalmer and Funeral Director.

He was not too happy about calling on Ollie, a cheerful man engaged in a profession especially harrowing when practised in the intimacy of a small community. Doctor Richardson felt that Ollie held up his cheerfulness as a shield that stopped one from going very deep into the man. He took pride in his work and in his greenhouse. No one else in the town could manage the magic he did with flowers; actually, the doctor had told himself, it was a congruent avocation if the man found satisfaction and relaxation among his bulbs, seedlings and cuttings, with their wonderful resurrection of plant life.

The doctor's main concern now was that Ollie Pringle had one other interest besides his work and his plants – goose hunting. He did not hunt with Donald Finlay and Doctor Richardson, for neither was too sure the man owned the piano-wire nerves or the inner discipline needed in the goose pit. As he rang the Pringle bell the doctor reminded himself that he must handle it deftly and delicately if he was to accomplish his mission to Daddy Sherry's best advantage. If Ollie Pringle got in on the hunt the odds for success would have dropped greatly.

Yet it was with relief that he saw Ollie's friendly face when the door opened; he would have to work fast if a hunt was to be arranged for Daddy in the morning.

'Ollie,' he said when they were inside, 'I was wondering about the Athenium Book Club tea last Saturday – their decorations – did you have a hand in that?'

'No – not really.'

'Not the decorating itself but the way they had the front of the hall . . .'

'. . . like a garden with all those flowers . . .'

'The grass. Seemed to me it looked familiar like those grass rugs you use . . .'

'. . . for the later service. I think they borrowed them from Mayor Frazer at the Bon Ton – it's used a lot for window dressing as well.' Ollie looked at the doctor questioningly.

'What I – it's Daddy Sherry actually . . .'

'He hasn't – he's not taken a turn for the worse!'

'No – no,' the doctor assured the undertaker. 'He's fine – just fine.'

'Oh.'

'Matter of fact – just a week ago – he was wishing he could go on a goose hunt.' As well as he could the doctor tried to say it as though it were the most ridiculous thing in the world.

'At his age! It would – why he'd – the cold fall air drawn down into those delicate lungs – wilt like bean plants in the first frost – dampness of lying in a goose pit would strike right into the core of his thin old body . . .'

'Well – I don't . . .'

'Kick of a shot-gun against his shoulder – who ever put the notion into his head of going on a goose hunt!'

'Nobody – really – '

'I should hope not. Glad to hear he's fine. Now – what about this artificial grass?'

'I wondered if I could – if it would be possible to . . .'

'. . . borrow it . . .'

'Thanks,' the doctor said stiffly. 'I'd like it for . . . well – Donald Finlay . . .'

'. . . wants it for the church . . .'

'No – no. He and I have a hunt lined up for . . .'

'. . . ducks.'

'Geese.' He instantly regretted having blurted so indiscreetly.

'You have! You did! How many! Wavies? Greys! Where . . .' Ollie stopped as he realized that his eager interest had betrayed him into the gaffe of prying into another man's hunt. 'That is – you do have them spotted?'

'Mmm-hmh.'

'Exact field?'

'Mmm-hmh.'

'Seen their drop – their sign?'

'Well – yes,' Harry admitted reluctantly. Whether he wished it or not he knew that in the end Ollie Pringle would be participating in this hunt. 'They're feeding on the green so it's – '

'. . . touchy – they're always touchy on summer fallow . . .'

'Green feed,' the doctor corrected him. 'That's why – for camouflage I wondered . . .'

'Oh . . .' Ollie looked disconcerted as he realized the unusually secular use Harry had in mind for the grave grass.

'I know the stuff's expensive – if you think it might get damaged . . .'

'No – no – it's *intended* for outside use. It just doesn't seem fitting – I mean – well – if it were for something in the church – '

The doctor could see that he was honestly distressed. 'I wouldn't have asked for it if it weren't in a good cause, Ollie. It has to be a large pit and it's the only possible way it can be managed – no other way. It *is* a goose hunt for Daddy.'

'Really!'

'Don't worry – we'll be taking every precaution – he'll be dressed warmly – we're going to line the bottom with heated rocks. There's no need to – after all I am his physician.'

'Yes.'

'He'll be just as comfortable in his rocker there as he would be in his own home. But it isn't going to be easy to lower that rocker and Daddy in it down into the pit — with just Donald and me. If you could bring the grave grass out with you in plenty of time in the morning and give us a hand with the rocker . . . You could look on it as — as though I were prescribing . . . it's . . .'

'. . . Doctor's orders.' Ollie's face had cleared. 'Very generous of you to invite me on your hunt.'

'Yes,' the doctor agreed wryly. 'Donald is captain,' he added firmly. 'We're in it for Daddy and the idea is to hold our fire so that he has first shot and knows quite clearly that he's knocked down his goose — after that it's every man for his selfish self.'

'I'll be there.'

'We'll be digging the pits — including Daddy's excavation — starting about midnight. Donald spotted the geese. He's to be captain of the hunt,' Harry reminded the undertaker.

'I understand,' Ollie said.

Doctor Richardson had cleared it with Belva Louise Tinsley; he knew that she had suppressed her disapproval only because he was Daddy's doctor, but her restraint was not quite enough to damp the look which said that he and the minister were idiots. Daddy's prune face kindled instantly with glee.

'Have to get out old ten-gauge Grampa!'

'Just a minute, Daddy,' the doctor protested.

'Ain't gonna hit 'em with a shovel. Got to have my gun!'

'We've arranged that,' Harry said firmly. 'Your shot-gun . . .'

'. . . has knocked down more geese than you'll ever see! I shot geese an' ducks an' prairie chicken with her — why, I had her so long as I can remember havin' a shot-gun . . .'

'That's just it,' the doctor explained. 'It's too old . . .'

'If she's too old — I'm too old. . . .'

'She — it is too old but I don't think you're too old. . . .'

'Finest Damascus twist barr'l made . . .'

'That's right – and that fine Damascus twist barrel with a modern shell could blow up and wrap itself right round your neck. . . .'

'I just point her like I point my right arm – never miss – I'm used to her. . . .'

'Donald has a spare gun – his twenty-gauge upland game over and under . . .'

'Twenty-gauge!' Daddy was outraged. 'You want a ten-gauge for geese! You got to throw a bedspread of lead at a goose – hell, it ain't partridges comin' down on us at dawn tomorrah!'

'A twenty-gauge can be just as deadly as . . .'

'. . . a goddam pea-shooter.'

'Daddy!' Harry's patience broke. 'Don't finish my sentences for me! You go on this hunt it'll be with Donald's twenty-gauge. Only difference between that and your ten-gauge Damascus twist is that you might finish this hunt alive.' He waited for Daddy's reasonable agreement. When it was not offered he added, 'Also, you'll have to shoot much more accurately with Donald's gun – get your goose in the centre of the smaller pattern – no fluke shots with a twenty-gauge.'

'I never fluked a goose yet!'

'All right – then!'

The darkness had diluted along the horizon till now the torn edges of low cloud there had kindled orange. The new day's birth chill struck right through Harry Richardson, confined below earth level, shot-gun between his legs and over his shoulder, knees folded almost up to his chin. He was feeling a little ashamed now of his earlier reluctance to invite Ollie on the hunt, since the undertaker had picked and spaded almost twice his share of concrete clay for the great ditch in which the old man was now buried. It had quite taken the strength of all three to lower a swaddled Daddy and rocker to the floor of warm rocks below. Ollie had thoughtfully brought the long black hearse, its floor lined with tarpaulin onto which they had thrown the spoil to be driven away so that it would not mound round the lip of the gaping hole and betray the pit.

The emerald grave grass had proved perfect, two spreading rugs of it overlapping generously at Daddy's neck so that at a distance it looked as though the old man's decapitated head had been carelessly dropped among the shrill ribbons of young green feed. With the decoys set out the doctor had bent over Daddy, feeling the pit warmth kind against his cheek as he lifted the edge of one of the grave blankets over Daddy's head like a bonnet.

His cramped right leg had begun to jump and jerk under the stimulus of cold and anticipatory excitement; both knees were stiff and aching. He tried to ease them with a turning movement but the tight embrace of earth would not yield. He felt the pelleting trickle of dirt down the back of his neck and for just a moment he envied Daddy rocker-snug in his warm nest; then instead there was a surge of sympathy for the old man with his thin blood and his frosted testicles. Daddy would be all right, he reassured himself, though he wished it were not so near flight time so that he could go and check on him again. Particularly he would have liked to see whether or not the hot-water bottles, the warm stones, were exhaling visible steam; if they were, the hunt was doomed.

He was sure that Donald would call it right – not too soon – not too late; he wished he could be just as sure of Ollie's will power and obedience to the categorical imperatives of the goose hunt.

With a pang at his heart he noticed that the light had strengthened enough now so that he could see within the pit. A glossy, tea-coloured bug appeared at his right shoulder, angling up the steep earth wall ribbed by the delving spade. Slowly it threaded the thin white worms of grass roots hanging from the line that described the narrow zone of top soil. Astonishing – ludicrous that he should be interred here beneath the earth's surface by careful and deliberate appointment. But it would be frightening as well if he were laid out flat on his back. Hell – this foetal crouch was more ancient – the most primitive mode of all – kinked legs – inclined head – chin on knees. The start and the end.

Faint as the sound was, it broke his morbid reverie in the twilight of his earth crypt. He could not be certain actually that he had heard it at all – whether it was muted with distance or faintly imagined in the mists of his subconscious. He strained to capture it again, caught only the dry sigh of morning wind through the oat blades over his head. He swallowed twice to erase the blood tingle ringing in his ears, then realized with surprise that he was not cold at all now. The sun's strength must be a warm fact in the upper world of light.

The sound was borne to him again, but he could not tell what it was – a rooster's arrogant announcement or perhaps a farm dog rude to the young day. His heart had hastened, urgent at his throat and temples; his mouth was dry with tension. Against his pant legs he tried to rub the sweat from the palms of his hands. He wished that he had remembered to relieve himself last thing before climbing down into the pit.

The barking sound had drifted nearer – not one dog but as though many of them were coursing in the distance. Not dogs at all! A first flight of geese must have lifted from the water in noisy assault against the sky. Each moment would bring them closer- and he must sightlessly wait for them, submit to each tick of time, each second a turning of the screw. With an inner eye he could see the thin and uncertain filament lift above the far horizon, losing and finding itself against cloud and clear sky. Now stretched out the time of terrible waiting, of undulant and elastic advance. Now they could be drifting off course till the sky had quite dissolved them; now they would have made their correction to come on glacier slow; now they must be individually revealed as their wild calliope thrilled the sky.

Down the wind they came, closing on the field with such falsetto fury it was hard to say whether man stalked goose or goose stalked man. High over the still decoys and the buried mortals they trailed hysteria, circled lower and returned up-wind – shrill hell loosed for recess – wild – wild – bagpipe wild. Once more they would leave, Harry Richardson knew, and then, drawn by Donald's hoarse plaint on the caller, wooed by the Judas decoys, they would return for the moment of truth.

Halfway into the field they hushed except for an occasional conversational GRONK, came on with a pulsing rush of hoarse wings in the steady rhythm of galley oars.

Donald Finlay's whistle violated the air.

All burst from their pits.

The minister had called it beautifully; the rectangle of men pocketed a flight of almost a hundred birds with feet lowered, momentum drained to the skim of speed that barely kept them aloft. The field was bewildered with wings frantic for leverage on the unbuoyant air. In the flapping, shrieking anarchy Harry saw one goose, lower than all the others, as though the extra weight of his body had brought him down to earth sooner and he must lift the heavier cargo slower than lighter ordinary geese. The doctor heard the deep call then, as though this shaman goose chided the others for their panic, or as though he grunted with the effort of working the great sickle wings.

The deep demi-call came again and there was no mistaking it at all; Old Croaker hung a hundred feet off Harry's right, the wing shot he seldom missed. He felt his gun leap to his shoulder, but his trigger finger stayed. How fitting that this grand gander should fall to Daddy Sherry's gun. It was directly over Daddy's pit now.

Harry eased the gun butt from his shoulder, waited for the flat *whap* of the light twenty-gauge, waited for the old honker to plummet earthward. He saw Daddy, head back, up to his navel in grave grass, gun barrel cradled in one elbow.

'Shoot! Shoot, Daddy!' he screamed.

But Daddy made no move to lift the gun-stock to his shoulder.

Old Croaker slipped sideways across the wind, came over the pits of the minister and undertaker, both staring up to him as they kept their pact to wait for Daddy's fire. The goose was lifting, had gained full flying speed as he passed over the far pits. He veered again and visibly caught the boost of the wind. Ollie's restraint broke then. Without any aim whatsoever, he machine-gunned the three shells from his automatic shot-gun.

Old Croaker flew on.

Donald Finlay emptied his gun.

Old Croaker flew on.

Harry Richardson felt his Greener kick for each barrel.

From the ancient rear end of Old Croaker two bits of down separated themselves and drifted lazily to earth. In beautiful range, at a slow target twice the size of any ordinary goose, the three men had fired seven shots and the honker had not hiccuped in his steady flight. Unable to believe their defeat they stared after the receding line of reprieved geese and the one large speck well behind the others. As they watched, Old Croaker's basso taunt drifted back to them – deliberate – quite derisive.

Then Harry heard the honking behind himself. He looked back to a half-resurrected Daddy Sherry. The old man had lifted the bright green grave grass over his shoulders like a shawl. He was laughing. Two old ganders laughed in unison.

They laughed at the doctor.

They laughed at the minister.

They laughed at the undertaker.

Chapter 8

Well past midnight and long after bung and banter in the beer parlour below had died, goose hunt and Scotch bottle finished together. There came a light knock at the door; the night man whispered that Doctor Richardson was wanted at the hospital. Harry looked at his watch.

'Probably a false alarm – she's at least two hours early but I'd better drop over.' He handed out a small flat plastic box to David. 'You might try these.'

'What are they?'

'Pretty effective ulcer pill – just a sample.'

'But how did you know I . . .?'

'You do have – or you have had one?'

'Yes – hasn't troubled me for quite a while – but how did you . . .'

'The antacid bottle on your dresser helped the diagnosis,' Harry said. 'Those are just a slight refinement of the same thing – belladonna and added sedative. If you're eating at the Bluebird Café you can use it.' He paused with his hand on the door. 'You know – you'd be better off at a boarding-house – believe

I heard that Helen Maclean and her mother are thinking of taking in a boarder . . .'

'Keith's mother.'

'It would be nicer for you, and Mrs. Clifford is a wonderful cook in a town full of good cooks. I can speak to her for you.'

'Well — ,' David hesitated, 'it's such a short time.'

'Ulcers and a room over a beer parlour — meals at the Bluebird Café — your time will be short.'

'I don't like to impose on anyone,' David explained. 'Move in — then right out.'

'They haven't had boarders before — they might forgive your short stay if you can forgive their inexperience. I'll mention you to Mrs. Clifford.'

'Thanks — oh, and thanks.'

'It was a nice evening,' the doctor said as he opened the door. 'Too bad your work didn't bring you out here in fall.'

'I'm sorry it didn't, but tonight must have been just as good as a real goose hunt.'

The doctor stepped out into the hallway. 'Nothing — including intercourse — is as good as a real goose hunt.'

When he had closed the door after the doctor David went over to the typewriter on the dresser. It was four-thirty when he stopped to undress for bed.

The noontime gaiety of the beer parlour woke him. If he'd had any reservations about boarding with Mrs. Clifford, they were dispelled by his late breakfast at the Bluebird Café, which ignited a gastric fire that still smouldered stubbornly after three of the pills the doctor had given him the night before. At the desk he asked for directions to the Clifford house.

As soon as she had opened the door David realized that Mrs. Clifford had been quite worthy of Daddy Sherry's steel at the time of the flying trapeze episode. Though her clear and direct eyes said she might be sixty, it was hard to be certain; she could be anywhere between that and seventy-five. Her firm voice and manner were not warming but they did suggest a well disciplined vitality. David imagined that she reached decisions with sensible economy — much more light than flame. He was sure that never

– ever – in her life had she yearned to be a flying acrobat.

She seemed to have made up her mind about him before he had called, for she took him up to a room at the front of the house minutes after he had introduced himself. Dinner, she warned him, was at six o'clock. He sensed that she expected him to be on time for meals – just as much as she would Keith or anybody else.

The room could have been one in the boarding-house his mother had kept when he was a boy; he had then known linoleum to shine like this; the oak veneer dresser with its serpentine drawers, and the righteous brass bed with pineapple-patterned spread, tolled him back. Almost a third of the ceiling was bent to conform with the pitch of the roof.

'It's a nice room,' he said. 'I wonder – my work – will it bother anybody if I use the typewriter rather late at night?'

'No.'

She had gone to the window to pull aside the net curtains and for the first time he realized that her hair did not show the slightest grey. It was superlatively black until she turned her head in the generous sunlight; then it glinted copper highlights. How contradictorily frivolous of her; hair hue and skin tone did not complement each other, but the failure did not lie in the complexion, which was fresh and almost young; the dye was to blame.

As he packed shirts, socks, pajamas, toothbrush and shaving kit just before checking out of the Cascade Hotel, he wondered briefly what Mrs. Clifford's daughter would be like. The odds were for a younger, practical and school mistressy version of the mother, he supposed.

Later – when he met her just before supper – he was asking himself incredulously how she could possibly be the daughter of her mother. His first response was the conviction that she was the most attractive woman he had ever met. His next and almost immediate feeling was one of wonderment: how in the world did she manage it? Her features did not have the bland regularity that work the magic of beauty; her mouth was too large, her cheeks too wide and high – and God Almighty, she was lovely! Just look at the surprising blue of her eyes with their almost Asiatic cast – the dark skin with its dusky under-flush of rose – her head-back dignity. But her mouth spoiled that; even in repose it held a slight lift at the corners as though a secret smile had not made it – quite. And when she did smile, the sun cleared cloud, fife and drum struck up, it was the Queen's birthday and if we don't get a holiday we'll all run away!

Through dinner he had to be deliberate about keeping his eyes from her at least for some of the time. Part Egypt – part gamine. Discipline couldn't possibly be one of her strong teaching traits. English – and she probably taught it with enthusiasm and intensity enough to fire even her grade-twelve louts with interest in poetry. She'd be a Keats girl – a Yeats and de la Mare girl – not Housman at all. David wished that he had known her for years; he wished that he were not staying here for only a few weeks. Toronto was light years away and instant infatuation was just as ridiculous as spontaneous generation, but oh, it was nice to know it could still happen when you were near forty – even though it was idiotic!

He tapped away at Daddy Sherry for almost four hours that night.

The next morning he did a piece for his column, a rather satisfying I've-left-the-pavements-grey-to-return-to-the-scenes-of-my-childhood thing, in which he compared the tempo of Yonge with the leisurely saunter of a foothills main street. He was just a little surprised that 'nine bean rows' and a 'bee-loud glade' had finished much stronger than he had anticipated. When he went to the post office to mail it he found the morning raw, for an Arctic front had slipped south during the night. Before he had got back to the house, snow had begun to fall.

After lunch a phone call to Miss Tinsley gained him permission to visit Daddy Sherry again. He found her more receptive than she had been the day before, perhaps because she had paused in her spring house-cleaning, perhaps because she could accept him more easily now that he was a boarder at the Clifford house, perhaps because it was the way of people in a small western community. He made a mental note of that as a possibility for the column, just the sort of thing to please western readers and sting eastern ones – score twice. Almost as good as eulogizing the cat and demeaning the dog – wait a year then praise the dog and to hell with the cat.

The pyramid-roofed cottage stood amid the thinning fall of snow-flakes melting almost as soon as they touched the earth. It would soon be over, Miss Tinsley felt; the noon weather report on the radio had promised her. 'It's our altitude,' she said. 'It gives us chinooks during the winter but it gives us frosts early and late in the year too. Actually I'm relieved.'

'Relieved?'

'Usually, this time of year he *wants* to be out – even if it's raining he'll go out to the porch and take his walk under the shelter of the roof, then sit in his rocker. I haven't been able to understand why he should be staying in bed – his appetite poor. Now this explains it – the snow – he must have sensed it was a false spring. He's generally right. A lot of people in the district put in their crops by him.'

'Oh – does he predict the weather?'

'No. It isn't that – that clear for him – he *feels* it – but he seems to be only partly aware of it himself.'

'I see.'

'It's more like sap rising in a tree – or leaves yellowing and turning brittle in the fall.' She turned back to him at Daddy's door. 'He's still in bed, you know, but it doesn't worry me so much now. He had a big lunch – for him – soup and two soft-boiled eggs – three pieces of toast. Also he's not talking silly. Daddy!' They stepped inside the bedroom. 'Mr. Lang to see you!'

The dandelion head turned toward the door.

'Feeling better today, are you,' David said and right away he knew that Daddy had no recollection at all of the earlier visit. 'I'm David Lang – I'd like to do an article about you . . .'

'Sure – sure – sure.'

'Won't involve much,' David explained. 'A few visits – talks . . .'

'I know. Belva already said. Belva!' Though the house-keeper still stood only twelve feet away in the doorway, he had trumpeted her name.

'Yes, Daddy.'

'This fellah – Mr. . . .'

'Lang,' she supplied.

'Doin' a story about me.' His eyes slid to David. 'Straight or water?'

'Hmh?'

'Your Scotch.'

'Oh – water.'

The eyes turned to the door again. 'Make mine like always.'

'You've had it,' Miss Tinsley reminded him, 'not an hour ago.'

'I know I have. Can't let him drink his alone. Ain't polite . . .'

'But I don't think you should have another so . . .'

'An' a couple Senate House cigars . . .'

'You had the last one at lunch.'

'No – I didn't.'

'You took it out yourself,' she said, 'so you saw for yourself it was the last one . . .'

'. . . in the box – yes – but you go take a peek in that walnut sewin'-case – lift up the spool tray – whole han'ful of 'em under there. Bring us two, then you can take an' hide the rest.'

Without any change of expression she turned away and David admired the woman; what a rain of irritation and annoy-ance she must stand under day after day, and what a fine sense of emotional proportion she must have.

'She must be up to her ass in cigars,' Daddy said confiden-tially to David.

When she returned with David's Scotch and water she also brought a small shot glass which Daddy took in both hands to his breast. Like an ancient humming-bird at a blossom he sipped at it quite delicately, just touching the tip of his tongue to it now and again. And he seemed to relish this visit as much as he did the whiskey. He answered David's questions clearly and directly.

He had been born in a log farm-house three miles east of the town of Bayfield in Huron county, Ontario. He had David pull out a great Bible from the shelf under his bed table; there on the inside of the puffed leather cover David read: John Felix Sherry – May 17, 1849. Daddy told him that he could check as well the vital statistics records in the court-house of the city of Goderich.

At the age of eighteen he had come west by the American route to Pembina. Quite vividly he recalled for David the Fort Garry of 1867 with its mud and saloons, where he had taken up freighting with his own team and wagon. In the summer he had gone west with the buffalo hunt into what was now the province of Saskatchewan.

'May,' he told David, ' – first I ever seen the Qu'Appelle valley – middle May – she was lovely – lot like Paradise Valley west of here – only without the Rockies liftin' behind her – an' I seen it again – that was the middle April – spring of eighty-five.'

In March of that year the Saskatchewan Rebellion had broken out; there had been the Frog Lake Massacre and the exiled Louis Riel had returned from Montana to help his Métis people, the same Louis Riel who had fifteen years before starred in the Red River Rebellion. History had selected him for the riddle of wild and tame, of east and west, fur trader and farmer, church and state, nationhood and colony, conservative and liberal. A classical scholar and University of Montreal graduate, born into a non-nomadic Métis family on the banks of the Assiniboine, he was still seventy-five years after his death a mystic riddle, whose only answer, if there had ever been one, was gone for ever with the shrieking wheels of the Red River carts, the cry of prairie wind compelling grasses low, the thunder of buffalo hooves. Perhaps Riel had come closest to the answer in the fall of eighteen eighty-five when the deputy sheriff on the Regina scaffold asked him if he had anything to leave to his people. 'Only my heart and I gave that to my people fifteen years ago.'

In April John Sherry had joined up with the Batoche column, starting out from Winnipeg. The men had sung as they marched over soggy prairie in fine early spring weather. Sloughs were slopping; patches of winter snow lingered. Just before the Qu'Appelle Valley the officers called a halt. Among the others, John Sherry's name was called out – the fifty men picked for their fine marksmanship to go ahead to feel out the enemy.

With five other soldiers he had climbed into a Bain wagon, sat on the box rim, facing in. Over faint prairie trails, through virgin prairie wool, past clumps of moose hay, the wagons rolled west, and he could feel the tremble of the wheels telegraphing through the box side and up his spine. Above him the April sky was stainless and the prairie unmarred by human habitation, staked with upright gophers; now and again a meadowlark dropped its bright and hasty notes, or a coyote trotted sideways. John Sherry wondered when they would come across the enemy.

The sky had clouded over and then, just as they neared a large bluff, the fickle April afternoon loosed a snow-storm. It blinded them with great soft flakes, but it saved their lives, for with it came the ululating falsetto of Indian war-cries. But for the snow they would have ridden into ambush.

For three-quarters of an hour he crouched in the shelter of the box with his rifle at the ready. The snow ceased as suddenly as it had begun and he lifted his nose cautiously over the wagon side. Mounted Indians milled around in front of the bluff.

'Like a goddam red ant pile kicked open,' Daddy said. 'Bullets buzzin' an' rickoshayin' – wagons was titherin' an' totherin' in all directions!'

The Indians had disappeared into the trees; wagons, horses, men took after them at full gallop. The bluff exploded. From it rocketed hysterical prairie chicken, crows in hoarse panic, jays and magpies, a bounding lynx, a bolt-eared army of jack rabbits, gophers and field mice, ground squirrels and coyotes. Behind them billowed smoke and then the flames of the fire the Indians had started.

'That was the first time the Batoche colyum closed with the enemy,' Daddy told David. 'We was lucky – luckier'n we was later at Fish Crick an' at Batoche.'

'I suppose,' David said, 'in the sixties – when you were at Fort Garry – you must have seen Riel.'

'Nope.'

'Oh.' David's voice showed his disappointment. 'He came to St. Boniface in 1868 – then in sixty-nine during the trouble . . .'

'Yeh-yeh – but our trails never crossed,' Daddy said. 'Then.'

'Then?'

'Later – after Batoche. I seen him after when the party was all over an' time for General Middleton to put down his skirts.'

'Did you!'

'Me an' Lennie Parsons – when Howrie an' Armstrong brought him in – after the charge at Batoche – wasn't any fuss – just walked up to 'em an' says how do you do I'm Louis Riel polite as anything an' they brought him in.'

'Yes?'

'Put him into a tent an' me an' Lennie was on guard duty – daytime – that was where they held him – well – they didn't exactly *hold* him because he didn't intend goin' anywheres – shootin' was all over by then.'

'What was your impression of . . .'

'Him an' his people lost. Just in this tent till they'd take him south to Regina jail. That's where they hanged him.'

'Yes – I know.'

'1885 – November.' Daddy sighed. 'I guess they hanged worse fellahs.'

'Do you think they did?'

'Huh?'

'What was your opinion of Louis Riel?'

'Ohhhhh – I'd need more to go on – hear he had a good education – lawyer or somethin' . . .'

'What about his mission – the Métis cause – ' David waited for Daddy to answer him. 'Would you say he was a – a dedicated man?'

Daddy shrugged.

'You must have given it a little thought – other soldiers must have expressed an opinion . . .'

'Hell – they wasn't soldiers – hardware an' shoe an' grocery clerks out for a whizzer – ribbon an' ladies garter drummers – plough-boys an' choir leaders – takes more'n one summer to make soldiers outa them.'

'Perhaps it does,' David agreed, 'but the other – men – putting down the rebellion – your friend on duty over Riel . . .'

'Lennie.'

'What did he think . . .'

'Only he didn't get called Lennie much – Ramrod was what he went by.'

'You ever hear him express an opinion about Riel – the Métis . . .'

'He was a miller – started out to be a miller in Ontario – Waterdown. By God, he was a fine fellah! Best friend I ever had!'

'Was he . . .'

'Yeh-yeh-yeh – nobody could fault a horse or a man better'n him.'

'Did he ever fault Riel?'

'Him an' me changed off with a couple other fellahs. Alf somebody – Bunbury – Bainbridge – they wrote him up down in T'rontuh just a few years back – you know what he done after he mustered out?'

'No,' David said, 'I don't.'

'You ever run acrosst him down there in T'rontuh?'

'Not that I can remember.'

'Blocky – dark complected fellah – before the rebellion he worked in the market down on Front Street. After – you know what he done after?'

'No.'

'Mary Pickford.'

'What?'

'Actress – she got to be famous.'

'Well – yes – I know.'

'When they invented movies. Beautiful child with long sausage curls down to her shoulders.' Daddy looked at David for a moment. 'You probably never run acrosst her either. Little T'rontuh girl . . .'

'Yes – I know . . .'

'She'd be a pretty big girl now . . .'

'What has she got to do with the Riel Rebellion?'

'Not a goddam thing I know of.'

'Then why do you mention her if . . .'

'I don't suppose she was even born time of the Saskatchewan Rebellion . . .'

'Yet you associate her with the rebellion,' David persisted.

'I don't. You do.'

'Do I . . .'

'I associate her with Alf – whatever his name was – fellah done guard duty with this other fellah an' they changed off with Ramrod an' . . .'

'Yes – I know – I know.'

'I didn't know him very well – just when him an' his partner come on or when they went off – never seen him before or after that – never clapped eyes on him from then till right now.'

'Didn't you . . .'

'Why should I. He went back to T'rontuh – me an' Ramrod headed for the foothills an' started up our horse ranch together – that's a long time ago.'

'I know it is.'

'1885 – hell, me an' Ramrod we didn't know they hanged Riel till half a year after – they done it late fall – we was up Paradise Valley all that winter – snowed in till late April – lived off muskrat for a month – outa salt – tobaccah. I tell you there's where you know a fellah's your friend and you're his friend – no tobaccah an' no salt an' he doesn't chew your ass out an' you don't chew his out. God, he was a nice fellah! Outa all the men I ever known . . .'

Daddy's voice had broken. David saw the lower lip tremble; the narrow shoulders moved almost impatiently under the shawl. 'He stank, you know.'

'Did he . . .'

'Ramrod an' me was together for – from when I first met him – three years we was on the ranch – the one we trailed beef to the Klondike – Boor War – eighty-five to spring of six an' seven

– over twenty years. All that time I never knew him to change his socks or his underwear till they come off of their own free will. Stank like a spring bear! He stank of willah smoke an' he stank of Black Judas Chewin' Tobaccah – horse an' cow an' sheep – he stank of all the hides the Lord ever wrapped around – Ramrod ever skinned off of – a critter – an' besides all that he stank of hisself. You know – he never did look dirty – an' he *was* dirty – them blue eyes his – that blond hair an' beard – must of been Swede somewheres back in him. Lived dirty – died dirty – claimed washin' was unhealthy the way it sluiced off the natural oils. Mind you, he wasn't careless or lazy . . .'

'Wasn't he . . .'

'Nope. Natural oils. He could of been right,' Daddy said charitably. 'He could sure stand cold – when he died the spring of six an' seven – I – aaaaaahhhh . . .' Daddy's voice fainted down to a hoarse and prolonged sigh. He leaned his head against the rocker's high back, closed his eyes; the thin lips moved in silent inner colloquy. David thought he caught the words: 'Scatter-piss Annie.' After a moment the old man's voice surfaced again though the eyes remained closed.

'. . . be alive today . . .'

'Ramrod?'

'Yehyeh-yeh – I buried him . . . Wolf Willah Crick – not a bud ner a leaf.' In the corners of the hooded eyes clear tears had formed; they spilled over, slid down past the liver blotches, found their channels in the creases of the cheeks, met and joined under the wattled chin, dropped deliberately one by one to the shawl caught together with a safety pin. 'Thin – thin – topsoil was thin – I never washed him.' The eyes were still closed. 'Buried him where the wolf willah blows.' Daddy opened his eyes and new tears released, coursed down his cheeks. 'Dead,' he said, 'he didn't stink anymore – when he stopped – it stopped.' He wiped at his eyes with the back of his hand. 'We was talkin' about Riel.'

'Yes.'

'Little I seen of him he wore a suit – dark – that heavy wool them breeds wore all the time – all rumpled – he'd been through the siege of Batoche – funny – all durin' the campaign before we ever seen him – leadin' all them half-breeds an' Indians – had a sort of pitcher of him in my mind – great black slashin' fellah – but he wasn't . . .'

'Wasn't he . . .'

Daddy shook his head and snuffed up a last tear. 'He wasn't short but he wasn't tall either – an' another thing about him made me feel kind of sorry for him – Captain in charge of Riel – in the tent with him – had a cot there with an ammunition box turned on end for a table – they'd got Riel some writin' tablets an' pencils – he was writin' all the time except – oh – every fifteen minutes maybe – the Captain would holler out – "Soldiers the guard," – me an' Ramrod we'd march in smart. Captain would say, "Fall in – by the prisoner." We would. Then he'd say, "Forward march!" No – ' Daddy corrected himself. ' "Quick march!" We would, with Riel between us – maybe a couple three hunderd paces from the tent – but still right out in the open, "Halt!" Then: "Stand easy whilst the prisoner moves his bowels!" '

'Oh.'

'Me an' Ramrod would – gun-stocks restin' on the ground – Riel squatted with his trousers puddled around his ankles – had the diaree – Way I figgered – even if you're gonna hang a man for treason you oughta let him do that in private. Every fifteen minutes – we wasn't on nights but this Alf fellah said all night whilst he was on too. Janitor.'

'Pardon?'

'Back in T'rontuh he ended up like a janitor of a big playhouse there. Years after the rebellion – lookin' after the stage door – that was how he discovered Mary Pickford.'

'Did he . . .'

'Little girl got sick in this play an' he went an' got another child – that was Mary Pickford – that was how she got started. I try to see all her pitchers – knowin' Alf that way – his discoverin' her . . .'

'That's interesting,' David said, 'but tell me – you say you felt sorry for Riel . . .'

'Feel sorry for anybody got that stuff – vi'lent – I even felt sorry for General Middleton when he got it – everybody – some bug – maybe Glaubers' salts in our drinkin' water – war and the diaree goes together,' Daddy mused. 'By God, lots of times right now I wouldn't mind a pinch of Glaubers' – loosen me up . . .'

'I was wondering . . .'

'An' some of Ramrod's natural oils – keep me warm. Main thing is to keep reg-lar – stay outa draughts – drink now and agin to – you know that rebellion was fought sober!'

'Was it . . .'

'That goddam mutton-chopped Methodisty English bastard at the lake head . . .'

'Who?'

'Middleton – General Middleton – teeth chatterin' in forty below at the end of steel – "Let 'em drink tea," he says. I bet that's the only goddam war was ever fought on tea – before or since!'

'You may be right.'

'What about him!'

'What about him?'

'He didn't fight it on tea! No, sir! Look what Gabriel Dumont an' his breeds found after they nailed our hide to a fence post at Fish Crick!'

'What?'

'Middleton's baggage – we outa there leatherin' both sides an' left everything behind an' the breeds got Middleton's trunk. You know what was in that trunk?'

'No.'

'Extra britches an' tunic – dress uniform – vest made outa bobcat fur some grateful folks give him back in the Qu'Appelle Valley for comin' to save 'em from Indians an' brandy – fulla brandy bottles! He didn't fight it on tea! Dumont an' his men took it back – give Riel the bobcat fur vest – an' then they drunk Middleton's health in his own brandy. Aaaaaaah!' Daddy shook his head with remembered disgust. 'Madder'n hell when we charged Batoche,' he muttered, 'then tickled to take all the credit when we pulled it off – aaaah . . .' His voice trailed off as though the outburst had wearied him. '. . . all them prime furs – poor war,' he mumbled, '. . . amacher – piss poor amacher war.'

'Was it . . .'

'For us. Them half-breeds wasn't – Boors wasn't either. I guess we always been amachers.'

David waited a moment, wondering just how he could tease out of the old man some observation a little richer historically than alkali-induced diarrhoea in the poet, mystic, and martyr who had been a fifteen-year thorn in the political side of Prime Minister Sir John A. Macdonald, at the same time known and respected by Sir Wilfrid Laurier, and General Grant during his presidency of the United States. 'The cause the Métis were fighting for . . .'

'Huh?'

'They felt they were fighting for their land – for their recognition . . .'

'Was they?' Daddy seemed surprised.

'What did you think they were fighting for?'

'Me? I don't know.'

'Didn't you wonder?'

Daddy shook his head.

'Some time during the campaign you must have . . .'

'We wondered about keepin' warm – keepin' fed – with them half-breed snipers mainly we wondered about keepin' alive.'

David felt sad. The pity of it was that longevity had ordained Daddy with apostolic succession, but it had bequeathed him such a wistful fragment of historic truth to hand on.

'Smell it – smell it now – sweet an' strong!' He was drawing in great draughts of air through distended nostrils. 'That's wolf willah, boy! What a bonny perfume!'

'Yes,' David agreed. 'It is – it is, Daddy.' As he saw the fresh tears well in the old man's eyes this time, he felt like crying himself.

Chapter 9

- -

When he had come out to the living-room after his interview
with Daddy, David saw that Miss Tinsley had a visitor, a tall,
spare man with grey hair, who rose from a chair near the front
window. Miss Tinsley introduced him as a Mr. Dalgliesh. He
seemed vaguely familiar, and when Miss Tinsley said that he
was in real estate and had called about the Daddy Sherry
Anniversary preparations, David remembered him at the organ-
ization meeting when he had agreed to be head of the Finance
Committee. He had the covert nickname of Title Jack Dalgliesh.

Mr. Dalgliesh had just arrived and after the introduction he
continued with his explanation that donations were already
pouring in and being pledged to his committee, enough to have
become rather embarrassing, for the expense of the birthday
party was limited to the cost of the hall, the refreshments, and
the birthday gift itself. Quite obviously, before they were through
they would find themselves with a fund much greater than they
needed. Ordinarily, he said, this would have made up a purse
for the honoured person, but since Daddy was already well
fixed, the committee felt that such a cash gift was out of place.
At the same time the Finance Committee did not like to refuse

people in their generosity and had decided that further donations should be accepted and turned over to some worthy cause in Daddy's name. Three had suggested themselves: the Activarian Club's Old Folks' Home building fund, the Athenium Club's cemetery landscaping project, the Eastern Star's furnishing and decorating of the Old Timers' Room in the Community Centre. Mr. Dalgliesh had called to sound out Daddy on his preference.

'Was he still awake when you left him?' Miss Tinsley asked David.

'Yes.'

'He's generally dropped off before now,' she said. 'I'll just check.'

As she went in to Daddy's room, Mr. Dalgliesh turned to David. 'I can kill two birds with one stone, Mr. Lang. I wanted to see you too. How long do you think you'll be here?'

'Another ten days or so,' David said.

'Yes-yes-yes.' Actually the repetitive affirmation was just an indrawn breath with the finest edge of voice to it, a gentle and almost absent-minded agreement. 'We were wondering – the club service committee in Rotary – if we could have you for a speaker at one of our meetings.'

'Oh,' David said.

'We meet every Thursday – in the Bluebird Café diningroom. This is Tuesday and it's hardly fair to ask you for this coming Thursday on only two days' notice. But a week Thursday?' He held up his hand as David was about to reply. 'We know you're a busy man and we appreciate you're not here on holiday – we wouldn't take it amiss if you felt you couldn't spare us one of your evenings.'

'Well,' David started to beg off on the excuse that his work would hardly allow him time for the chore.

'And I'm afraid our dinners aren't up to what you're used to on speaking engagements down East, but I assure you it would be a red-letter day for Shelby Rotary if you could possibly...'

'He's dropped off, Mr. Brown.' Miss Tinsley spoke from Daddy's bedroom doorway.

'Yes-yes-yes – well – there's no hurry, Miss Tinsley – it's not something for him to decide in haste. Perhaps you could mention it to him when he wakes up. That way he could consider it between then and when I drop in on him – perhaps tomorrow.'

'I will.'

'Yes-yes-yes,' said Mr. Dalgliesh. 'I've just been trying to prevail upon Mr. Lang to speak to us at Rotary. I imagine it's an imposition he's well familiar with.'

'Oh – it's not an imposition,' David lied politely.

'Nice of you to say so – but it is the price of being famous and if you can't see your way clear Shelby Rotary will understand.'

'I think I can,' David said.

'Wonderful. You can expect a big turn-out, for we planned to make it a Rotary-Anne night as well.'

This information made David revise his opinion of Mr. Dalgliesh; though his first impression had been one of an indecisive and negative individual, he saw the man now as an adroit master of the soft sell, achieving his target with reverse English.

'Are you on foot?' Mr. Dalgliesh was saying.

'I'm just down the block,' David said, 'at Mrs. Clifford's.'

'Just thought I might give you a lift.' He turned to the housekeeper. 'Thank you, Miss Tinsley.'

As they went down the Sherry walk the real estate man said, 'A wonderful woman. Mr. Sherry pays her well, but she more than earns it. She saved his life you know . . .'

'Did she!'

'Spring of nineteen fifty-four.'

'The flood year.'

'Yes-yes-yes. If it hadn't been for her he wouldn't be with us today.' Mr. Dalgliesh paused with his hand on the car door. 'You might almost say – a dedicated woman.'

'She seems quite sensible and efficient,' David said. 'You know, Mr. Dalgliesh, you're the second person to mention the spring of nineteen fifty-four, I'd like to hear about it – '

'Oh – I'm afraid I wouldn't be much help to you there,' Mr.

Dalgliesh said. 'I've heard about it all right – pretty hard not to in a small community like this – Daddy going round the Horn . . .'

'Round the Horn?'

'Town joke – I think your best person for a true and detailed account of that would be Miss Tinsley herself. Must have been a harrowing experience for her but all's well that ends well and I'm sure she'd be only too willing to tell you about it. My association with Daddy has been pretty well limited to business – handling his hail and fire insurance renewals – farm rental agreements – income tax returns and . . .' Mr. Dalgliesh stopped suddenly with an expression of consideration. 'It was very gracious of you to accept my invitation to speak to Rotary when you're right in the middle of your story on Daddy.'

'Glad to,' said David, still trying to understand why he had agreed.

'I suppose all of us at one time or another have had something to do with Daddy that's – well especially between ourselves and – and Daddy. And I suppose that's the sort of thing you want.'

'Yes,' said David, not quite sure what Mr. Dalgliesh meant.

'And it wouldn't be very – ah – grateful of me – after what you're doing for me – this is almost the end of my year as President of Rotary,' he explained, 'and it means a great deal to me – having you as a speaker – comes as a wonderful climax to my year. I certainly appreciate it and it just occurred to me that I might be able to help you.' He looked at his watch. 'Three o'clock – coffee break time. Let's go down to the Bluebird Café . . .'

April in the foothills was a time of renascence, farmers seeding and ranch herds calving; it was a month which consistently brought Ollie Pringle the least business of any in the year, a convenient annual lull for him since the greenhouse was then urgent with sprouting bulbs, cuttings and seedlings. For Title Jack Dalgliesh it was a harried month of fiscal hell, bringing – in addition to the usual insurance renewals – new farm lease agreements, the handling of car and drivers' licences for the district, and the feverish scramble to complete the personal and corporation income tax returns of his clients. Taking part of an afternoon off for David Lang at this time of year had been an act of genuine gratitude.

He was essentially an unselfish man, donating a great deal of his time to charitable drives; it was unthinkable that anyone else should have been chosen head of the Daddy Sherry Anniversary Finance Committee. His ethics, his files, his person were impeccable; he was respected by the community for his efficiency and for his dignity, a quiet and unfailing balance which was the result of a complete lack of a sense of humour.

The tragedy of Title Jack's life was that he had never been afforded the opportunity to study law; that he drew up wills, leases, agreements for sale, handled estates, did the work of most small-town lawyers, yet must be contented to be a Commissioner of Oaths rather than a Queen's Counsel. The most satisfying achievement of his life had come to him seventeen years before when he had acted as arbitrator in the contention of Mooney versus Dixon.

Len Mooney was a choleric extrovert, who raised pure-bred cattle nineteen miles west of Shelby, his lease lying next to that of Harry Dixon. The particularly bitter winter of 1942-3, Mr. Mooney spent the months of January and February in Laguna Beach, making arrangements for his neighbour to take care of thirty Hereford bulls.

Two citrus-scented months, lolling under palm fronds, had refreshed Mr. Mooney, his holiday all the sweeter when he read about the foothills weather in the forwarded *Shelby Chinook*; the thermometer had dropped to forty below and stayed there for five weeks on end. But on his return Mr. Mooney found that Mr. Dixon had not discharged his responsibility towards the bulls; he had allowed thirty thousand dollars' worth of pure-bred Hereford cods to freeze. An explosively-tempered man, he demanded that Mr. Dixon make good the sterility damage or he was instructing his Calgary lawyers to sue. Mr. Dixon said that the weather was not his fault, the seminal

110

calamity was an act of God, and what had Mr. Mooney expected him to do – wrap the testicles in tea-cosies?

Title Jack was quite proud that he had been able to persuade Mr. Mooney to consider arbitration, Mr. Dixon to make out a certified cheque for thirty thousand dollars, to be placed in Mr. Dalgliesh's safe until a settlement agreement had been reached. Mr. Dixon had chosen Mr. Dalgliesh as his representative on the arbitration board; Mr. Mooney selected Milton Abercrombie, the Royal Bank manager; both agreed finally on the third member, Dr. Plunkett, the district's veterinarian. There had followed almost two weeks of bitter wrangling, painfully lacking in dignity, Mr. Mooney braying with tiresome regularity, 'A bull with no balls is no bull!'

The first break in the emotional impasse had come with the agreement that it was unlikely all or none of the bulls had sustained or escaped sterility, that fifty per cent was a fair estimate, whether it be one hundred per cent damage to fifty per cent of the bulls or fifty per cent damage to one hundred per cent of the bulls. Mr. Dalgliesh then proposed that Mr. Dixon buy half the herd at a thousand dollars a head, the selection of bulls to be made after the calf crop of that year and to include all of established sterility.

As it turned out, only two were; pure-bred stock went high at the Calgary bull sale that year and Mr. Dixon made a two-thousand-dollar profit.

But Title Jack could not look back with satisfaction upon his experience five years before with Daddy Sherry; at the time it had upset him terribly, for he had felt that in some way he had failed Daddy; the affair still haunted and puzzled him. Until his talk with David Lang, he had not discussed it with anyone. He still did not know what he might have done differently, though immediately after the event he had been on the point of getting in touch with the Attorney-General's department, quite convinced that senile decay had ended Daddy's years of self-determination and sound judgment, that in his own best interests he should be made a ward of the government.

But he had not taken this distasteful step, for he was not

sure that he had the true answer to the matter. There were certain abiding things in life; the sanctity of property was one of them; a utilitarian faith that his fellow man was decently concerned with the steady and safe increase of his wealth was another. Daddy Sherry had shaken his faith; even more than that, he had frightened Title Jack Dalgliesh.

Mr. Spicer had alerted him first on an August morning when he had gone in for a haircut.

'Every morning,' the barber said, 'in here every morning for a shave – hasn't missed the mint freshness of a shave five mornings in a row – so I guess he's been in Shelby that long anyway. After that he has his facial. Follows his shave like night the day.'

'Who?'

'This fellow – bird of passage. Affluent bird of passage I'd say. I guess I don't give more than two facials a year – when I was younger – full of beans – first came to Shelby – ambitious. Hair to the south. Used to make a bid every time for a shampoo – facial. Young and ambitious – I felt I could pay the rent out of shampoos and facials alone.'

Mr. Spicer traded the clippers for scissors; he kinked his knees slightly and said into Title Jack's neck, 'Chit-chat. Snippets conversation. Five days now and I'm no closer to knowing what he does than the first day he stepped into my shop. No closer. Snippets. Surrounds himself with secrecy . . .'

'That's his privilege,' Mr. Dalgliesh observed.

'Time and again I've given him the opportunity with leading questions. Failed to take the hint. Then a couple days ago I asked him outright. "What's your line?" I asked him. "What line you in?" Outright.'

'Yes?'

'Pause,' the barber said. 'Noticeable pause before he answered me.' He indicated the pause. ' "Mr. Spicer," he said to me, "bit of a rush this morning – we'll just miss the facial." '

'What's unusual about that?'

'Coming right after my direct question it was a threat. What you might call a veiled threat. I have not asked him again since.' The barber cleared his throat. 'You – ah – you haven't heard anything around, have you?'

'No, I haven't.'

'Piques a person's interest – sticks in a fellow's mind like spear grass. Isn't so much he's a stranger in town – isn't so much wondering where he's from – but why he wants to keep it so quiet. Secrecy of it – shrouded secrecy.'

'He probably has his reasons, Merton.'

'Mm-hmh. They say he isn't using the Cascade sample room – stayed too long to be a bank inspector – little dusty there.'

'What's that?'

'Clean scalp's a healthy scalp. If you wanted a shampoo . . .'

'Not this morning, thanks.'

Though he had not said so to Mr. Spicer, Title Jack's interest had been piqued as well, but it was with more than the barber's idle curiosity. He was quite fond of Shelby and wanted nothing more than to see the community grow and prosper; it was a boom province, no longer dependent entirely on agriculture, for there were oil and gas and pipelines now; it seemed to Mr. Dalgliesh that all towns but his had progressed. Shelby alone seemed to resist. From the number of estates he managed for farmers' and ranchers' widows, who had moved into the town, he suspected where Shelby's conservativeness lay. As he left Spicer's barber shop he felt that he should find out what he could about the laconic stranger; secrecy sounded like a property deal of some sort; property was the basis of new business, and new business meant growth for Shelby. He would call on Mayor Fraser.

The man's name was Suttee, the mayor said; in a casual way he had been discussed after council meeting the night before.

'We came to a sort of conclusion about him,' Mr. Fraser said, 'felt he must be looking the town over for possibilities.'

'What possibilities?'

'Industry. Small industry.'

'It would have to be small.'

'Be a great thing for Shelby,' the mayor said. 'Pay roll. Bring in new money and purchasing power . . .'

113

'Has he approached your council?'

'No – he hasn't . . .'

'Wouldn't he?'

'Not necessarily. He might be just getting the lay of the land. He might feel that as soon as he started dealing for property up it would go – double the price . . .'

Title Jack was a little disappointed in Mayor Fraser and his councillors; optimism was a fine thing but it must have *something* to feed upon.

'The way things are moving today,' Mr. Fraser was saying, 'it could be anything. Look at the pre-cut building industry – small houses – he could be from an outfit like that – looking for a spot.'

'Why?'

'Like a lot of industries these days – want to get away from the big cities. Taxes – overhead. And we have both railroads. Shipping is an important factor.'

'I know it is,' said Title Jack. 'But I don't understand just why you should think that . . .'

'Another thing is mustard.'

'What about it?'

'We have a lot of wild mustard in this district and that might be it. Mustard seed industry. They use it for paint and varnish – there's a lot of money in mustard seed reclaiming . . .'

'Yes-yes-yes – but so far it sounds like a lot of wishful thinking – everybody in the dark about him . . .'

'Not exactly. We arrived at our conclusion reasonably – by deduction.'

'Yes-yes-yes,' said Title Jack.

'Negative deduction. Nobody knows this man – he has no relatives in Shelby. He doesn't travel in groceries – dry goods – canned goods – automobile accessories – hardware – ladies' wear – small wares. He isn't in fruit – stationery – drugs – embalming supplies – tombstones – caskets. He is not an inspector for the bank – the schools – the government – boilers – income tax. He doesn't sell roofing – insulation – insurance – life or casualty – peddle bonds – stocks – beer or sets of books. He doesn't play the musical saw.'

Sometimes Title Jack wearied of Mayor Fraser's light approach to everything.

'. . . sing tenor – bang the marimba phones – blow a cornet to drag folks into the Community Centre – so – he isn't one of these travelling evangelists – this is the time of year for them. . . .'

'Yes-yes-yes.'

'First thing I thought of when I saw him dressed in that expensive double-breasted suit, driving an automobile as long as a grain freight. But I gave that up when he didn't take out a two-page ad with Matt in the *Chinook*. Also he hasn't been rolling through the business and residential sections blaring through a P.A. system and telling people to come hear him preach and pray and play the musical saw. Negative deduction. Town council . . .'

Neither man heard the door at the front of the shop open.

'. . . intend giving him every co-operation.' Mayor Fraser had dropped the jocular vein. 'We all want to see the town grow and become diversified . . .' He stopped and looked beyond Title Jack. 'Good day, Mr. Suttee.'

'Mr. Fraser – a carton of Senate House cigars.'

The man was American; he came from a south-western state. The mayor introduced him to Mr. Dalgliesh, saying, 'Mr. Dalgliesh is in real estate, Mr. Suttee. I'm sure he'll be glad to give you any help or information you may need. You'll find town council willing to co-operate too – in any way.'

'That's nice,' Mr. Suttee said. 'And there is something you could do for me.'

'Certainly,' said Mr. Fraser.

'Yes-yes-yes,' said Mr. Dalgliesh.

'I would like to get in touch with Mr. John Sherry. I'm not sure where his house . . .'

Title Jack had waited until he was sure that Mr. Suttee would have finished his visit with Daddy, before he called in at the Sherry house.

'He's just had another visitor,' Miss Tinsley told him. 'He didn't stay long and I had to get the clothes in, so he was just leaving when I got back. He said something about calling again.'

'Relative of Mr. Sherry's?'

'No. Daddy hasn't any – alive. I don't know just why . . . go right on in, Mr. Dalgliesh.'

The room was wreathed with cigar smoke, an opened Senate House carton on the bedside table.

'Who the hell was he?' Daddy greeted Title Jack. 'Never seen him in my whole life before – what's he bringin' me a carton of cigars fer?'

'I don't know, Daddy. Didn't he tell you?'

'Maybe he did. Maybe he did. I kind of slipped off on him. Eases me. Like takin' your boots off. Aaaaaahh – what's the temperture out?'

'Lovely day,' Mr. Dalgliesh said. 'Almost eighty.'

'Eighty above an' I'm cold – still cold – what do you want?'

'Just called for a visit – pass the time of day.'

'Them tax forms bounce back yet?'

'No – I don't think they will.'

'Aaaaaaahh – never square with the gover'ment – live over a hunderd years an' they'll always have you where the hair's short. Old days they left a fellow alone now an' agin – nowadays they make a hobby of it. Never bothered me an' Ramrod up Paradise.'

'Yes-yes-yes,' Mr. Dalgliesh said a little wistfully.

Daddy sucked in a shuddering breath. 'Lighter'n dandruff – except for ought six an' seven – that was what made her lovely – light snow. Me an' Ramrod was warm up Paradise Valley. Grass up to your belly. Juicy. Ready for market right off of that grass an' they wintered well with them soft chinooks blowin' down – tit soft – aaaaah – yi-yi-yah – aaaaaahh . . .'

'This Mr. Suttee, Daddy . . .'

'Ramrod's burried there – under the wolf willah . . .'

'. . . was it property that he . . .'

'. . . good old Ramrod! I told him to stay away from her! Be alive today – sure he would – she killed him – Scatter-piss Annie give him the pox! Bad – had to keep this rock by the windah ledge next his bunk. Agony – agony! Cold – cold – cold

rock so's he could reach up an' take it down an' lay it agin him
– take himself down . . .'

'Yes-yes-yes.'

'Layin' under the grass in Paradise Valley – aaaaaah – lucky
ol' Ramrod – put me beside him . . .'

'Yes-yes-yes,' promised Title Jack.

'All I want – all I ever want!'

Title Jack returned from his fruitless call on Daddy to find
Mr. Suttee waiting for him in his office.

'I understand you handle most of Mr. Sherry's affairs for
him,' Mr. Suttee said.

'Yes-yes-yes.'

'Then perhaps I should have come to you in the first place.
I'm a land man, Mr. Dalgliesh.'

'I see.' The man's earlier reticence was instantly clarified for
Title Jack, now that he knew Mr. Suttee's profession: a drilling
company bird-dog, casting over the province for the scent of
oil; finds were rare for such men now that there had been three
decades of intensive development, and competition among them
was keen, secrecy paramount.

'Mr. Sherry owns the mineral as well as the surface rights on
two sections west of here.'

'Yes-yes-yes – Paradise Valley.'

'Mm-hmh. Well – now – I – ah – represent Federated Petroleum and – ' Mr. Suttee stopped, tapped a fingernail reflectively
against his front teeth. 'This is just a little delicate, Mr.
Dalgliesh, but I'm going to rely on your discretion – I have to.
Federated have been drilling a wildcat on Flat Top.'

'Yes-yes-yes.' Like everyone else in Shelby district, Title Jack
was quite well aware that Federated Petroleum were drilling
high on the crest of the truncated mountain that formed the
west wall of Paradise Valley. Mr. Suttee had not yet been in-
discreet.

'Been my experience that fairness pays dividends – so I'm
going to give you some information that's important to Mr.
Sherry. There are some land men who might not – might feel

that it wasn't very shrewd dealing. I'm not interested in shrewd dealing – I'm interested in fair dealing. I want you to remember that.'

'Yes-yes-yes.'

'What I'm about to tell you is in the strictest confidence – you could use it for your own personal benefit – I have no objection to that but I must ask you not to mention it to anyone else. We've blown in a dandy with Flat Top Number One.'

'Gas?'

'Crude. Tests nine hundred barrels a day – we've got into what could be the richest pool in the D Two in Alberta. It could well be another Redwater field and Mr. Sherry's offset not much more than two miles away – mind you, more than half of that is straight up, so that in distance that counts he's barely a mile off.'

'Well,' Title Jack said.

'I need your help and while that may not cut much ice with you – Mr. Sherry needs your help.'

'Yes-yes-yes.'

'I hadn't realized before I called on him that it – that he would prove so – just who in hell is Mary Jane?'

'I don't know,' Title Jack said. 'I don't think anybody – except Daddy – knows.'

'There was once there I thought I was getting through to him and then we were romping off with Mary Jane and a lighted lantern. Can you help him – can a deal be made with him?'

'Yes-yes-yes,' Title Jack said. 'He has his good days and he has his bad days.'

'Fine – all we have to do is pick a good day and . . .'

'Just a minute, Mr. Suttee. I'm quite agreeable to act in the negotiations – but for Daddy – he's my first interest.'

'That's right.'

'Now that the mineral rights on Paradise Valley are – look – ah – interesting – there will be other companies besides your own. . . .'

'That's right.'

'So that perhaps Daddy's best interests and your best interests may not coincide.'

'Oh – I'm not asking you to accept my offer because you like the way I part my hair.'

'Why do you expect me to accept your offer for – or rather recommend to Daddy that he accept your offer?'

'Because it will be a fair offer. Because I sense that you're a just man and will take into consideration that I have made the first offer, giving you at the same time important and confidential information – which actually I might have withheld so that I could make a better deal for my company.' He stood up. 'You think it over, Mr. Dalgliesh, and you compare me and my offer to the others.'

'Others?'

'Within the week you're going to be up to your – navel – in land men.' He took a paper from his pocket. 'Look this over at your leisure – show it to Mr. Sherry if you think you'd care to – on one of his good days.'

'Yes-yes-yes.'

Mr. Suttee had been right in his prediction; before Saturday five had called upon Title Jack, each having first visited the Sherry house, where Miss Tinsley on Mr. Dalgliesh's instructions had sent them down to the real estate office. All were ebullient with good will toward Daddy's representative, one of them setting a blunt price of ten thousand dollars' worth of escrow oil shares on his esteem, another inviting him to the Cascade Hotel for drinks, his preliminary reconnaissance not having uncovered for him that Mr. Dalgliesh was passionate in his abstinence; three of them within minutes had addressed him affectionately by the detested nickname of 'Title Jack'. All had withheld the information that Federated Petroleum had got bingo on Flat Top. Title Jack sent for Mr. Suttee.

In three sessions with the land man, he succeeded in raising Mr. Suttee's original offer from a thirty-five-thousand-dollar cash payment to one hundred thousand, the royalty from net to gross and from ten to twelve and one-half per cent. He was quite sure that this had not been a false victory pre-arranged for him by Mr. Suttee; except for the astronomical amount of money involved he had played in an old duet no different from his many deals in grain or beef or town and country property. His perfect pitch told him he had not played a wrong note; it had been necessary for Mr. Suttee to phone Tulsa for confirmation.

But their first try together at Daddy had coincided with a bad day. He had seemed fine when they had first entered his room, but Mr. Suttee unfortunately mentioned oil in almost his first sentence.

'That's right – fulla coal oil! Lantern fulla coal oil an' the loft fulla tinder-dry hay – but she has to take that lighted lantern into the barn all the same!'

'Mr. Sherry,' Suttee said firmly, 'some people are driving Cadillacs these days – and if we could get out of the fog for a minute – come to an agreement – you could be riding in one too.'

'Aaaah . . .'

'What?' said Mr. Suttee. 'What's that?'

'Queen always lay back in the harness . . .'

'Look, Mr. Sherry . . .'

'If they come they come,' Daddy said. 'They may take London – may take Hamilton – may even take Guelph – but as long as there's breath in a Sherry, they'll never take Zorah township!'

'What in the world . . .'

'Fenian Raids,' Title Jack explained. 'We've lost him back in sixty-six.'

'The fife an' drum is out, boys! When you hear that bugle blow assembly – come a-runnin' belly to the ground! Fire away, boys – don't matter if you don't see the red bastards! Fire away! She's the York Rangers every time. . . .'

'He still in those Fenian Raids?'

'No,' said Title Jack. 'He's made it ahead twenty years to the Riel Rebellion.'

Daddy muttered something.

'Did he say – poor war?'

'Boer War. We'd better try him another time, Mr. Suttee.'

When they called on him the next day Daddy was fine. He

listened to Mr. Suttee's offer with great interest. 'Oil? Oil. Oil!'

'That's right, Mr. Sherry.'

'Hunderd thousand dollars.'

'And an over-riding gross royalty on all wells at twelve and a half per cent.'

'Yes-yes-yes – you've struck it lucky, Daddy,' Title Jack said.

'All we need is your signature, Mr. Sherry.' Mr. Suttee had spread out the agreement on the bedside table, was holding out his pen to Daddy.

'Hunderd thousan' dollars.' Daddy mumbled to himself for a moment. 'Yep! Sounds all right to me!'

'It's a fair contract,' Title Jack assured him. 'Mr. Suttee and I worked it out for you. I'm sure you won't get better terms anywhere else.'

'Nice juicy grass – rollin' – rollin' – finish nice an' hard right off the grass . . .'

Mr. Suttee shot a stricken glance towards Title Jack. 'You'd better sign it, Daddy,' the real estate man advised him.

'Of course – of course,' Daddy said. 'Never said I wasn't – who said I wasn't?'

'Nobody,' said Mr. Suttee.

'Where do I . . .'

'Right along that line,' Title Jack pointed out. 'I'll sign as your witness.'

'You understand clearly,' Mr. Suttee said.

'My hearin's good. I heard you when you read out them clauses. I got it all. You want this oil outa Paradise Valley an' you're gonna pay me a hunderd thousan' dollars an' twelve an' a half barr'ls oil outa every hunderd barr'ls oil you get.'

'That's right,' said Title Jack. 'Just the mineral rights. The grass in Paradise Valley is still yours. Mr. Suttee's company will pay you for anything they do to the surface rights.'

'Huh?'

'Acidizing,' Mr. Suttee explained. 'Any damage from oil when we blow in – we pay you . . .'

'Hold on – hold on now. Now – that's the best grass this continent.'

'Mm-hmh,' Suttee agreed. 'If you sign right here . . .'

'Finest valley in the country – Dominion – whole world . . .'

'Well, it's certainly one of the richest in crude oil,' Suttee said.

'Let me read that clause.'

'What clause?' asked Title Jack.

'Surface – surface – where is she?'

'It's simply that if we do any damage to the surface . . .' Suttee started to explain.

'Oil – oil – blowin' like a whale,' Daddy said a little wildly, 'spoutin' like a fountain!'

'That's right,' said Suttee, 'blowing high in sixty days.'

'All over Ramrod!'

'If it comes in and we hope it does . . .'

'Hundred foot in the air – black stinkin' oil outa all them wells – spreadin' an' stainin' an' killin' that grass – filthy black oil outa filthy black derricks . . .'

'Just a moment, Daddy,' Title Jack tried to soothe him.

'Soakin' down through the top soil! Oh – no you don't! Git outa here an' leave Paradise alone! She's mine – she's mine an' she's Ramrod's. Ramrod's layin' there under the sweet wolf willah an' you ain't gonna vomit your black oil all over him. . . .'

'But we can't drill if we don't . . .'

'Damn right you can't!' When he spoke again Daddy's voice was low and plaintive; he did not speak to the men in the room at all. 'She's all right – she's all right. They won't. I ain't stinkin' it up for you – ner for me neither. Move over, Ramrod – you git over now. I'm comin' down beside you soon. Is she blowin' – is she blowin' sweet an' gentle – is she? Aaaaaaaaaaaah – she's honeycombin' the snow now – chinook – chinook. . . .' He lifted his voice in a phlegmy scream that made the insides of Title Jack's elbows go cold. 'Noooooooooo! They won't! Head 'em off, Ramrod! Head the sons-of-hunyaks off! She's our valley! She's ours!'

They had not tried again, and strangely, it had been Mr. Suttee's wish that they did not.

'As land men go,' he said to Title Jack, 'I'm long in the

business. I've bought up oil rights from Texas to the Mackenzie, handled young and old, dealt with every kind there is. Nothing new for me when the dollar sign comes up. If they're human I always figured they like money. Some of them reach further and harder for it than others. Some take it sure – some want to gamble. I've seen every response to oil there is. How old is he?'

'Hundred and six.'

'Would have been the same if he'd been twenty-six. I think so. Anybody ever figure out how come he's lived so long? I suppose they've all got an answer for it. Me too. Now. You know what I think? It's because he just doesn't give a damn for unimportant things.' Mr. Suttee stared at Title Jack for a moment. 'Things like half a million dollars.'

That was what had frightened Title Jack Dalgliesh.

Chapter 10

David could not recall an article assignment when so much had
come to him in such a short time; though he had been disappointed at first in Daddy's reminiscences of the Red River and
Riel Rebellion, he knew now that he had expected more than he
should have from the old man, who had been too immersed in
living to build historical significance out of his days. And when
he went over his notes, he realized that he had a wealth of
sensuous detail; rough as they were, the prairie perfumed them;
the foothills sun had warmed them; ever so faintly one could
catch the gay and martial impudence of fife and drum; this was
the sort of material to stain his narrative with immediacy. But
it was also difficult to bring to order; for three days he had
worked to persuade it, and he knew that many more days would
be necessary. He was sure, however, that another week would
see all his groundwork done.

His second Saturday he wandered from the house and out to
the Clifford yard, telling himself that he might run across young
Keith and that together they might try the river. The boy would
be pleasant and relaxing company and he was an authority on
Daddy Sherry. He also had a lovely mother, of whom David

had seen very little, for she was gone to her classes long before David came downstairs in the morning, left again almost immediately after lunch, and seemed busy in the evenings correcting papers or preparing her next day's lessons.

As he walked over the lawn towards the back of the house he noticed that the grass was showing green response to the snowfall of a few days before; then he caught sight of Keith's mother on her knees by a wire netting trellis that ran along the back of the lot. He walked over to her, saw that she was working with a trowel in a narrow trench there. She seemed to welcome the interruption, turning round, still in kneeling position as she looked up to him.

'I thought Keith might be out here,' he said. She was quite trim in shirt and faded levis.

'He was — until about an hour ago when he and Chief headed towards the river.' She brushed at her face with the back of a hand and left a smear of loam down one cheek. 'Have you a cigarette?'

'Yes.'

'I left the house without mine and once I start on these sweet peas I like to get them over with.'

'Here you are . . .'

'Thanks. They were supposed to be in two weeks ago. Sweet peas planted by Good Friday is generally the way it's done in Shelby.' She sat back on her heels as David bent down with a match for her cigarette. 'I'm noted for my grey thumb, but I have had some luck with sweet peas — last year they were way over that netting — the bloom wasn't much, mind you, but there was a lot of foliage. Do you like sweet-pea' she exhaled, 'foliage?'

'It's green,' he conceded.

'Mmmh. And it does show I've tried. How are you and Daddy coming along with your sweet peas?'

'Fine. I've left him alone for three days now — trying to consolidate what I have.' He resisted an impulse to wipe off the dirt smear for her. 'And there's a lot — enough for a novel actually.'

'Oh — do you — have you written a novel — novels?'

'No,' he said and it was not quite so difficult now to resist the impulse to wipe off the smudge. 'I'm just a journalist.'

'What do you mean – just?'

'That I'm not a novelist.'

'Yet?'

He shrugged. 'There's a little matter of talent involved. Anything I can do to help?'

'Do you really mean that?'

'Yes – I think I do.'

She looked through the fence and towards a partly dug patch beyond, where a spade stood with handle aloft. 'Keith started out strong this morning. I made a bet with myself that he'd get up to that post and no farther. I lost it – he got one and a half rows beyond. I don't blame him so much as the worms.'

'Worms?'

'The rainbow run has started below the bridge.'

'I see. Pretty rough turning up worms with every spadeful of dirt and knowing the rainbow are running.'

'That's right. Seems to me you might have had trout in mind when you came looking for Keith.'

'I might have,' he confessed. 'How far do you think I might make it?'

She looked up to him, her eyes squinting with calculation. 'Well – now – I don't know. No reason you should do any digging at all – if you'd rather go fishing.'

'I haven't any rod or tackle.'

'We can fix that – you can use mine.'

'Oh – you fish?'

She shook her head. 'Most boring thing I ever tried. The rod is a fine one – just been used twice and you're welcome to it while you're here.'

'But why do you . . .'

'It's left over from being Keith's mother – or rather from when I thought I should be more than that. Fishing was one of the things I felt I should share with him.'

'Oh.'

'I don't know whether it was harder on me or harder on

Keith. I realized that when I reversed it. I'm a great one for reversing things. Sometimes it makes them clearer.'

'How?'

'Well – in this – I simply imagined I was Keith and he was me. It was immediately quite silly – embarrassing to be a little girl and your father skipping rope and playing jacks and dressing dolls with you. I don't breathe down his neck any more – try to give him too much or take too much.'

'I don't imagine that's too easy to manage,' said David, who was remembering his own mother.

'Oh – it's not so hard. Part of the restraint is just selfishness. That's half the battle in being a good parent.'

'Being selfish?'

'Mmm-hmh. Most selfish people I know have fine children – the self-sacrificing ones have hellions.'

'So it's good for children to put in an apprenticeship under miserable and inconsiderate parents?' David said.

'If you want unselfish and considerate children it is,' she said.

'You may be right,' David went along with her, 'but I'd say that Keith – the odds were that Keith would grow up into a selfish and inconsiderate man.'

'I can always look forward to lovely grandchildren.'

'Just when did you see the light?'

'One Saturday night about a year ago. I'd run his tub. He asked me to leave the bathroom. I haven't done his neck or back for him since.'

'For a boy his age he seems quite considerate of Mr. Sherry,' David observed.

'Oh yes – but Daddy does a lot for him too.'

'I can see that he would.'

'For one thing – I'm pretty sure Keith swears – beautifully.'

'And cleanly.'

'Mmm-hmh. Next to Ramrod Parsons I think Keith's been the most important person in Daddy's life. I love him for it. He's made up for a lot of things Keith's been gypped out of.'

'Yes – I know.'

'You said that in a special way.'

'Did I?'

She did not pursue it. 'You haven't seen Daddy for a few days.'

'No.'

'I was talking to Belva Louise this morning. She's worried about him. He's still in bed – has a slight cold now. If he doesn't shake it there are going to be quite a few people worried.'

'You mean the celebration.'

'It's barely a month away. I'm not so sure it was a good idea – all their committees – a birthday party shouldn't be so – so *public*.'

'But Daddy's a public figure, isn't he?'

'Yes,' she agreed, 'but somehow it's as though his – they'd gone ahead without consulting him about his wishes in it. Oh – I don't blame them – he might quite likely have spoiled it for them. I'm just wondering.'

'What?'

'You don't suppose – that couldn't be why he's taken to his bed – retreat from all the fuss about his birthday?'

'You know him better than I do,' David said. 'But I don't think so. He's been in bed since – before their plans – first time I called on him.'

'That's right,' she said. 'And besides – it isn't the way he'd do it. He'd just tell them to go to hell.' She considered a moment. 'He has his ups and downs. This seems like quite a long down for him and Belva's right to worry. A cold at Daddy's age can be a major thing. Now.' She looked up to him. 'Which is it? The rod or the spade?'

'The spade. The typewriter doesn't do much for stomach muscles.'

She continued to look up at him in his slacks and sweater. 'From here,' she observed, 'I could see that.' Her smile was lovely and friendly.

Her remark had nothing whatever to do with his spading the entire garden plot; he found a mild satisfaction in the steady rhythm of plunging the shovel into earth soft with spring, lifting

it, turning it to drop and break apart its burden. As he felt the
sweat start, he took off his sweater, hung it on a post, rolled up
his sleeves, took up again the soothing repetition of digging
with the sun's warmth constant upon his back and shoulders.
Halfway through, some of his satisfaction left him, for she had
finished her sweet-pea planting and gone; he missed the soft arc
of her kneeling figure just beyond the wire fence. To be honest,
he told himself wryly, he had taken on this chore as much to
be near her as for anything.

When he had finished, he realized that the sun had been more
amorous than he had bargained for; his forearms were showing
a slight blush of burn and there was sting in the rub of his shirt
collar across the back of his neck. He found her when he had
rounded the side of the house, hosing down screens; for the next
two hours he took off storm windows, stacked them away for
her, put up the screens in their place. It was a job, she told him
over iced tea in the kitchen, that would have taken her and
Keith at least two Saturday afternoons to complete. 'It's nice
to have a man around the house again,' she said.

'Well, it's got your garden dug and your storm windows
changed.'

'I don't mean that, though it was nice of you to do it. I just
hadn't realized the difference – seven years – like a seasoning
missing – you know – a trace of cigar or pipe smoke on the air
– the smell of shaving lotion. The house is different for having
a man in it. Crisper – and at night the darkness isn't so – so
dark. If Mrs. Sorenson has waited till after midnight and for a
west wind to light up her refuse barrel in the alley and I wake
and smell smoke – it's just trash burning – the house isn't on
fire at all. All the machines in a house work better with a man
around.'

'Do they.'

'The furnace fan whirs now.'

'Didn't it always?'

'No – whenever it went on it grunted. . . .'

The phone on the wall by the doorway interrupted her. It was
Miss Tinsley, Helen told David, asking that she come over right

away; the housekeeper had already phoned for Dr. Richardson and for Donald Finlay unsuccessfully.

'They've heard about the rainbow run too,' she said on their way to the Sherry house.

David was surprised to find Daddy much the same as he had been on any of his other visits – no better – no worse. The housekeeper had met them at the door, obviously upset, ushering them directly into a bedroom drifting with cigar smoke, then leaving immediately for the railroad bridge where Helen had suggested she might find both Doctor Richardson and Donald Finlay.

'Now – what is this, Daddy?'

'Hell of a winter – hell of a winter.'

'Nice day like this – geese flying north – sap rising – I thought you'd be out and around.'

'Not this time,' Daddy said. 'Made up my mind.'

'To what?'

'Good a time as any.'

'For what?'

'Hunerd an' eleven. No point in overdoin' it.'

'Overdoing what, Daddy?'

'Livin'. I made up my mind – Sort of decided to die.'

'You have not!'

'Yeh-yeh-yeh . . . he can come for me now – any time.'

'That's ridiculous!'

'No it ain't. Like the old man in spring to get the horse outa pasture – panna oats out in front an' a halter hid behind. "C'mon, Daddy," he'll holler sweet an' coaxin', "C'mon, boy . . ." them oats whisperin' in the bottom of the pan . . .'

'Now – look here, Daddy,' Helen began.

' "Here, boy – here boy – ain't gonna bother Doc Richardson ner nobody – jist you an' me an' away we go . . ." '

'That's enough of that,' she said sharply. 'You aren't going to do any such . . .'

'Hell I ain't! My own business. You can lay me down in Paradise Valley . . .'

'We'll lay you down there when your time comes,' she promised him.

'She's come.'

'That isn't for you to say.'

'Who else?'

'It isn't that easy to die, Daddy.'

'I can do it — I can do it with one arm tied behind my back.' His eyes slid from Helen to David then back again. 'An' I am!'

Helen looked over to David. Her blue eyes were asking for help. 'She's right, Daddy,' he said. 'You can't just pick up and leave.'

'Why not?'

'Well — it's not something a person does on the spur of the moment. You aren't even ready to . . .'

'Ready! I had a hunderd an' eleven years to git ready! How ain't I ready?'

'Have you made arrangements?' Helen asked him. 'Your will — how long is it since you've . . .'

'By God, you're right,' Daddy said. He turned his head to David. 'Go git him for me.'

'Who?'

'Title Jack,' Daddy told him. 'Title an' me ain't chewed that will since before Christmas. You go git him for me.'

David could tell from the look and the nod Helen directed toward him that it was best to humour the old man in this. He found Title Jack in his office, explained to him as they drove back to the Sherry home. The real estate man had protested at first, without making a dint in Daddy's determination.

'. . . upsetting all the plans for the celebration — all the committees organized . . .'

'They can un-organize 'em,' Daddy said. 'Read off that list we made up — who's to git what.'

Reluctantly Title took a long paper from his pocket, unfolded it. 'First there's the house, of course.'

'Mmm-aaaaah — '

'Daddy, pay attention to Mr. Dalgliesh,' Helen disciplined him. 'You got Mr. Lang to bring him all the way up here.'

'Oh — yeh — yeh — aaaaah — first there's the house an' that's to go to Belva — you read 'em out an' I'll listen for anything we left out.'

'Yes-yes-yes.' Title Jack went over the bequests which meant little to David, for they were mostly farm and ranch properties whose value he could not assess. He did note that Paradise Valley was to be left to Keith.

When Title Jack had finished, Daddy said, 'Rocker – rocker.'

Helen said, 'What about it?'

'One Title's settin' on. Walnut – black walnut – that ain't listed.'

'Yes-yes-yes. Who's to get it?'

'My gold watch an' chain an' fob – not just the watch – give him the watch.'

'Who?' asked Title Jack.

'Him.' Daddy pointed a thumb at David. 'He went an' got you for me.'

'Watch and chain to Mr. Lang,' noted Title Jack.

'Just the watch. Let him buy his own chain. Chain can go to – aaah – to Roy Teetsworth – Roy helped thrash me in twenty-one. Thrashed me before he thrashed hisself when there wasn't a man in the district to help harvest. You give Roy the chain – no – the watch. Give *him* the chain. So – aaaaah – Sarah.'

'What?' said Title Jack.

'I want Sarah to have that rocker.'

'Sarah who, Daddy?' said Helen.

'She's all dowelled an' pegged.'

'She very well may be,' Helen said, 'but who is she?'

'Not a nail in her. Black walnut – alla the fence posts an' rails was black walnut too. Give her to Sarah Spencer.'

'Spencer!' said Title Jack. 'Sarah Spencer died thirty years ago.'

'Let her have it – let her have it!' Daddy said impatiently. 'Many's the time she's come acrosst the fields with a new . . .'

'Daddy,' Helen interrupted him, 'Sam Spencer's wife, Sarah, died in nineteen thirty-one.'

'. . . comin' acrosst the fields with a new loaf of bread she just baked. Brought it acrosst herself – fresh bread.'

'But Sarah Spencer isn't alive to get your rocker,' Helen explained to him.

'Don't let Florence Allerdyce get it. She can just keep her hooks off that rocker. Anteek – oold anteek – two hundred years old. Don't let Florence . . . oooohhhh!' he exclaimed as though in pain.

'You all right, Daddy?' Title Jack had half risen from the rocker.

'Cuff links! We forgot about my gold nugget cuff links. Only thing I brought back from the Klondike when me an' Ramrod . . . aaaaaaaaah – give them to Sarah Spencer too.'

'But she – she's a woman,' Title Jack said. 'What would she do with cuff links?'

'Aha – ha – said she was dead thirty years ago but just as soon as I mention them gold nugget cuff links she comes back to life quick enough – don't she? She'd take 'em too. All right – put her down for the rocker but she ain't gettin' them cuff links into the bargain. Her bread wasn't all that good. The rocker.'

'How can he put her down,' Helen protested, 'if she isn't . . .'

'I noticed she never thought to bring over any buns when she was bakin',' Daddy said.

'Yes-yes-yes. The cuff links – '

'What cuff links?'

'The gold nugget ones,' Title said. 'The ones you *don't* want Sarah . . .'

'Lost 'em at the Ranchmen's Club in a game of Seven-toed Pete. I raised Dennis Cayley an' he raised me an' I raised him again an' bang went the whole . . . kicked him out a month later when they found out about the pricked cards but that didn't get me back my gold cuff links. You got Sarah Spencer down for that rocker?'

'Daddy – Sarah Spencer is no longer in the land of the living,' Helen said slowly and carefully.

'No!' Daddy's face stilled with sudden sadness. 'Poor Spence. When did it happen? What did she die out of?'

'Thirty years ago,' Helen told him. 'And I don't know.'

'Who's over there lookin' after the baby?'

'Molly's grown up and married, Daddy – with babies of her own – living in the East . . .'

'Poor motherless child. I know – give her the rocker – put

133

Molly Spencer down for that rocker.'

'Yes-yes-yes.'

'For when she's growed up. An' the pitcher.'

'What picture?'

'Alma Tadema,' said Daddy.

'For Molly?' asked Title Jack.

'Florence Allerdyce.' Daddy leaned back against the head-board of the bed and closed his eyes; his chest and shoulders laboured for some time before the dry and wicked laugh was born. 'Wouldn't have it in her house! Indecent!'

'Even the standards of indecency can change with the years,' murmured Helen.

'There's some others,' Daddy was saying. 'Put down these ones — figger out who gets 'em afterwards.'

'Yes-yes-yes.'

'One with them girls — in their nightgown an' tossin' that ball back an' forth — playin' catch in front of the pillars an' the blue sea beyond 'em. They got their hair piled up. Greek girls.'

Title Jack wrote it down.

'Then there's — she's — settin' on a rock. Always hated that one,' Daddy said. 'She's blind an' she's settin' there whimperin' with her busted harp an' the sea gulls is flyin' overhead.'

'Hope,' Helen said.

'. . . or Faith or Charity — one of them girls. Stranded on this rock with a busted harp. Give that to Florence Allerdyce too — she'll hate it the way her shirt's pulled down clear off of one — give her Hope but not the rocker. Not the rocker.'

'Yes-yes-yes.'

'That's about all for now. I'll send for you if I think of anything else — well — hello, Doc.'

Still in fishing clothes, Doctor Richardson stood in the bed-room doorway, Miss Tinsley behind him. Title Jack and Helen and David left, Title Jack with perhaps the greatest alacrity.

At least Keith had enjoyed a successful afternoon, for supper that evening was one of three rainbows he had caught below the bridge, magnificent steel-head-type trout, all of them just over five pounds. Mrs. Clifford had cooked it properly in butter and lemon juice so that none of its delicate flavour had been masked in the frying.

'Skin's the best,' said an expansive Keith, and David agreed with him.

He would have enjoyed the meal more if it hadn't been for the afternoon with Daddy. He could not assess how seriously he ought to take the old man's determination to die. There was the indulgent approach of Title Jack and Helen towards the announcement, but on the other hand Miss Tinsley was obviously not taking it lightly at all, and Daddy Sherry's stubbornness, once he had made up his mind, shouldn't be underestimated. If he were successful in keeping his promise, it was going to be awkward, as Title Jack had pointed out, for the Daddy Sherry Anniversary Committee and all their plans. It was going to be rough on David Lang as well, with an article in the works; dead – there were lots of people older than Daddy by many thousands of years. He told himself that this was a selfish and calloused attitude and that it was not his main concern at all; the cross-willed old human had completely won him, and somehow – if Daddy were to die now – their relationship would have failed to complete itself. There was something else that Daddy had for him, David felt, besides a gold watch – or rather a chain; all that was needed was more time, not much more, he thought, not a great deal more at all!

There was no great reassurance from Helen when he talked with her the next morning; in spite of her off-hand manner he saw that she was just as concerned as Miss Tinsley. She said that she was sure Daddy would be all right, that he had been finding life a bit dull lately and simply wanted to stir things up a bit.

'I don't know,' David said.

'Surprise – that's his secret – his life has been full of surprises.'

'Well, this one's a dandy.'

'I think it's the most remarkable thing about him,' Helen said thoughtfully, 'not that he's lived so long but that he's kept alive

135

his appetite for surprise. He doesn't subscribe for a minute to the principle that there's no new thing under the sun. *Everything* is a new thing under the sun. Maybe that's the secret of eternal youth. It's the most wonderful thing about being young, isn't it?'

'One of them.'

'When you're young you're doing things for the first time – most of the time. Daddy comes to everything as though it were fresh and new – like a poet.'

'I hadn't thought of him as a poet.'

'In a way – with him each day and each experience and each emotion – each cigar and each glass of whiskey is unique and his own because it's new and – and surprising.'

'That's another one for my collection,' said David.

'Another what?'

'Sherry explanation – Harry Richardson gave me the lucky egg – Mr. Spicer – life-prolonging desiccation of pure western air – Mr. Dalgliesh's oil friend – contempt for material things – yours is surprise. . . .'

'But it's the essence of all life!'

'Surprise?'

'And unpredictability.'

'Well – let's hope you're right and that he goes on surprising and being surprised.'

'Yes,' she said fervently. 'It would be forlorn without surprise and without Daddy!'

Chapter 11

'Extreme age has a way of preparing its nominees for death,'
Harry Richardson had said, 'with a sort of relaxed acquiescence
– a willingness to accept that it's a personal fact now. I mean
the very old. Often there's a natural and mild anaesthesia and
a conviction that they are approaching a quite normal event.'

The doctor had dropped into the Clifford house the evening
after his angling had been interrupted by Belva Louise Tinsley.
'Not that I think Daddy's ready for a rendezvous – yet,' he
added quickly. 'He's in good shape, except for this cold of his.
Once he's over that we'll have him up and around again. In the
meantime Belva is giving him lots of liquids – a whiskey occa-
sionally. I'd feel happier about him if we could get him out of
that bed and into his rocker. I've told her to encourage him to
have visitors for their therapeutic value.

As much for this reason as any, David called on Daddy the
afternoon of the next day. He found Miss Tinsley not nearly so
optimistic as the doctor; Daddy was not eating well at all, nor
was he sleeping as much as she would have liked him to. 'I don't
care what Doctor Richardson says, he's made up his mind, Mr.

Lang. He *intends* to die the same way I might set out to bake a cake. And if it doesn't happen soon, it won't be his fault. That's why he's not eating – on purpose – and sleeping – He knows he needs sleep and he hasn't taken his afternoon nap for five days now – I can't tell how much he's getting at night but I'm sure it's just as little as he can manage. He's been picking at me to phone Mr. Pringle for him. I've been putting it off since day before yesterday but I've run out of excuses and these tantrums weaken him. I should have done what he asked right at first – now I can't get Mr. Pringle on the phone and if I go in and tell him he'll think I'm just thwarting him again . . . Would you do something for me?'

'Go in and tell him you can't . . .'

'No – Sunday afternoon – Ollie's out in the greenhouse – that'll be the reason the phone doesn't answer – if you could . . .'

'I'll drive down . . .'

'He won't answer the door bell,' she predicted. 'Just go along the south side of his place till you come to the greenhouse and tap on the glass. Tell him to bring his catalogue with him.'

'Catalogue?'

'The casket one – that's the reason he wants to see Ollie.'

She had been right, for through the glass of the lean-to greenhouse at the back of the funeral home, he saw the undertaker within, busy over an end bench. David tapped for his attention; Ollie made a wide gesture directing him to the back of the building. He opened the door to David there and led him across the embalming room, then through another door opening into a sunny and humid jungle that overwhelmed with botanical life. Ollie Pringle moved ahead of him between the tables with an automatic hunch to avoid the overhead baskets and pots of ivy-leaved geranium and hanging petunias. To David's left flourished a bed of snowball chrysanthemums; at the far end he saw a stand of red and yellow talisman tea-roses in bloom; his eye picked out the scarlet of poinsettia bracts, the macaw brilliance of crotons, the purple and gold of bird of paradise blossoms in stilled flight, a tall congregation of gladioli. He saw the plumes of young palm trees, glossy gardenias, the flame of bougainvillea and hibiscus, a table devoted entirely to orchids sheltered from full sun by a canopy of muslin. There were plants dormant, plants budding and blooming, plants in tables, pots and flats, plants sprouting from bulbs and corms, rhizomes and tubers, monopodial and sympopodial – terrestrial and epiphytic orchids, ferns and monocotyledons and bicotyledons and succulents and vines. With pride Ollie drew his attention to one bench. 'I have them grouped together,' he explained, 'because of their popular names.' He identified them for David: Jerusalem Cherry, Moses-on-a-Raft, Twelve Apostles, Angels' Trumpet, Passion Flower, Wandering Jew, Star of Bethlehem, Prayer Plant, Crown of Thorns. The Creeping Charlie and Brazilian Fire-cracker, he explained, did not belong; they had been moved there only temporarily from their own secular table to make room for the bedding-out flats at this time of year.

He said that he would come up to Daddy Sherry's just as soon as he had finished the flat of lobelia he was pricking out. David stayed and watched him deftly transferring the seedlings with their pinpoint green heads and their hair-fine roots. When the flat was filled he measured out a teaspoon of ruby liquid from a small bottle and into water, staining it pink as though with blood. With this he sprayed the flat.

'Damping-off,' he explained. 'It's much better than flowers of sulphur for damping-off fungus. Last year I lost hardly any – only the corner of one flat of snapdragons.'

Just as they were about to leave the greenhouse, he stooped down and came up with a seedling from under the bench. He planted it in a two-inch pot.

'What sort of plant is that?' asked David.

'I'm not sure. Could be a seed dropped from that guava – or the Passion Plant there – it might be a citrus – yes – I ate a tangerine in here just after Christmas and I must have dropped one of the seeds under the bench then. When it's volunteered like that it's a shame to waste it.'

Miss Tinsley was profuse in her apologies to Ollie for taking him away from his greenhouse on a Sunday afternoon – and for the purpose that Daddy had summoned him. The undertaker was cheerfully gracious about it. 'Quite all right, Miss Tinsley. I understand perfectly. Have to humour him when he's under the weather – only glad to have the chance to help.' And as David seemed about to leave, he said, 'You might as well come in with me, Mr. Lang – you were going to visit him anyway before you came down to get me for Miss Tinsley.' David would not have passed up the invitation for anything.

Daddy wasted little time in preliminary greetings. 'Let's see 'em, Ollie – open her out.' Ollie laid the catalogue on Daddy's lap, wet his thumb and turned back the cover.

'Aaaaaaaah – mmmmmh,' Daddy stared down at the casket illustrated on the first page. Shrewdly enough, the print under it was in large and heavy upper case. 'Solid mahogany – massive bronze corners,' Daddy read out. 'That cloth – what's she – '

'Lined with . . .' Ollie leaned forward and tilted his head, '. . . diamond art silk.'

'Aha – nice-nice-nice.' Daddy flipped over the page. 'Same thing over here – what's the difference?'

'Hundred dollars,' said Ollie. 'That first one was mahogany but that one you're looking at is selected quartered oak. You go ahead and look them over, Daddy. Full range there and at the back there's a selection of hardware and casket sundries – you want it custom then we can put anything on anything you like.' He settled back into his chair. 'Those in the first part of the book are pretty high priced – further towards the back the . . .'

'How much,' Daddy said, 'for the . . .'

'. . . mahogany one? Eight-fifty.'

Daddy looked at him with wild surprise. 'Eight dollars an' fifty cents!'

'Eight *hundred* and fifty,' Ollie corrected him and cleared his throat delicately, 'dollars.'

'Aaaaaaah – oh – ' Daddy snuffled and reached for the tissue on the bedside table as he turned another glossy page. 'Um-aaaaaah – Venetian bronze corners – fumed an' . . .'

'. . . varnished finish. Five-sixty.'

'Hinged panel – brocade silk – hey!' He pointed with outrage. 'Pillah – no pillah!'

'If you want one – we can put one in,' Ollie assured him.

Daddy blew his nose and turned the page. 'Gold rose, copper handles. This one's got a pillah,' he said brightly.

'Four-fifty.'

'Oh now – now! Tossels – tossels – tossels!' he exclaimed with delight. 'All covered with cloth – nice black – '

' – broadcloth. Three-seventy-five.'

'Handles – she's got handles to her!' He looked up to Ollie. 'Silver?'

'Nickel.'

'Looks like her whole side lets down – uh – how much does . . .'

'. . . it cost? – three-seventy-five.'

'Three dollars an' seventy . . .'

'Three *hundred* and seventy-five – dollars.'

For a long time Daddy stared down at the casket illustration, muttering to himself. He slapped the page. 'Yep! Tossels an' all – that's the one I want!'

'When your time comes,' Ollie said.

'Uh-huh. Right now. Put my name on that one – that pillah ain't extra, is it?'

'No.'

'All right – now let's see the other one.'

'Other casket?'

'No – catalogue – where is she? Let's see her.'

'I just brought that one, Daddy.'

'Gotta have a stone, don't I? Wanta see what you got in the line of tombstones – you was supposed to bring it – why didn't you bring it! You dangle back down there an' get it. . . .'

'That's enough for today.' Miss Tinsley spoke from the doorway.

'He only brought the one,' Daddy told her. 'I wanta look over his stones. I don't want somebody else to pick out my stone for me . . .'

'Some other time,' Belva Louise said firmly. 'It isn't fair to Mr. Pringle – and – and it's Sunday.'

'All right then,' Daddy said to Ollie. 'First thing tomorrah – I wanta see that tombstone catalogue an' pick one out. I'll give

141

it back to you,' he promised, 'when you come back tomorrah with the other one.'

As David left, he was certain that he agreed with Miss Tinsley's more than he did with Harry Richardson's optimistic prognosis.

He went up to his room, intending to do some work, but the Sherry article did not appeal at all, and after several false starts at possible column pieces, he gave up. He found Keith in the kitchen.

'Thought you'd be down at the bridge.'

'Nope.'

'Your mother says I can use her rod – maybe we could . . .'

Keith shook his head. 'I don't feel very much like it.'

'Oh.'

'I was over to see Daddy.'

'I see,' David said.

'It was Grandma's idea. She said it might cheer him up. It didn't. Didn't cheer me up so much either.'

'Didn't it . . .'

'He's got – he's got his coffin all picked out – showed it to me in this book he got from Mr. Pringle. He's going to die.'

'Oh – I don't know about that, Keith.'

'Says he is. Generally does what he says he's going to do. You know – when I was fishing yesterday – when I walked back along the tracks from the railroad bridge – I saw a cat.'

'Mm-hmh.'

'Dead cat across the rail. I don't think the train killed him. He was all in one piece and just laying across the rail. Maybe somebody threw him there. Just when I came to him a cloud of flies lifted up off of him real quick. He had his paws out in front of him – like when a person prays?'

'Yes,' David said.

'His eyes were open. Beads. Black – dead beads. I didn't feel so good.'

'Well – look, Keith . . .'

'Why does stuff have to die?'

142

'The way it is,' David said.

'I know it's the way it is – but why is it the way it is?'

'Because there couldn't be any life if there wasn't any death.'

'I don't see that.'

'If animals – people – lived for ever – there wouldn't be room – even if there were – there'd still have to be death for life to keep on . . .'

'Why?'

'Well – the plants we eat – to keep us alive – they die – the trout you caught yesterday – '

'They don't count like *humans!*'

'There's another thing about it. Supposing everybody lived for ever . . .'

'Yeah?'

'They'd go on being just the same as they are for thousands of years – making the same mistakes – no chance for improvement – every new individual that's born to replace one that's died – is a – a fresh start.'

'Take a lot to improve on Daddy!'

'I agree with you.'

'Get born and then quit. What's the use?'

'Well,' David said, 'a lot of people like it in between.'

'They'd like it a lot better if there was more in between,' Keith said.

'I think Daddy has some more left to him.' David hoped he sounded as convinced as he tried to.

His visit to Daddy the next afternoon coincided with Ollie Pringle's return engagement. David had barely seated himself by the old man's bed when the undertaker arrived with his tombstone catalogue. Daddy made his choice quickly.

'. . . an' I don't want her polished – I want – '

' – rough red granite,' Ollie said, not cheerfully at all.

'Now – aaaah – how high is she?'

'Top part's five feet two inches wide – ten inches thick – two feet six inches high . . .'

'That from the ground?'

'No – total height including the base – three feet two inches.'

'What's she weigh?'

'Ah – ,' Ollie ran his finger along the bottom of the page. ' – thirty-six hundred pounds.'

'What do you think of that?' Daddy said to David.

'Of what?'

'Aaaak . . . thirty-six – um – take way two thousan' once – an' sixteen – over a ton an' a half – almost two ton,' Daddy said proudly. 'Now I want her rough,' he warned Ollie again, 'just polished where they – where she – hold on – hold on . . .'

'Yes?' said Ollie.

'What goes on the – '

' – front of it – the epitaph – that can be worked out,' Ollie said a little wearily.

'Damn rights it can – right now – my name – when I was born – what's next Friday?'

'What do you mean?'

'Date – date . . .'

'Twenty-ninth . . .'

'May seventeenth, eighteen forty-nine – April twenty-nine nineteen sixty – an' then there's gotta be – aaaaaah – short – short – I want her – '

' – short. There's a list of selections in the back of the booklet,' Ollie said.

'Good – let's hear some of 'em.'

'Usually the epitaph is a – it's a sort of tribute,' Ollie explained.

'I know – I know. But I want her short.'

'Ah – "Resting where no shadows fall",' Ollie read out.

'Aaaaah-um,' said Daddy noncommittally.

' "A noble example was his life".'

'Go on – go on.'

' "Kind, loving and faithful".'

'Um – nope.'

' "None knew thee but to love thee".'

'Hell they didn't! Short an' – an' – kind of truthful.'

' "Until the day break",' Ollie said.

'Huh?'

'That one – "Until the day break" – doesn't pin you down much – commit you . . .'

'Mmmmmh. What else?'

'Look,' Ollie protested, his distaste quite evident, 'I'll just leave it with you and you can look it over at your leisure. . . .'

'Hold on a minute,' Daddy ordered him. 'What's the shortest one there?'

Ollie consulted the book for a moment. ' "At rest".'

' "At rest".' Daddy savoured it. 'Yeah – yeh – yeh – she's short all right – but that's all you can say for her. Keep readin' 'em.'

' "Gone home" – "Gone to rest",' Ollie took up the dreary and didactic list, ' "Rest in peace" – "Deeply mourned" – "Sweet as the rose" – "To memory ever dear" . . .' His voice was slightly hoarse when he had come to the end. '. . . "His life an ideal" – "His memory an inspiration".' He closed the book-let and said shortly, 'Take your pick.'

'Aaaaaah – leave her – leave her – I'll look 'em over. . . .'

'You will not!' David was startled by the blunt impatience of the undertaker's contradiction; Ollie had exhausted the reserve of patient cheer which had seemed infinite. 'I'm not going through it with you a third time – it isn't fitting! You make your pick now.'

Daddy stared up at him for several long seconds. 'All right, Ollie,' he said mildly, ' "At rest".'

Ollie rose from his chair, began to gather up his catalogues. 'You can leave 'em for me – '

' – to pore over – no, I can't,' Ollie said shortly. 'It's morbid.'

When the undertaker had left, David said, 'I'd better be going too, Daddy.'

'Not so fast – not so fast. Which one?'

'Which one – what?'

'Which one do you like?'

'Of the epitaphs? To tell you the truth, Daddy, I don't like one single one of them.'

'That so! That so!' Daddy was stung. 'You got anything better

– you're a writer – maybe you can think up somethin' better . . .'

'Oh no – for what they are – they're all right. . . .'

'I didn't pick on that one – didn't ask for it short just because she's fifty cents a letter . . .'

'I know,' David said.

'What's your objection then?'

'Epitaphs aren't my favourite reading. None of them looks good to me at all – particularly if I were considering them for my own tombstone.'

'You figger it's morbid too.' When David nodded Daddy said, 'For you or Ollie, anybody else. Not for me, it ain't. You can git out now – time for my nap.'

'Oh,' David said, remembering Miss Tinsley's earlier concern, 'certainly – I wouldn't want to keep you from sleep . . .'

'You wouldn't – it's just easier to concentrate on *not* havin' any when I'm alone.'

Chapter 12

Helen Maclean's husband had been dead for eight years; a young geologist with an independent oil company, he had been killed one July night when his car had turned over on a foothills trail in to a drilling site. With Keith a child of three to be supported, she had turned to teaching barely a month after Murray's death, for at the same time there had come an opening on the Shelby High School staff in English, Dramatics and Social Studies, the subjects she had taught before her marriage. It seemed to her now that she and Keith had always lived with her mother and that the four years in Calgary with Murray had been simply an interlude away from home, sandwiched between childhood and the present. It bothered her that her married years had lost their clarity, for she had loved her husband very much; they had been happy ones in a relationship that was to have lasted for ever — not stepping-stone years like the three at University or the two in her first school — but vivid at the time and dim against her will now.

She suspected that her mother had played a large part in the regrettable fading, trying to help at first in the only way that her undemonstrative nature permitted: tactfully and surely ignoring her daughter's widowhood, never referring to Murray, quickly reasserting the quiet dominance Helen had known in girlhood. She would have conducted herself in much the same way if her daughter had come home to recover simply from a broken engagement – a long and serious one perhaps but to a man whom Mrs. Clifford had never met. In the beginning Helen had talked to Keith about his father in an effort to keep the boy's memory of him fresh, but in time she had dropped the deliberate regularity of such talks, feeling that they succeeded only in underlining the child's loss.

From their first meeting, David Lang had interested her as no other man had since Murray's death; it was an attraction of surprising strength for the short time she had known him. He was not one of those who proffered themselves directly and without contradiction; his solid, dark bulk and deep voice should have been accompanied by the benign arrogance of most large males. They were not, yet he was a confident man, she thought, or rather, self-sufficient in the manner of contemplative people – and, she decided, lonely ones. She was sure that he had been a quiet and serious child, that some special condition of his early boyhood had made him so. She wondered why he had not married; it was a shocking waste.

The thing she liked most about him was his willingness to listen; it flattered because it was done without self-congratulatory ostentation: 'I'm listening and I value what you say even though you are a woman.' It was all the more flattering from a man who was frank, who obviously did not suffer fools gladly. It inspired an answering frankness.

'I don't go out much,' she had told him a couple of evenings after their visit together to Daddy Sherry.

'Don't you . . .'

'Small towns are rough on single women – spinsters.'

'But you're no spinster . . .'

'I qualify,' she said. 'Oh – I'm invited – but I seldom go.'

'Why not?'

'It's not nice being extra.'

'But you have your friends.'

'My age – they're married – people are intended to be in pairs.'

'And they all are – except you.'

'I have had friends – women my own age – several – but in time they've married. They're the worst.'

'What do you mean?'

'It's as though they had resigned themselves to the alone state and can't get used to it – can't get over the wonder of finally having someone – a male. They flaunt him. What I mean is – it's so much more evident with them than with others. . . .'

'I wouldn't think a man could make all that difference.'

'It isn't because he's a man – damn it – you aren't all that important – it's because a woman is a woman.'

'What's that mean?'

'Being what she is it means that she's only – she's not whole without a man. It's her nature to want response and attention and affection and not from another woman but from a man. Without it she isn't completely a woman.'

'But surely there are – there are men for friends . . .'

'Oh yes – there are men. I'll tell you something about men and about myself. I'm in favour of them. I warm to them more than I warm to women. I was born with candles inside me that light up just for men. It doesn't matter who he is – his age – his personality – the important thing is that he's a man and not a woman. Now – do you know what happens?'

'When you light up your candles?'

'I can see it going through his head – here is an experienced and unattached woman – doesn't matter that he's attached – the important thing is that here is an unspoken-for woman and she's fair game. Know what happens then?'

'I'm a man,' he reminded her.

'I've had more passes – covert and overt – thrown at me than any other female in Shelby and greater Shelby district.'

'I'd say that was response.'

'It's not good enough – not nearly good enough. It's not that primitively simple. I wish it were. But it isn't.'

'Just what do you want from them?'

'I don't want anything from them – not a single thing.'

'But you said that you . . .'

'I said that I was not complete and that no woman's complete without a man. I shall probably spend the rest of my days just that way – incomplete.'

'What have you done – taken a vow?'

'In a way.'

'And what have you gained?'

'It isn't what I've gained – it's what I would have lost if I hadn't – that's what counts.'

'Well – that sounds as though it makes sense – even if it doesn't.'

'It does,' she assured him. 'There hasn't been another Murray. Accepting anything less than what we had together – and what I've been offered has been tremendously less – would be to admit that what we had was nothing much after all. What happens between a man and a woman is nothing but a casual and fragmentary – you see I'm in one hell of a state . . .'

'It's called limbo.'

'It could be worse. I have Keith. Keith and teaching. What's yours?'

'My what?'

'Reason for existence.'

'I'm not sure.'

'Welcome to limbo. Only not really – you have your work – it must be very exciting and satisfying.'

'Not nearly so much as it seems,' he said, 'or as I used to think it was.'

'But you're making a definite mark.'

'Not so definite.'

'When did you discover that?'

'I'm not sure – I was too busy writing to notice that I was being followed.'

'By whom?'

'The fellow who erases what I've just written. I write and he rubs it out and I write again and he rubs it out again and I'm getting a little tired of it.'

'Any idea who he is?'

'Time.'

'He's always been rough on journalists.'

'Yes.'

'Have you written anything that might offer more resistance to the eraser?'

'Years ago. Some poetry.'

'I thought so,' she said. 'But why not any more?'

'I didn't do it well enough. My sprung rhythm leaned more and more towards an unfortunate enumerative quality — as though the margin release of my typewriter had become stuck.'

'Well over to the left?'

'Yes.' He laughed. 'Some day — as they say — I'll try a novel — in the meantime I'm giving the old boy something to rub out with great regularity — which is better than giving him nothing to rub out.'

'But this doesn't put you in limbo.'

'It's one foot — and I'm extra too, you know.'

'Oh. I've wondered why you never married.'

'There was a war, then there was apprenticeship — for a writer it's at least ten years and they're damned uncertain ones even when there's just yourself.'

'Mmm-hmh. It isn't just your writing the old boy's interested in,' she cautioned him.

'I know that,' he said. 'Now.'

He was stopped in the Sherry article and he knew that he was badly stopped. In the first place the old man's intention of dying on Friday, April the twenty-ninth, which David was inclined now to take rather seriously, made it impossible to conduct fruitful interviews. Miss Tinsley's distress at Daddy's promised death kept David from bothering her for an account of what had happened in spring of the flood year of nineteen fifty-four. But these were not nearly so important as the internal impediment; he had put up what he hoped was a fairly accurate biographical scaffolding, had assembled a great deal of lumber, but he had not yet found the key that would let Daddy into the house he was building for him.

In the middle of the week he had called on the Reverend Donald Finlay. The minister had recalled much of his fifteen-year association with Daddy. He seemed to sense that David's quarry was too elusive for anecdote.

'Daddy is a man who has not only lived an astonishingly long life,' the minister said. 'He's lived it fully – intuitively.'

'Is that living life fully?' David asked, hoping the man was not given to the rounded clichés of his profession. Good stewardship had not been mentioned so far.

'Well . . .' Donald Finlay considered, 'whether we like it or not intuition is nearer to life than intellect – or science . . . That's why we have the arts, isn't it?'

'I suppose.'

'It's one of the reasons I'm a minister.'

'Just what do you mean by living fully?'

'Expressing your whole potentiality – taking advantage of every bit of elasticity life offers and stretching it to your profit.'

'What sort of profit?' David pressed him.

'Liberty – freedom. It isn't easy to do. Freedom's a rare thing in our lives. With qualifications, I believe in free will,' he said, 'and in Mr. Sherry as a personification of it.'

'Well, aren't you – couldn't a person interpret that as meaning that he's spent a long and selfish and – licentious . . .'

'Oh no – that's the most restricted life of all – to be a slave of appetites – it invites the worst kind of restraint – that of others – of society. However naïve and primitive it may be, he has a code and remains his own master. A lot of men in his generation did.'

'What sort of code?'

The minister reflected a moment before he answered. 'I'd say honour meant a great deal to him and he places loyalty high. I've heard him say he wouldn't "hire a disloyal man to haul guts to a bear." Not too discriminating a sense of loyalty but a fervid one. And pride. Pride has been held in consistent disrepute by my profession through the ages, but that's because there must be several brands of it, I think. Surely it's only false pride that goes before a fall. His isn't false; it's quite admirable

152

and an important part of his dignity. Then there's honesty –
that seemed to flourish in his day. . . .'

'That sounds a little cynical?'

'You know – Harry Richardson once accused me of being
cynical – but I don't think I am – I believe in revelation and
intuition and they wilt under . . .'

'I didn't mean in a philosophic sense,' David said.

'Or in the other. When I said that honesty flourished in his
day I should have added – and in his part of the world. I think
it does so in an inverse proportion to the number of individuals
and the distance between those individuals. Distances were long
then and people – few.'

'Why should that affect honesty?'

'Dishonesty has to have an audience – doesn't it – someone
against whom to direct it?'

'What about dishonesty with one's self?'

'I'm not sure about that. There has to be a voluntary quality,
and dishonesty with yourself is most apt to be involuntary –
wouldn't it be self-delusion – instead?'

'What I had in mind,' David explained, 'was – a compliance
with the accepted notion of honesty – but a dishonesty accord-
ing to the ethics of the kingdom within.'

'I see. Yes. The more modern kind – at least there's perhaps
more of it now. In Mr. Sherry's day and his sort of life I
imagine the kingdom within and the kingdom without were
more like each other and that made it easier. Are you interested
in hearing . . .'

'Indeed I am.'

'I see a man like Daddy alone in all that wild space and I
can't see that he could *afford* to be dishonest.'

'Why not?'

'Dangerous – so few other humans to turn to for aid that a
man couldn't waste friendship or jeopardize it through dishonesty. That would account for loyalty too.'

'Judging from television there seem to have been quite a few
train robberies – stage hold-ups – rustling . . .'

'I'm sure there were.'

'But in the past fewer people to spread it out over.'

'I'm not saying there was no dishonesty.'

'Less opportunity and fewer people to direct it toward – aren't Harry Richardson and I right? Isn't that a rather cynical explanation?'

'No – because cynicism argues a lack of faith in man's capability for improvement. I have no way of measuring the resistance he is putting up against dishonesty today but I have faith that he's improved – even since Daddy's youth.'

'Wait a minute now – that isn't consistent with . . .'

'More honesty then and less opportunity for dishonesty – ' the minister summed up; 'less honesty now and more opportunity for dishonesty – but in the end a net gain – men more *capable* of honesty.'

'I see.'

'Our Indians were generally good at honesty for the same reasons but weak against the pressure of civilization. I did mission work with the Bloods when I was younger. It was for long enough – and long enough ago for me to see it happening.'

'Harry Richardson told me that you – that a number of years ago Mr. Sherry contemplated marriage.'

'Yes.'

'The doctor also said you'd rescued him.'

'I did. She was a quite terrible woman. I hadn't realized she was – at first – when I was instrumental in getting her into Daddy's house as his housekeeper. She came to my congregation – a Mrs. Holloway – from somewhere in the north of the province, and she fooled me with the first impression she made – a hearty, jolly woman. Quite wicked. I believe in wickedness,' he said. 'She had planned and schemed it deliberately – used me to get into his house, though she hadn't needed to – really . . . Up until Miss Tinsley, Daddy's turn-over of housekeepers was staggering – they never lasted more than three months. She was – this one was almost successful in her harpy designs – but not quite. That's about all there was to it.'

'Except for one thing,' David said.

'What's that?'

'The doctor said you had queered it. Just how did you manage that?' He saw a look of embarrassment appear on Donald Finlay's face.

'I'm not proud of the means I used,' the minister confessed, 'especially since all our talk about honesty.' Diffidently then he went on to explain to David that he had made a last attempt to persuade Daddy to call off the wedding just the day before the ceremony. It had been one of Daddy's bad days, so that the task of getting through to him was almost hopeless. The fifth time that the minister spoke of breaking off the engagement to Mrs. Holloway, Daddy answered him angrily.

'No engagement – no engagement!'

'But there is, Daddy – tomorrow afternoon.'

'I tell you – no engagement. Didn't even get in range of 'em! I was there . . .'

'I mean your marriage tomorrow . . .'

'No casualties – surgeon – he got drunk the night before an' fell through the open basement. Then the sergeant got kicked in the face – grey in his team kicked him – he had an engagement. Bust his jaw.' He wheezed up a laugh. 'Engagement with the grey's hind hoof.'

'But you are getting married tomorrow . . .'

'Eh!'

'Marriage – marriage!'

'Sure – sure – her – Saturday – good day for it – was a Saturday when them officers come down the ranks after we fell in – handed out cigars. Down they come – boxes opened. Every man got a cigar. My stummick was on edge an' I never did smoke mine – how can a fellah smoke a cigar when he's goin' in to fight – Fish Crick – aaaahaaaaah! *There's* your engagement. . . .'

'No, it isn't. . . .'

'Took an awful whippin'. She was an engagement all right – wounded tryin' to crawl back outa line of fire – Darcy got hit – horses gut shot! Oh, God – what an engagement!'

155

'Daddy – I want to ask you not to marry . . .'

'Mary – Mary Jane,' Daddy muttered. 'Told her not to. Over an' over I told her – over an' over . . .'

'Mary Jane took the lantern into the barn,' the minister said carefully and distinctly.

'Damn rights she did!'

'Mary Jane Holloway.'

'Fulla hay – loft fulla hay an' away she went – fire – fire – always been scairt of fire . . . why should Mary Jane . . .'

'. . . Holloway.'

'Hah!'

'Mrs. Holloway – the woman you intend to marry tomorrow – Mary Jane Holloway . . .'

'. . . horses screamin' – an' – aaaak . . . Mary Jane . . . Mary Jane . . .'

'Next time,' the minister warned him, 'it won't be the barn – it'll be the house – Mary Jane Holloway. . . .'

'No – no – no!'

'If you marry her tomorrow . . .'

'Git her out – git her out! Git it off her – '

'What, Daddy?'

'That goddam lantern,' Daddy whispered.

'All right – all right, Daddy. Are you marrying Mary Jane Holloway tomorrow?'

'No – no – hell, no! I ain't marryin' nobody!'

When he had finished, Donald Finlay had not asked David to refrain from using the anecdote in his projected article. David could imagine how a priest must feel after hearing confession; nor had the minister any more reason to worry than a penitent would that his confidence would be violated.

Later in the afternoon David ran across Harry Richardson in front of the Bluebird Café. 'I'm a little worried about him,' he admitted to David. 'It's bronchitis – there's a relative frequency of pneumonia in the aged and the worst of it is, it's difficult to tell when bronchitis becomes pneumonia. He's running a slight fever today – if it lasts longer than four days we'll know for sure.'

'Isn't there anything to – you can give him?'

'No point in chemotherapy – the infection isn't caused by bacteria. Mind you – it's just a possibility – there's no râles, though he is short of breath – but the signs and symptoms are generally vague. It's difficult to tell whether pneumonia occurs because a patient is dying or whether the pneumonia causes the dying. What I don't like is the possibility of his – I wish to hell he'd help some!'

David had walked down town and on his way home he overtook Keith in the middle of the road, half-heartedly kicking a stone along ahead of himself. The boy joined him on the sidewalk, Chief stalking behind them.

'I guess there's a lot of things that scare humans,' Keith said.

'I guess there are, Keith.'

'And dying would be the worst of all.'

'Yes.'

'Doesn't make sense.'

'Dying?'

'Daddy dying . . .'

'You mean deliberately – because he's made up his mind to?'

'No – I figure most the time he can do anything he sets his mind to. I mean the time for it – now.'

'What about it?'

'Isn't the time of year I'd pick. I'd wait till harvest – fall – when frost had killed everything. I sure wouldn't pick spring.'

'Wouldn't you . . .'

'Mm-mmm. Spring isn't any good for that. Kind of puts a person out of step with everything.'

'Yes,' David said. 'It does, Keith. You – ah – got anything planned right now?'

'No.'

'Let's you and I have a little visit with him.'

'Look at all the stuff you get with spring,' Keith said as they walked toward the Sherry house. 'Chicks and calves and colts – gophers coming out again and crocuses . . .'

'Yes, Keith.'

'Meadow larks again – I don't mean all that's so hot but they do happen in spring and that's why it doesn't seem right he should decide to die now instead of in fall or winter. . . .'

'I agree with you – untimely.'

'The pussy willows are out and yesterday when I came home from the bridge . . .'

'Save it – save it.'

'Huh?'

'Till we get to Daddy's.'

'Oh,' Keith said.

'We're going to tell him about a little trip we're taking.'

'Trip?'

'Drive – west – you and I are going to visit Paradise Valley.'

'Are we!'

'Well – some time – perhaps Saturday when you have no school. . . .'

'Gee – that'll be great!'

'Mmm-hmh – the great thing about it – I'm hoping – well, we'll see. Wouldn't hurt to tell him about your rainbow – anything – ah – spring-like that occurs to you – but we are going to go to Paradise Valley and we do want him to know about it.'

In the cottonwood before the Sherry home David noticed an untidy nest on a low branch, and as they went down the walk a matronly robin was shopping for a worm in the dark earth below Daddy's bedroom window.

He was shocked at the change in Daddy since he had last seen him; he had visibly shrunk; he opened his eyes just for a second when the two came into the room, then closed them, their lids even more transparent-looking than usual, his skin as white as the pillow. He was breathing in short quick gasps.

'Well, Daddy.' David took the old man's limp hand in his.

'Ah-yah-yah-yah.' With tired faintness it came from deep inside the man, the mouth flaccidly ajar, the blue lips unstirred.

'Lovely spring day.' When he released Daddy's hand it dropped to the bed; the skin had been hot and dry. 'Sort of day a man wants to be outside.'

'The hell it is,' mumbled Daddy.

158

'Hell it isn't,' David contradicted. 'Nearly seventy above.' He looked meaningfully over to Keith.

'Sure — sure — maybe eighty,' Keith said quickly. 'That way for three — four days now. Rainbow are running, Daddy.' The old man did not comment. 'I caught five in two times — one of them,' he looked anxiously at Daddy, 'almost six pounds. Should of seen her eggs — she was ready to spawn.'

'We had it for lunch,' David said.

'So she won't spawn now, will she?' Daddy did not open his eyes.

'Little stuffy in here.' David went to the window, began to raise it.

'Mr. Lang's going to take me up to Paradise Valley,' Keith said.

Back in his chair, David saw that Daddy's eyes were open.

'You want to come with us, Daddy?' Keith asked him.

The pale old eyes stared. 'If you feel up to it,' David said.

'What for?'

'Oh — see it — perhaps visit Ramrod's grave.'

'When you goin'?' Daddy said.

'Saturday,' Keith said. 'No school.'

'Not much point. You're goin' Saturday. I'm goin' Friday.'

'Suit yourself,' David said and he knew that the invitation had been shoved at Daddy much too quickly.

' 'Longside the south end of our house mother's tulips . . .' Keith began.

'That catalogue,' Daddy said.

'What catalogue?' Keith said.

'Casket catalogue on top the table. . . .'

'Ollie Pringle took them with him,' David said.

'Oh — yeh-yeh. . . .'

'South end of our house,' Keith tried again, 'mother's tulips . . .'

'Real nice broadcloth,' Daddy said, 'with tossels.'

'. . . they're up real green. . . .'

'Her whole side lets down on hinges. . . .'

'. . . not just the tips showing,' Keith explained a little desperately, 'but they unfolded a whole leaf an' you can see . . .'

'. . . right inside of it without havin' to peer down from up above.'

': . . green buds inside.'

The old man mumbled unintelligibly.

'I guess spring's pretty lovely in Paradise Valley,' David said.

'Sure is!' Keith said.

'Aaaak . . .'

'Mallards all paired up on the beaver dam – deer – ' Keith enthused, 'we may see fawns and the calves . . .'

'Too damn soon for calves,' Daddy said.

'No – it isn't! Rita phoned mother from the L7 and they already had thirty-six. Gophers,' Keith said to David, 'sittin' up all over like tent pegs – and crocuses – '

'Yes, I know,' David said.

'The hell you do,' Daddy said. 'What do you know about it?'

'Oh – I was born south and east of here,' David told him. 'Of course, spring generally came there earlier than it does here – by a couple of weeks. Warm nights. Had most of the seeding done before now. . . .'

'We generally got seeded in plenty of time,' Daddy said.

'Our trees would be in leaf by now and the grass . . .'

'Short grass. That's short grass country.'

'I know it is. Short grass for good beef.'

'For goats,' Daddy said. 'Cattle wants long grass. . . .'

'Short grass is harder,' David said.

'Who told you that! Wanta raise cattle go where the grass is long – that dry short-grass country they shrink more pounds rustlin' for food than they can put back on when they do get it!'

'I don't know, Daddy – that prairie wool . . .'

'Ain't any left. You wanta see real grass you go up to Paradise.'

'We are,' David reminded him. 'Saturday.'

'Take our rods,' Keith said. 'If the river's clear and low – those cut-throat – can we – will we have time to . . .'

'Sure,' David said.

'They ever go for a nymph! I got this little fur nymph on a

ten hook – Mr. Cameron ties 'em – muskrat belly fur – dry it doesn't look like much but when it's wet it's juicy looking – to a cut-throat anyway. They really fight when you get 'em on a . . .'

'Two ton,' Daddy said. 'Over two ton – red granite – he's gonna leave her rough . . .'

'Keith and I aren't very interested, Daddy.'

'Huh!'

'In your black tasselled coffin and your red granite tombstone. We'll take summer fallow steaming under the sun with the killdeer crying behind the drill – over your black broadcloth – the crocuses in Paradise Valley say a lot more for us than the longest epitaph in the undertaker's book – your two-ton stone isn't worth one single pussy-willow bud . . .'

'Aaaaaaah . . .'

'What a hell of a time you picked for it!'

'Aaaah . . .'

'You take the sound of Donald Finlay's voice as he tells the mourners all about your long and sinful life, Daddy, and then you take the pure song of a meadow lark . . .'

'Hold on – hold on – you ain't heard – there ain't any meadah . . .'

'Been here for over a week,' Keith said. 'Tar-tar-diddly-boo! Yellin' it from every straw stack an' off of every fence post an' telephone wire . . .'

'Stuffy in here,' Daddy said.

'A little,' David said.

'Open that windah then.'

'It is open,' David said.

'Meadah lark – meadah lark – an' quit squeakin' that goddam rocker!'

'I'm not squeakin' any goddam rocker,' Keith said.

'I said she was stuffy in here,' Daddy complained. 'Open up the windah.'

'It is,' David said again. 'Any room's stuffy this time of year.'

'There you go again – I told you to quit squeakin' that rocker!'

It was not only Daddy who had his good days and his bad

days, David decided; this must be a Lang good day; the bird perched on the window-sill had to be the plump one he and Keith had seen as they came up the walk to visit Daddy. And bless the heart under her rusty breast she was a loquacious robin. 'Turn your head, Daddy – to the right – it isn't the rocker chirping.'

'Well – now!' Daddy stared at the robin. 'Ain't she – my – ain't she the brassy one!'

David caught Keith's eye, made a gesture with his head towards the doorway. The boy got up.

'. . . an' what a husky outfit – just as much beef on her as Belvah . . .'

'Keith and I have to be going,' David said.

'You just come.' Daddy turned his head back to them. The robin flew off. 'What's your hurry?'

'I've got work to do. Keith has to finish digging his mother's garden – put up the screens.'

Outside, Keith said to David, 'Garden's all dug and the screens are . . .'

'I know.'

Belva Louise Tinsley phoned Helen Maclean at noon the next day. When she had come into Daddy's bedroom that morning he had been standing in his night-shirt in the middle of the floor.

'Get back into bed – your bare feet on that . . .'

'Pants,' Daddy said.

'Pants?'

'Where the hell did you put my pants an' my shawl! She's spring out! Spring!'

'But – I thought you were – on Friday . . .'

'Spring's a hell of a time to do it in. Man can't go an' die in spring.' He took a few stiff steps toward her. 'Ain't decent!'

Chapter 13

Daddy's lightning recovery had been welcome as a reprieve, but not without cost, David found. In a sense he had lost a week of time and he knew that he could not possibly meet the deadline he had set for himself; but he was not greatly disturbed and he had phoned the producer of his programme to tell him that he would have to miss an additional show. In the middle of the call he did some quick calculating and begged off two shows; it gave him three more weeks in Shelby and included the Daddy Sherry community birthday party. There was no trouble with Earl at *Mayfair*; 'Be our guest in Shelby for three weeks longer,' the editor said, 'but hang onto your vouchers and receipts and bring back a good article.'

On Saturday David kept the promise he had made; with Keith, Helen, and the miraculously restored Daddy he drove west through the foothills swells; on either side of them brisket-fat Herefords lifted white faces to stare; calves tossed their heads, to go rocking off with tails high. Just before Paradise Valley they stopped for the picnic lunch that Mrs. Clifford had made up for them; after they had eaten, Daddy took his nap in the front seat of the car. Keith came back to the car with a handful of crocuses. Daddy stirred, sat up. They were on their way again.

It was truly a lovely valley with the main range to the southwest now, a parade of rock still caped with snow. Directly ahead they could see the truncated bulk of Flat Top, Daughter of the Mist, remote and stately. Daddy pointed out the ploughsharing curve of Lookout and, to the north, Chimney Mountain. He knew the land, the brands, the people who owned them. He spoke of ranchers by first name and by nickname. Suddenly he slapped David's knee.

'Hold up – hold up.'

'What's the matter?' David said.

'Falls.'

'Binestettner's Falls,' Keith said.

'Yeh-yeh – take him over an' show him.'

Daddy remained in the car while they walked across the open field; they could hear the roar of the falls long before they had reached the cliff edge of the river. There they looked down to the tarn a hundred feet below, filled by the stream spilling down in an anguished web of mist and spray. Helen clutched the back of Keith's collar as he leaned forward for a better view.

'Careful, Son.' Then to David, 'Ask Daddy . . .'

'What?'

'Ask Daddy,' she raised her voice to be heard over the thumping thunder of the falls, 'to tell you about Binestettner – man the falls are named after!'

When they had started on their way again, Daddy lit up a cigar and told David the ballad-sad story of Joe Binestettner. 'He was a railroad man from Philadelphia. Come to the Valley in seventy-three. Had some of his trouble before he come here.'

'What kind of trouble?' David asked.

'Women. Treated 'em too well. From what he told me – there was this Spanish woman – married woman – in Philadelphia and he – was seein' her. Called on her one night – night she shot her husband – kind of surprised him findin' her like that, with a smokin' Smith an' Wesson in her hand an' her husband dead at her feet. Joe told her he'd take the blame for it if she'd give him time.'

Daddy puffed at his cigar a moment. 'She did. Joe, he went to the president of the railroad — still the days when a engineer could go to the president of a railway — told him the jam he was in, explained how he had to pertect the woman. President said, "Joe, you take seventy-nine from the roundhouse — I'll clear the track for you an' you get the hell outa Philadelphia."

'Just what he done. He high-balled west to the end of steel an' that happened to be five miles inside of a Snake Indian reservation. He left the engine where she stood, took up with a Snake woman named Sally Three-Persons, headed for the Canadian border, come up through the mountains where Glacier Park is — Boundary Lake. Took up a lease the other side of them falls — stretched clear up to Ramrod an' me. His home cabin was about five miles from ours. They had four daughters; one of 'em died of T.B. — two of 'em died in the typhoid epidemic.'

'What about the other one?' David asked.

Daddy did not answer him right away, then he said, 'She died too.'

'In the typhoid epidemic?'

Again there was the pause before the answer. 'No.' Daddy fell silent for so long that David thought he was done with Joe Binestettner. 'He was fond of her — "Slep' thirty years with a Snake an' never got bit," Joe used to say. She died in the typhoid epidemic along with two of the girls.'

'Joe was broke up. He sorrahed an' he pined. Then one day he drunk a dipper of gopher poison. He jumped from the suspension bridge used to be acrosst the pool — rope aroun' his neck. He pulled the trigger on his gun when he jumped with the barr'l in his mouth. Rope broke. Ramrod found his body the next spring — caught in a beaver dam ten miles down-stream. He shot hisself — poisoned hisself — hanged hisself an' he drownded hisself. I sat on the inquest the Mounties held in Fort Macleod. Unsound mind. Dead by his own hand. Me — I'd of changed that to dead by both han's. Paradise Valley folks figgered pool an' falls oughta be named after him. Fittin'.'

As Daddy had told the sorrowful legend of Joe Binestettner, the car had rolled through Paradise Valley; now Helen directed David off the road and onto a rutted trail that angled south. To the north ran a tan line of hills bunched with buck brush, for all the world like the clump bodies of distant buffalo fixed in the act of grazing.

They came soon to a clearing high with cured grass and the stalks of wild delphinium, here and there a stand of black birch or cottonwood. In a moment they saw the small cabin. Keith was first out of the car, his rod already jointed.

'Comin' down to the river, Mr. Lang?'

'Didn't look very promising to me,' David said. 'High and murky back there. You go along – I'll give your mother a hand with Daddy.'

'I'll just try it anyway.' He was off.

With Helen, David helped Daddy over the rough ground to the cabin. 'Ramrod an' me built her in the fall of 'eighty-five – God, he was good with a axe – couldn't get a cigarette paper between his mortishes.'

You could now. The cabin was quite derelict; foundation logs had given way and the lurching weight of the structure had pushed the fireplace into a pile of stones; the sagging ridge had broken so that one whole end of the roof was bare to the pole bones of its rafters; the rotting shingles were furred with moss. They stepped through a doorless opening and into the incredible stillness of abandonment, dust-moted bars of afternoon sunlight slanting down to bare earth. 'Used to be a floor here,' Daddy explained, 'but she went, board by board – big-game hunters invitin' theirselves in an' too lazy to rustle their own firewood.'

It was like viewing the remains, David was thinking, without benefit of the embalmer's art; from here just as undeniably soul had departed.

'She was warm,' Daddy reminisced. 'Nothin' like two-foot logs for warmth. We was cosy – even in six an' seven. Look at her now – give a packrat's ass the heartburn.' He stirred impatiently. 'C'mon – c'mon – let's go.'

A few hundred paces back of the cabin they came to budding wolf willow thick along a stream bank. 'Wolf Willah Crick,'

Daddy said. 'Flows into the Spray quarter mile east of here.' He sniffed the air deeply. 'Smells lots stronger later on . . . aaaaaaah. . . .'

It was a small plot embraced by a low rail fence. David was startled to see that there were two wooden crosses within. They stood by the old man in the warm and drowsing afternoon for the short while that he chose to commune with his dead. 'I told him – I told him – alive today . . . Victoria – aaaaay-ah.'

When he was ready to leave they went directly to the car; David helped him into the back seat; Helen placed under his head the pillow she had brought. 'You get the rest of your nap now, Daddy.'

'Sure-sure. . . .' He was asleep.

'Keith won't be too long,' she said to David, 'with the river high. Come with me.'

She led him a short distance from the car to the top of a gentle rise; through a break in the cottonwood trees one could look down the length of Paradise Valley. 'This is the view I love,' she said.

For several moments he looked out over meadow and willow bluff, lifted his eyes to the mountains beyond, great glacial facts against the afternoon sky, presenting first a vista of dark pine, then spined and rocky disorder barred with shadow and fluted with radiance, finally the snow-pure peaks themselves gauzed with cloud. 'It's perfectly lovely.' He turned to see that she had seated herself on the grass.

'It's Daddy's valley.'

'And Ramrod's,' he said as he sat down beside her. 'Who else?'

'Who else?'

'There were two crosses.'

'Oh.' Her arms circled her knees; her head up and back as she looked down the valley; the stirring breeze laid a strand of dark hair across her cheek. 'The valley's mine too – partly.'

'How?'

'Remember the day Daddy went over his will with Title Jack Dalgliesh?'

'It would be hard to forget it.'

'Keith is to get this Paradise Valley land.'

'Yes, I know.'

'No — you don't. Not really,' she said. 'Beyond loving Keith, Daddy has another reason for leaving it to him.'

'Has he . . .'

'Daddy told you that Joe Binestettner had four daughters. There was one — the youngest of them — who died. . . .'

'But not in the typhoid epidemic — he seemed reluctant to explain further . . .'

'She died in childbirth — in 'ninety-one. Victoria Binestettner. Half Snake.'

'Did the baby die?' David asked.

'No — that was Sally — named after her grandmother. She was raised actually on the Three Walking Sticks — that's south of here in Happy Valley — by the Rundlemans. They virtually adopted her. When she was sixteen she married the foreman of the Rocking L. She was quarter Snake. Sally Clifford.'

'Oh.'

'She had one son — Keith Clifford. He was my father. I never knew him — a horse and a badger hole killed him in nineteen twenty-nine — the year I was born. Sally died in nineteen thirty-one in the sanitorium and of the T.B. that didn't get my great-grandmother. All that makes Daddy Sherry Keith's great-great-grandfather.'

'Well,' David managed, 'that's surprising.'

'Why?'

'All the time I've spent in Shelby — the people I've talked to . . .'

'You mean not knowing before now. No — it isn't surprising. You see it not only makes Daddy my great-grandfather — it also makes me one-sixteenth Snake Indian. . . .'

'But I don't . . .'

'Of which I am very proud, and of which my mother, I suspect, would not be.'

'What do you mean — *would* not be?'

'She doesn't know. I believe my father simply let her think his mother was a Rundleman.'

'How did you . . .'

'Daddy told me – when I was Keith's age – it was the most wonderful and exciting day of my life. He made me swear an oath not to tell my mother and I've kept it. It's hard to say why he didn't want her to know – whether for her sake or for his – whether he was considerately keeping from her the knowledge of a quarter Snake mother-in-law or a blanket-marrying old grandfather-in-law.'

'Do you really mean to tell me that your mother doesn't know . . .'

'Let's put it this way – officially she doesn't know. Certainly she had not and she hasn't any intention of ever explaining to me my black hair and my Asiatic eye-fold. Mother is a great one for facing up to things – except some things. She might have had to – if Keith had been a girl.'

'Why?'

'I would have called her Sally.'

Somewhere in the bland afternoon a crow fled cawing, the raw call fainting in the distance and taking some of David's heart with it. 'Well,' he said, 'thanks.'

She turned her head to him – slowly – deliberately. 'For what?'

'Telling me. Seems an important confidence. Makes me one of three who know – officially.'

'You inspire confidence, David.' He felt the soft brush of her hand against his, and instantly aching sweetness stormed him. Blue almond eyes dazed him with inner release – kind – oh, gentle and kind! He took her in his arms and kissed her.

As they walked back to the car she said, 'Actually four, you know.'

'Four?'

'I told Murray too,' she said.

And David was thinking that four had been the number that afternoon: the dead cabin and Ramrod and half-caste Victoria and now the most awkwardly lively ghost of them all – Murray Maclean.

Chapter 14

The Spray River had its birth high in the Livingstone Range, Helen had told David, with the marriage of two nameless streams; these gin-clear glacial trickles lived only till August when mountain run-off failed. But in its precipitate course under the high sigh of jack-pine, spruce, and fir, the Spray was fed by many creeks, among them Wolf Willow; a slender aquamarine ribbon at first, it twisted tortuously through hundred-foot-high canyon walls of shale and limestone, paused and broadened where beavers had been at work through Paradise Valley, splintering often into a glinting network of water strands. All came together to flow eastward, curving round the foothills' flanks and out to the prairie beyond.

In the rare mountain air it was a young stream, spawning-grounds for rainbow, cut-throat, and Rocky Mountain whitefish; by the time it reached Shelby it had achieved a smoother, more leisurely middle age. Here it had historical past. The shallow ford just west of the town was known as Stony Crossing and had been the scene two centuries before of a Blackfoot massacre; beaver trappers and wolfers and whiskey traders had splashed through here, as well as cattle herds trailed up from Texas and Wyoming; and in the early seventies, the first detachment of the new North West Mounted Police. Today there was Piney Dell with its peeled-log camping kitchens, tables and benches and outdoor toilets for the convenience of the Girl Guides and Boy Scouts, for the chosen who came to summer revival meetings to be washed and saved. Here the hundred-yards dash, the three-legged, the egg-and-spoon, and the potato-sack races were run at annual Sunday School picnics. The Rotarians held their steak fries where the beaver men had rendezvoused a century before, just east of the stone rubble marking the location of old Fort Stagger where whiskey traders had carried on their business.

Most of Shelby's young had learned to swim in the Spray. The twenty-fourth of May signalled the official opening of shrill and merry hell along its slippery banks with: 'Last one in's a monkey's uncle,' 'Petey-Petey – see the moon rise', 'I can bottom it – I can bottom it!' On the river road virginity had been lost many times, first with cow ponies grazing near, then with buckboard or phaeton or buggy standing by, finally with moonlight glinting from chrome and enamel. In late March of nineteen twenty-seven something more precious had been lost when ten-year-old Jimmy Sangster had gone through rubber ice, to be found far downstream in a back-water, blood-suckers over his body, his arms outflung and his head in Metherall's bearded barley field.

After Shelby the river flowed through the towns of Conception and Foxhole and Tiger Lily, much wider, much slower, its tepid waters shunned by trout and populated by mud-inhaling suckers, carp and gold-eye, scummed and tea-coloured, stinking of marsh gas, its edges reedy; an old and sluggish river, it slipped over the American border at One Star, Montana.

Each year with the glacial run-off late in May the Spray threatened Shelby with flood, and in 1925, in 1931, in 1945 and in 1954, property damage had been high. Now an earth and gravel breakwater protected the community, and most people felt that never again would their homes and stores be awash.

'It was wonderfully exciting before the breakwater,' Helen recalled. '1954 was the worst year of all – they used canoes and row-boats on Main Street. All of Mrs. Sorenson's chickens were drowned in spite of the Shelby Emergency and Disaster Relief Committee. It did frighten Mayor Fraser and his council into action and they had the breakwater built – it diverts the Spray from its natural course through the business district – and from Daddy's cottage.'

The last flood had taken place two years after Helen had returned to live with her mother and to teach in Shelby High School. Daddy Sherry had been one hundred and five that spring, had put in a winter uneventful in regard to health or to personally created incident. The last week in April, Helen had gone into Mayor Fraser's store, the Bon Ton, to settle her month's bill for groceries. She always paid by cheque so that she had a record, but Mr. Fraser had insisted, as he usually did, on making out a receipt for her.

As he bent over the counter he said, 'And how are things in the Clifford household?'

'Fine, Mr. Fraser.'

'What's this we hear about Daddy Sherry?'

'I don't know,' said Helen, who had heard nothing.

'Hasn't eloped – held up the Royal Bank – dynamited the town hall – shot up the Cascade Beer Parlour.' Mr. Fraser enjoyed a benign split personality; in private life he took nothing seriously, in public – everything. 'There you are.' He handed Helen her receipt.

'Thank you. Just what is it you hear about him, Mr. Fraser?'

'Understand he's taken the notion to travel.'

'Oh? Where?'

'The South Seas.'

'To the South Seas!'

'That's right. Honolulu – Fiji Islands – Tahiti. Wants to lie back in a hammock, he says – rocked to sleep by the tropic breeze – listen to the idle strum of native instruments – waiting for the bananas and paw-paw fruit to drop into his lap. . . .'

'I suppose we all think about how nice that would be,' Helen said, 'sooner or later.'

'All he's been talking about for the past month. Miss Tinsley has been trying to get his mind off it. . . .'

'She isn't taking it seriously, is she?'

'She takes everything seriously,' Mayor Fraser said. 'I told her not to argue with him about it.'

'That's right.'

'. . . just sets him firmer. Of course – it's so ridiculous – I don't suppose there's any real need to worry . . .'

'With Daddy,' Helen said, 'you should worry in direct ratio to the ridiculous element in the situation.'

Mayor Fraser considered that for a moment. 'Yes,' he said, 'I suppose you're right.'

On her way home she called in at the Sherry house.

'He keeps muttering about long pig,' Miss Tinsley said. 'And he seems quite set on it. Imagine – a hundred and five – why is it? – always in the spring he gets these silly – well – brain storms.'

'You shouldn't pay too much attention to them,' Helen advised her. 'Just ignore him when he . . .'

'Ignore him! Have you ever tried it? He's out in the back-yard – you go on out there and see how easy it is to ignore him – in anything!'

Daddy was well wrapped against the early spring air. 'How are you, Daddy – what's this I hear you're plotting against the whites?'

'Aaaaah – day – day, girl – itch – itch – itch. . . .'

'Wait a minute – my time's valuable – can't waste it if you're not going to make some sense.'

'Set – set.' He indicated the empty chair on his left. 'Mrs. Doc Richardson.'

'You have the wrong girl, Daddy. I'm Helen Maclean – remember?'

'Didn't say you wasn't. Didn't say that.'

'What did you say then?'

'Mrs. Doc Richardson – aaah – Mrs. Allerdyce – Sadie's headed for La Jolly California – Florence Allerdyce's slouchin' aroun' St. Petersburg. . . .'

'Yes?'

'Me – I froze for ninety years on the prairies an' in these foothills – cold – cold – I ain't been warm since I cracked ninety!'

'That's too bad, Daddy.'

'I aim to get warm.'

'How?'

'Thin – I got real thin blood an' she's slow risin' this year – when she does come up she's gonna split the bark.'

'You'll be all right.'

'Nope. Nope. This is the year John Felix Sherry migrates.'

'Where?' she asked him, just as though she didn't know.

'Bermuda – Mexico – aaaah Tobango – Durango – Sumatra – I'm goin' wherever the tropical breezes blows me – Tahiti where the warm trade winds can kiss my thin old hide an' warm her good. . . .'

'Well,' she said, 'you can afford it – no reason you and Miss Tinsley . . .'

'Just what I told her . . .'

'. . . shouldn't go down south – like Mrs. Richardson and Mrs. Allerdyce – Belva Louise can look after you just as well in Phoenix or Laguna or . . .'

'. . . or Papeete – Easter Islands – Sandwidge Islands . . .'

'But those places are off the . . .'

'. . . eat that there bread fruit – kick yams outa the dirt an' watch them grass skirts swayin' – listen to them guitars – lay on the silver sands an' see the hot sun settin' on blue doubloons . . .'

'Lagoons.'

'Eh?'

'Lagoons – a sort of tropical slough.'

'Coral Islands. Eat long pig for breakfast an' dinner an' supper . . .'

'Might not agree with you, Daddy,' she said.

'How the hell will I know till I tried it?'

'And it's a little far at your age – you'd better settle for California or Florida . . .'

'Itch – itch.'

'You have the travel itch?'

'Underwear – underwear. I ain't been outa scratchy underwear for a hunderd years. I'm goin' where I can take it off. . . .'

'You can take it off in California or . . .'

'. . . peel to the hide – right to the hide.' He leaned forward, grunting with the effort. 'Gimme your arm.'

'Certainly, Daddy – you want to go back into the house?'

'You're gonna come down town with me,' he told her. Today's the day I buy the tickets.'

'Now – just a moment. . . .'

'Sposed to had 'em ready ten days ago, then she stuck her nose into it. Cancelled 'em. I'll cancel *her*! An' him! First-class ticket – train – air an' windjammer – high-ballin' outa this deep freeze like a scalded kiyoot. Ticket – ticket – ticket. Mr. Rossdance's got 'em ready by now – like an accordeen – when she's opened out she'll stretch from here to the correction line! No – don't you hold me – let me grab holt of *your* arm!'

Helen suspected from the twitch of the front window curtains that Miss Tinsley saw them leave for down town; she was relieved that the housekeeper did not intercept them, which was decent of her; an explanation could be embarrassing so soon after giving out the easy advice to ignore Daddy. It was not so much that Helen felt that she was giving in to him as that quite obviously a different sort of response was called for: a very cautious humouring.

Behind his wicket in the station, Mr. Rossdance looked a little guilty under his green eye shade as he handed out the tickets to Daddy and accepted the cheque. Helen imagined that the agent had no intention of cashing the cheque, that the tickets had no more value than stage money. Daddy was quite satisfied, however, insisted that they go into the Ladies and Escorts section of the Cascade Beer Parlour to celebrate the purchase.

When she got home there was an accounting to make to her mother, for Miss Tinsley had phoned the house.

'You didn't help Belva, you know.'

'Oh, Mother – the tickets aren't real tickets – Mr. Rossdance won't present Daddy's cheque to the bank. . . .'

'That isn't the point. It's encouraged him and made it harder for her. I don't understand why you – it's almost as though you – Daddy will take it as though you had approved. . . .'

'I don't disapprove of his taking a trip – a short one south – that may be how it ends up and it would be good for him. This is the time of year when he's likely to have his old bronchial trouble. I felt it wasn't wise – right now – to interfere. . . .'

'Sometimes it's our duty to interfere for the good of another person.'

'I've never seen the time, Mother, that people didn't interfere without justifying it as being for someone else's own good.'

'South Seas!'

'In a way,' Helen said, 'it's Belva Louise's own fault.'

'How can you say that! She's done everything to stop him!'

'That's just it – now it's time to try something else. A little delicate substitution. It would never have happened if she hadn't been reading him those adventure magazines – all about diving for pearls in tropical lagoons. . . .'

'That's all he'll let her read.'

'She'd better go easy on *Astonishing Scientific Stories*. . . .'

'It isn't funny, Helen.'

'I think it is – a little.'

'Well, it isn't. Not when he has to be protected against himself. Miss Tinsley and I are worried. . . .'

'I am too, but I know when it's no use to resist him openly in something. Perhaps if no attention had been paid in the first place, he might not have considered it such a fine idea.'

'Nothing whatever is gained,' her mother said, 'by not facing up to things.'

The flood anecdote, of course, was Belva Louise Tinsley's, and it was from her that David got the rest of the story. Very soon after Daddy had got his tickets from Mr. Rossdance, the housekeeper had been able to forget her concern about the projected trip, for a cold had settled on the old chest, persisted stubbornly to become bronchitis. Now she had a fresh worry, but at least she knew the old man was through with his notion of traipsing south, sailing round the Horn, and kicking up his heels in the South Seas.

That spring the Spray threatened the town again and by the middle of May everyone was remembering other flood years when train service had been disrupted, the north-south highway under water, mail and food deliveries almost impossible. Remembrance of past disaster thrilled all together with a sort of shot in the community veins, at a time when feeling ran a little sluggishly through the civic body convalescent, after the fever of spring seeding had cooled and calving was over. The possibility of flood gave the town a fillip of excitement. It was actually a welcome one.

But as the river rose with turgid urgency, consternation lifted within the hearts of the townspeople. Business men removed stocks from basement storage; every evening concerned groups of people clustered at the CNR bridge to gauge the rise of the waterline on the cement pilings. Potato sacks had come to be at a premium. Town council held an emergency session, was addressed by a worried Mayor Fraser.

'It has been brought to our notice that the Spray – due to the recent heavy rains coinciding with the glacial run-off from the mountains – has risen dangerously high in the past four days. I'm afraid we've made a – we've underestimated the threat to our community this year. We seem to be in agreement that we ought to – ah – it's too bad we postponed for another year the fill and dyking we intended doing from the CNR bridge to a hundred yards above Daddy Sherry's house. No use crying over spilt milk. We can congratulate ourselves that we did set up our Emergency and Disaster Relief Committee to handle just such a situation as might arise in the coming week. I don't think it will. However, I do think it well that the Emergency and Disaster Relief Committee – ah – should – ah – begin functioning – that they make sure their machinery of – action – is ready – to act.'

'Just what do you mean by that?' asked Ernie Fowler, who had been appointed head of the committee against his will the year before.

'Well, now, Ernie – it's your committee – flood is – can be considered an emergency – could be a disaster – '

'I know that,' Ernie said, 'but it still doesn't answer my question.'

'Well – for one thing,' Mayor Fraser said to him, 'sand bags and sand – these should be at hand and ready for . . .'

'They are,' said Ernie.

'And crews to work round the clock in shifts. . . .'

'They are,' said Ernie.

'Millie Clocker at the telephone office quite clear about the difference between the blue alert and the red alert?'

'She is,' said Ernie. 'My point is . . .'

'You might try a few trial runs,' Mayor Fraser suggested.

'On Millie! She touches off the town hall sireen – the Mounted Police Patrol cars and Ollie's ambulance come screamin' through town – St. Aidan's church bell tollin' – way nerves are in this town now, we'd have real panic on our hands!'

'All right,' said Mayor Fraser. 'All right. It was only a suggestion. If your key men are standing ready twenty-four hours a day – Tom Seeley in charge of shelter . . .'

'Tom Seeley's down with 'flu – Mr. Rossdance's at the coast on his vacation before the summer. . . .'

'Well – whoever you've appointed to act in their places – Harry Richardson – first aid – Hickory Bob Smith – flat-bottom boats – it's your committee, Ernie!'

'It's my committee,' Ernie said, 'but it isn't my flood! And if you remember last year it was me that tried his damnedest to get some action on that breakwater project and it was me that said bein' Fire Marshal was enough responsibility in itself without bein' saddled with the Emergency and Disaster Relief Committee as well!'

'You were the natural man for the job,' Mayor Fraser tried to soothe him. 'We have every confidence in you and in your committee – oh, there's one thing – the houses on the flats – those people – wouldn't it be a good idea if they were to . . .'

'They all been warned,' Ernie said. 'They're all ready to get out at a moment's notice – move in with friends or relatives – all except one.'

'And who's that?'

'One that's in the most danger – be under water first thing – right plock in the old river course – Daddy Sherry.'

'Well, get him out.'

'We've tried – suggested he move out now since he isn't – wouldn't be as spry as the others. He won't budge.'

'All right,' Mayor Fraser said. 'You'll just have to make certain he's moved out – in good time – '

'But if he won't co-operate . . .'

'If you have to – use force – take as many of your shelter committee as you need. Actually, I don't think it will be necessary. I don't share your pessimism. If this rain eases up there won't be any flood at all.'

But the rain had not stopped, and two days later with the water just a half-inch below the CNR bridge, the flats were evacuated; Mayor Fraser himself called on Daddy. He found the old man recovered from his bronchitis, rocking on the porch. Binoculars dangled from the strap round his neck.

'I ain't stirrin' from here,' Daddy said. 'Got a ringside seat right here on my porch.'

Mayor Fraser returned to his store to check the flood reports there. He found Ernie Fowler waiting for him. 'You just take two of your men,' he told Ernie 'some time this afternoon or this evening at the latest – move him out and over to Cliffords'. I've told Mrs. Clifford and she expects him.'

'All right,' Ernie said. 'The crest is expected through Broomhead some time between two and four – should hit us around midnight tonight. I need more trucks – more town sand – more bags. . . .'

'You'll get them,' Mayor Fraser promised. He looked at Ernie's haggard face; the sand-bagging shifts spelled each other off every eight hours, but he strongly suspected that Ernie had been going round the clock for the past two days. 'Sorry about that dyke last year, Ernie.'

At four o'clock, just as the crest of the flood reached Piney Dell, and only ten minutes after Headley McConkey had hooked the farm-hand onto his tractor to ride out to the south end of his earth dam, Ernie Fowler and Hickory Bob Smith went up Daddy Sherry's front walk.

'We're taking him,' Ernie said firmly to Belva Louise, 'whether he likes it or not.'

'Thank goodness,' said Belva. 'He's in the . . .'

Daddy stood in the doorway, his ten-gauge goose gun in his hands. Ernie Fowler saw that both hammers were back.

'You fellahs aren't takin' me anywhere,' Daddy said. 'An' you can get the hell outa here before I count ten.'

It was eight when Ernie Fowler and Hickory Bob Smith reached the sidewalk, still not certain whether Daddy's ultimatum meant the porch, his yard, or the entire block on which he lived.

Out of effective shot-gun range they turned and looked back; what they saw sent them running for higher ground. It was much too late now to rescue Daddy Sherry and Belva Louise Tinsley.

Three miles west of Shelby, Headley McConkey with the tractor had intended taking only a small bite out of his earth dam to drain the water flooding over his eighty acres of registered seed oats; within minutes the entire dam had crumbled and McConkey Lake rushed to reunion with the Spray just reaching its crest there. A quarter-mile above Shelby the CNR bridge, always a bottle-neck during flood season, resisted the onrushing water for only minutes, then gave way. Accurate reports were understandably confused and contradictory later, but many were agreed the wave that swept down upon the Sherry cottage had been at least six feet high. Even before Millie Clocker had sounded the Red Alert, the cottage was snatched from its foundation, carried past the river's curve and out into centre stream, where it began a surprisingly steady and balanced but slowly spinning voyage south.

She had never been so terrified in her life, Belva Louise explained to David, as she clung to the porch post and watched

180

the river banks slip past. It was not true, she said, that she had stayed to save Daddy or to protect him or to go down with him. It had happened so fast that she had been unable to jump clear. She could not swim a stroke and her only hope was to stay with the ship. As shock faded slightly she saw that Daddy was in his rocker, must have gone into the house and come out again since they had embarked, for he was wearing the white, visored and gold-braided yachting cap he had bought earlier in preparation for his intended South Seas voyage.

'Jump to them mizzen sails there – throw out the sea anchor – let her roar . . .'

Bracing herself against the tilt of the porch floor she made her way to the rocker, grabbed at the high back for support. 'We're going to be all right, Mr. Sherry – if we just don't panic!'

'Batten them hatches an' head for the squid jiggin' ground – Mary Jane's got the bit in her teeth – runnin' with the wind an' as soon as we lay our han's on Blackbird Teach there'll be keel haulin' – then for the South Seas. . . .'

'We've got to get inside – inside!'

'You go on below – I'll take her round the Horn myself. . . .'

'But, Mr. Sherry – if we hit – if we tip – there's nothing to stop you sliding right off the . . .'

'Get the hell off my bridge!'

But she had stayed to hold the rocker, hoping that the flood current would carry them close to one bank or the other, hardly able to gather her wits while Daddy raised his cracked old voice in sea chanteys, keeping time with his cane and returning always to 'Rule Britannia!'

They were almost saved a mile north of Foxhole when the house went aground on a sand-bar there, but the river had plucked them loose again before Hickory Bob Smith and his Flat-Bottom Boat Committee could launch a rescue. The entire Emergency and Disaster Relief Committee, with the RCMP detachment's four patrol cars, the Shelby Fire Department's engine and pulmotor, and Ollie Pringle's ambulance, followed their leisurely course down-stream, halting wherever the highway or side roads touched the river. In this way the house was

181

almost always in sight until darkness fell. The last glimpse had been at the rear of the Co-op Grain Elevator in Tiger Lily.

With nightfall Belva had managed to get the old man into the house and into bed, she told David. As she had tucked him in he had commented, 'I always heard she was rough, Belvah – but we made her round the Horn. You stay at the wheel now. Sing out if you need me – but only if you need me – smell that there sea air – nothin' like it to make a fellah sleep.'

It was perhaps an hour before dawn that she sensed an extra steadiness under her. She had ventured out onto the porch only to find darkness. She went back inside. She was quite sure now that they were aground, for she could feel no movement, hearing no creaking in the house, only the lapping of water, the pulsing shrillness of spring frogs. She had lain down on the chesterfield then, and, incredibly, fallen asleep.

She awoke to morning light streaming through the living-room window, went to it, looked out and up to see the Star-spangled Banner limp about a flag-pole a few hundred feet from the house. At some time during the night they had crossed the border, without visas, illegally after border-crossing hours, and smuggling in under cover of darkness one undeclared Canadian house with all its contents.

Even as she turned away from the window there was a light and questioning knock at the front door. She opened it to the olive uniform of the American Immigration and Customs Service. Before she or the two border officials could say anything, Daddy, still night-shirted, spoke from his bedroom door-way.

'Take me,' he said, 'to your cannibal chief.'

Chapter 15

In the last two weeks of his stay in Shelby, David took his time with Daddy Sherry, visiting the old man almost every other day, not deliberately for material but simply savouring the old man's company, carrying home with him now and then some fragment of the past or personality to be woven into the nest. He stayed on now only to attend the Daddy Sherry celebration. He had come to hope that this event might dissipate for him the feeling of incompleteness that still nagged him in the article.

Four days before the celebration he dropped into Merton Spicer's barber shop for a haircut. He found that Daddy had been there just before his own arrival.

'Now I don't know — have no way of telling,' the barber said, 'how long since he shaved before he came in here — into my shop this morning — but there isn't much to shave — never is. I suppose hair's like anything else — slows down with age like anything else — heart — breathing — growth — those whiskers of his been growing for a hundred and eleven years — well — almost — they'd tire too.'

'I suppose they would,' David said.

'Tired whiskers – tired.'

'How are the preparations for his birthday party coming, Mr. Spicer?' David said.

'Fine – fine – everyone pulling together – humming right along fine. Rather pleased with my own personal responsibility . . .'

'The gift committee.'

'That's right. In a way the most important thing about the – ah – about the whole thing – what we give him – we went about it very carefully – exhaustively – all sorts of suggestions – examined every one of them and discussed them – even Harvey Totecole's – wheelchair.'

'Mr. Sherry wouldn't appreciate that so much,' David said.

'Of course not. We felt that too. Discarded it. A gold watch was considered but we decided that was trite. Discarded it. A gold watch is nice but people are always getting gold watches. It was so usual that we threw away the gold watch – though not the spirit of the gift – because with Daddy we kept coming back to the same thing – over and over again.'

'And what was that?'

'Time. In some way we had to take time into account if our gift was to be fitting. We finally hit on the idea of giving him a clock – a grandfather clock – happy selection – symbolic and fitting.'

'Mmmh,' David said.

'Mind you, we had no idea whether we would be able to find one or not – just by chance that Mrs. Allerdyce discovered one in the city – Aunt Harriet's Antique Shop – just came in with a shipment of antiques from Scotland. Lovely old clock – chimes on the hour – tells the day of the month. It does now thanks to Herb. Herb took care of that.'

'Did he? . . .'

'Took it all apart in his shop – cleaned it – went over every single – those things that fit into things – pins – polished them with jeweller's rouge while the case is at Hickory Bob Smith's. Beautiful burr walnut case and Bob's restoring and polishing it. Wonderful gift.'

'What does Mr. Sherry think of it?' David said.

'Oh – he doesn't know. Hasn't a clue. Not a clue. That would spoil it. He's not to know until four days from now.'

'I see.'

'Up on the stage at the community centre – we're going to have it veiled – at the right moment – unveil it – ticking – and just before it strikes.' The barber sighed into David's neck. 'Daddy doesn't make it easy for a person.'

'No,' David agreed, 'he doesn't.'

'All the time I was shaving him – kept picking at me – picking.'

'Did he . . .'

'Never let up. Trying to find out what we were giving him. Before I even got the lather on . . .'

'What sort of a present you fellahs tryin' to sneak past me?' Daddy had said as Mr. Spicer tucked the sheet round his neck.

'Present? What do you mean sneak . . .'

'Nobody's said what I'm gettin' yet,' Daddy said, 'that I know of.'

'Oh.' The barber turned away to the instrument shelf, took up the shaving-mug and brush.

'Well?'

'I don't know, Daddy. . . .'

'You should – you're head of the gift committee, ain't you?'

'Yes. Yes. I am. I'm head of it.'

'All right then. What is it?'

'Oh – I couldn't – wouldn't have the right to – I can't tell you that, Daddy.'

'What is it? What is it?'

The barber bent over the old man, began to brush on the lather. 'Birthday presents are always surprises . . .'

'I don't want a surprise – I want a present.'

'You'll get one,' the barber assured him.

'I ought to know whether or not I want it,' Daddy protested. 'I got the right to know. Maybe it's somethin' I don't want – somethin' I don't need – somethin' I already got. . . .'

'I don't think it is.'

'. . . somethin' unsuitable – like – like if they was all set to give me – a – a – automobile.'

'Oh – ,' the barber laughed indulgently, 'it isn't an automobile – I can tell you that safely – it isn't . . .'

'There you are – '

'What do you mean – there you are?'

'Maybe that's what I want.'

'Huh!'

'Automobile. I want a automobile my own. If it isn't a automobile then I don't want it.'

'That's ridiculous.'

'Listen, young fellah – when I want somethin' – I don't care what it is but if I *decide* I want it then me *wantin'* it . . .' Daddy turned his head as Mr. Spicer went over to the sink. '. . . then it stops bein' ridiculous – right in its tracks.'

'Well it is, Daddy, all the same.' The barber wrapped the towel end round the hot-water spout and turned the tap on. 'No use telling you it isn't, because it is. It's the most ridiculous thing I've ever heard of.'

'Why!'

'It's – it's – an automobile is expensive – it's costly.'

'Oh-hoh – you're gonna give me a cheap present – all set to fob off a chimpy-skimpy-pimpy . . .'

'We are not! We have no intention of – what we've picked out is not a cheap present. . . .'

'What is it?'

'It's a very fine present.' The barber turned off the tap and began to wring out the towel. 'Suitable and fitting – quite fitting – and a surprise!'

'Won't give me no automobile,' Daddy said sadly. 'Don't care if I got my heart set on a automobile. . . .'

'Now – look here, Daddy,' the barber gave the towel a final and extra strong twist, 'you're just saying the first thing that came into your mind.'

'I did not.'

'You did so.'

186

'It ain't the first thing that would come into my head. If it would be the first thing that would come into my head then it wouldn't be a automobile – mmmh-dah-duh-daaaah – it'd be a ox cart.'

'Ox cart!' Mr. Spicer stopped, with the steaming towel held above Daddy's lathered face.

'Two-thirds my life I travelled by oxen before they ever even thought of automobiles – so a ox cart would come into my head first,' Daddy said, 'wouldn't it?'

'I suppose it would,' the barber said. 'That what you're trying to tell me – you trying to tell me you want one for your birthday present – you want an ox cart for a birthday . . .'

'No! I just want a present I want. I want a present that ain't a surprise present. I got no breath to spare for surprises. I can't stand still to wait for surprises. Can't hold my mind empty that long – got to know ahead of time so's I can touch her – cuddle her there – come back to her again and again and again like pettin' your dog.'

Quite unmoved, Mr. Spicer said, 'Sincerely – you sincerely want me to tell you we're getting you an automobile – an expensive, several-thousand-dollar automobile – that you couldn't drive yourself – that you couldn't possibly . . .'

'Nope.'

'You said an automobile – lay right there in that chair and you said . . .'

'Did I?'

'You know you did. You said . . .'

'You didn't have no witnesses.'

'Witnesses – what do you . . .'

'Nobody'd believe you if you was to tell 'em,' Daddy said, 'an' you proba'ly will.'

'Now look here . . .'

'I don't want no automobile. Cost a lotta money an' I don't want nobody spendin' a lotta money on a silly automobile for me . . .'

'We're not,' the barber said grimly. 'What we're getting for you . . .'

'Yeh-yeh-yeh?'

'. . . is a surprise.'

'Thirty-thirty.'

'What's that?'

'Rifle – gettin' me a bran' new rifle?'

'No.'

'Aaaah – gold spittoon.'

'Look, Daddy . . .'

' – billerd table – silver-plated saddle – glass case for my war medals . . .'

'Daddy, it's no use you . . .'

'. . . stuffed moose head – High-wyan gitar – gross French safes . . .'

Mr. Spicer dropped the steaming towel over Daddy's face.

'He does it deliberately,' Mr. Spicer told David, 'just to annoy a person – talks silly just to raise a person's shackles.'

'And generally he's successful,' David said as he got out of the chair.

'Well, with me,' the barber said, 'most of the annoyance is at letting him get me annoyed.' He stepped over to the till to get David's change. 'The present is still a surprise.' The bell rang as he punched the cash register. 'And when Friday comes – when he sits up there on the community centre stage – that lovely grandfather clock all covered with sheet – it will still be a surprise – till Urban Coldtart pulls the string – right till then.'

Two days before Daddy Sherry's birthday party Keith came to David in his room.

'You got a minute, Mr. Lang?'

'Of course, Keith.'

'You decided what you're going to get Daddy for a birthday present?'

'I've given it some thought. I'm not sure. Possibly a box of cigars.'

'Oh.'

David could tell that the boy was not terribly impressed.

'You see – I haven't known him as long or as well as you have – your mother – many – most of the people in Shelby. I thought a box of Senate House cigars would be about my speed.'

'Mmmh. Not too hard for you.'

'What do you mean?'

'Like you said – longer you known a person the tougher it is – got to be more careful.'

'I suppose you do.'

'You – I was wondering if maybe you had any ideas – for me.'

'I don't know, Keith.'

'I guess there's lots of things he'd like.'

'I guess there are,' David said.

'But there's a lot of things he wouldn't like.'

David said, 'The main thing, Keith – you're fond of Daddy, so you should know him well, and if you know a person well then it shouldn't be hard to think of a present for him.'

'That's easy to say,' Keith said.

'But it's right.'

'I got a dollar and twenty cents saved up.'

'There is one thing that might help you.'

'Yeah?'

'I have a feeling that he would get more pleasure out of something you made yourself than he would out of something you bought with your dollar and twenty cents.'

'Oh?' Keith looked up at him. 'Why?'

'He would.'

'Anything a kid like me would make – it'd be a hay-wire – shaganappi thing . . .'

'That isn't the point, Keith. Anything you'd buy would be something that anybody with a dollar and twenty cents could walk into a store and buy. If you made it yourself – then Daddy would know that you had – that it took you time to make it – and care. . . .'

'Uh-huh.'

'All the time you were whittling or gluing or sand-papering or hammering . . .'

'Gluing or sand-papering what?'

'Whatever you make up your mind – whatever you think he'd like.'

'Oh.'

'Some of your own time would be wrapped up in your present to him.'

'Uh-huh.'

'Does that help you any?'

'Not very much. Well – maybe it does in a way. I figure you're right – I ought to make it myself all right – only I still don't know what to make and it's harder to figure out a present to make for a person than it is to figure out a present to buy for a person.'

'I guess it is.'

'Bein' Daddy makes it twice as hard – maybe be the last chance I have to give him one.'

'Oh – I think you may have more opportunities, Keith.'

'I sure hate to fumble it. You got any ideas – something I might make for him – only three days . . .'

'I don't know, Keith.' David thought for a moment. 'You might find a length of diamond willow – make him a cane – varnished . . .'

'He's got six canes.'

'Oh. Well – a – a – tie rack?'

'He doesn't own a tie – never wears one at all,' Keith said. 'Anyway, it'd be a hell of a present.'

'Yes,' David agreed, 'it would be.'

'See what I mean,' Keith said. 'Isn't easy. Way I see it – ought to be something he'd get some fun out of.'

'Mmmh.'

'He'll get fun out of the cigars you're giving him. Maybe I could chip in my dollar and twenty cents on the box of cigars . . .'

'No – no,' David said quickly. 'That wouldn't be giving him a present at all. Now let's just think what he would get fun out of. . . .'

'He still gets a bang out of fishing,' Keith said.

190

'Tackle box . . .'

'He's already got one. Only kind of fishing stuff I could make would be a minnow net out of hay wire and an onion sack, and he couldn't use it anyway. . . .'

'I tell you what, Keith – let's just drop over and visit him – we might just pick up an idea.'

They found the old man on the porch, his rocker pulled almost to the edge to catch the full afternoon sun. They accepted his invitation to a drink of buttermilk, Keith going into the house for two glasses, pouring it from the great jug on the stand at Daddy's elbow.

'Three days you'll be a hundred and eleven,' David said. 'Here's to your long life and your good luck.'

'Two different things,' Daddy said. 'Two entirely different an' opposite things. Some fellahs is lucky – some ain't.'

'You're the luckiest fellow in the world, Daddy,' Keith said.

'How do you figger that?'

'Way you lived so long.'

'Anybody who's lived to a hundred and eleven,' David said, 'seems pretty lucky to me.' -

' 'Nother glass.'

'I haven't finished this one,' Keith said. 'You got more luck than anybody, Daddy.'

'Maybe – maybe.'

'I won't live to any hundred and eleven years,' Keith said.

'Jist keep outa draughts – keep reg'lar – lots buttermilk,' Daddy said. 'Don't give a whoop – be a dangerous acerobat – sail over the tops the circus crowds. Don't give a damn whether she rains or thaws or freezes – whether you live or die. Then you will.'

'Will what?' David said.

'Live to be a hunerd an' eleven. That's the way to do it. Like a drunk pitched off of a horse.'

'Huh?' Keith said.

'Live loose an' soople an' you'll come through without a scratch. Live careful an' you'll break your goddam neck. That's the secret – cuh-rock a day – keep reg'lar – don't give a damn an' you'll live an' live an' live . . .' He sighed. '. . . to be the unluckiest man in the world.'

'Luckiest,' Keith corrected him.

'Unluckiest. You wouldn't like it – enough to give a gopher's ass the heartburn. Twenty – last twenty . . .'

'Twenty what?' David said.

'Years. Shaganappi years – hoverin' over you – flingin' shawls over your shoulders – shovin' seats under your – ask anybody a hunerd an' eleven an' they'll tell you. Don't go one step past ninety.'

'We won't,' promised David.

'Dyin' ain't hard, you know. It's what they call universal – all sorts of folks do it without no practice ner no talent an' everyone of 'em does it right the first time.' Daddy laughed his dry-throat cackle. 'When I was a kid I was gonna live forever.'

'We all are then, Daddy,' David said.

'All the time you're coastin' down hill – from the time you're born – coastin' along an' you don't even know every hill's got a bottom to her.'

'Oh,' Keith said.

'Till you're around thirty an' then you start worryin' because you know some time you got to stop coastin' an' there's only one ride. She nags at you an' she nags at you for the next thirty – forty years – but when you get past eighty-five you couldn't care less. Get to ninety-five an' you're immortal agin – jist as immortal as you are right now – settin' there ten years old on the top my front porch step. . . .'

'Eleven.'

'Have another glass of buttermilk.'

'I got buttermilk sloppin' outa my ears now, Daddy,' Keith said.

'How you comin',' Daddy said to David, 'that story yours?'

'Fine,' David said.

'You might let me have a look at it – see how many things you got wrong.'

'Can't do that,' David said. 'I explained that to you before. . . .'

'It's me you got in your sights. . . .'

'I know.'

'Me that'll look like a damn fool if you're a damn fool.'

'You won't,' he promised and he was thinking how similar Daddy's argument was to that of the eminent psychoanalyst who had persuaded him on a first *Mayfair* assignment to turn over the profile article David was doing on him, simply for checking the esoteric and technical facts. He'd had many changes to suggest, or rather demand – deletion of such technical facts as his professional jealousy, his vanity, his age, his uneven temper, his inability to discipline his children, his height, his weight, his not so esoteric baldness. 'If you're really worried about it,' David said to Daddy, 'perhaps we can arrange to have it checked over, not by you but by Keith's mother – I'm sure she could set me straight.'

'Yeh-yeh-yeh – what's botherin' you fellahs today?'

'Nothing particular,' Keith said. 'Only a couple days till your birthday. . . .'

'You know what they're gettin' me?' Daddy said.

'I guess I do,' Keith said, 'but I can't tell.'

'All right – all right – I'm not tryin' to pry it outa you – or him – I'll find out. Sooner or later I'll get it outa Belvah.'

'Will you . . .' David said.

'She's weak.'

'Is she . . .' David said.

'Neither one of 'em.'

'Neither one of who, Daddy?' Keith asked.

'Belvah – Spicer – neither one of 'em would of made good acerobats.'

'Why not?' David said.

'He's too careful an' she hasn't got character. Got to have good character. Ever lay on your back?'

'Pardon?' David said.

'When I was a kid,' Daddy said, 'I'd lay down on the sod a lot – look up to the sky.'

'Yeah – yeah,' Keith said, 'I do.'

'Foxtails noddin' around you – wind dry in the grass . . .'

'Yeah,' Keith said.

'Still,' David suggested.

'Nope. Prairies an' foothills is never still,' Daddy said. 'Always a meadah lark – gophers squeakin' . . .'

'Grasshoppers clicking,' Keith said.

'Mmmmmmmmmm.' Daddy sighed. 'Look up there at the sky – pure – pure – clouds soft – soft . . .'

'A person gets to thinking the goofiest things,' Keith said. 'What would she be like if you were . . .'

'. . . up to the fetlocks in fluffy cloud. . . .'

'Just take a fast running jump and give a leap and sail through the air and land on a cloud,' David said.

'And bounce,' Keith said, 'and land on another one and bounce off of that one and . . .'

'. . . bounce from one cloud to another cloud to another cloud to another cloud,' Daddy said.

'When I was a boy,' David said, 'I used to dream I could float up off my bed and drift around the ceiling and then out the window. . . .'

'Me too – me too,' Daddy said. 'Slip my wishbone over the ridge of the barn – swoop down over the stock trough – then straight up – give the windmill a flip goin' past – straight up – straight as a arrah . . . kids fly kites any more?'

'I haven't,' Keith said.

'That's too bad,' Daddy said. 'Some time or another a kid oughta fly a kite.'

'Yes,' David said, 'some time or another. Keith.'

'Yes, Mr. Lang.'

'Pretty nearly supper time. . . .'

'But we didn't – we haven't – we came to . . .'

'I know,' David told him, 'but I think we have what we came for. . . .'

The old man's mumbling now surfaced in speech. ' – shot our own bullets back at us – wimmen an' kids went aroun' pickin' up our spent bullets offa the groun' – pebbles an' nails too – outa ammunition an' we didn't know it – poor war -- poor – poor war. . . .'

It disturbed him that he was not thinking clearly and effectively.

Only rabbit thoughts bolted from cover and into erratic flight, started now one direction, now another, circling back upon themselves without goal. At first he had assumed that his discouragement had its genesis in the unsolved puzzle of Daddy Sherry, but now he was not sure where it had begun at all. It might have been something said during his visit with Keith in the afternoon to see the old man; it might have been something later in the kitchen that evening; it might have nothing whatever to do with Daddy or with Keith. In some terribly important way the kite was part of it, but whether it was this kite, or whether it was another kite not quite dissolved by the years between boyhood and now, he could not be sure. In the end what was there that he could be sure of!

If only his mind would soar! If it could lift with the effortless grace of a still-winged hawk riding a foothills current to heights of ineffable detachment! Was that it? Their talk about leaping from cloud to cloud? Had their child-like reverie carelessly touched some profound truth, unaware? Whatever it was – was it of such faint and fragile substance that it would always elude him? God, it would be simply wonderful to have the hawk's high vision, if his understanding could tilt and hang against the rare sky, then with one superb slice fall upon the truth and hold it in sure beak and talon!

The night chinook grieved along the house eave, its dove lament failing now and again, only to find new and deeper sorrow as it caught and thrummed the metal edge of his bedroom window weather-stripping. From outside came distant percussion – decisive – rhythmic – concerto for unlatched back gate. He sat up in bed, lowered his feet to the floor, and found his way to the end of the bed. His hand discovered the bathrobe there; he slipped it on, went over to the table and turned on the desk light.

After he and Keith had left Daddy that afternoon they had called upon Hickory Bob Smith. They found him in the long shed behind his house, the shop interior redolent with wood glue, fruity with the perfume of shellac. For a few moments David had forgotten their mission as he stared at the grandfather clock by the window, a clock of slender grace and upright dignity. It was indeed as Mr. Spicer had said, a lovely clock, properly proportioned and without the overbearing look of so many top-heavy grandfather clocks; except for the filigree of the minute and hour hands against its china-white face, it was a chaste and puritan clock.

It had not gained or lost a second in the week since Herb had gone over it, Hickory Bob explained, was right on beat and clicking off the days in the date slot down-curved like a tragic mouth. Herb had replaced missing teeth in the master cog, cutting in new ones on his jeweller's lathe after Tom Seeley had filled the gap with welding brass. The works were crystal-lized with age, the carpenter said; the brittle case had been gaping at every dry joint until he had taken it apart and re-glued it. He had misted it with twenty-five coats of French polish and hoped to have done thirty by the time the presenta-tion would be made; if they thought the burr walnut grain was nice now, just wait till he was all done.

They asked him if he had any wood suitable for building a kite and he carefully pulled out a six-foot length from a mound of scraps. 'How about this?'

'Fine,' David said.

'Straight grain – spruce. Make a pretty fine kite for you, Keith.'

'Isn't for me,' Keith said. 'We're making it for – not for me. We'll need another piece, won't we, Mr. Lang? For across?'

'Here you are.' Hickory Bob stooped for another strip.

After the carpenter they had called on Mayor Fraser at the Bon Ton for string and for paper. Keith had wanted to start on the kite right away, but David had suggested that they wait until supper was over, when they would have the kitchen table to work on.

After supper, with the kitchen to themselves, they got down to the job.

'What do you think, Keith – how big shall we . . .'

'Biggest we can,' Keith said. 'The longest stick is six feet. . . .'

'Don't forget it's for Daddy,' David warned him.

'Sure – and he'll want the biggest kite he can get. . . .'

'Yes – but a six-foot kite is awkward to manage – it can be too big, you know.'

'Oh – how big do you think we ought to build it?'

'Four feet would make a good kite,' David said.

'You think five would be too big?'

'Maybe not.'

'I'm four foot six,' Keith said. 'We made it five feet then it would be taller than me.'

David looked into the spare and intense face, the blue eyes serious with the problem of the kite's dimensions. 'We'll make it four foot eight inches,' David suggested. 'A good two inches taller than you. We'll need a table knife, Keith.'

'What for?'

'I'll show you.'

When Keith had brought him the knife from the kitchen drawer, David laid the cross-piece on it, shifting the stick back and forth to find the balance point. 'Got to balance exactly, Keith,' he explained, and the words came to him of their own accord, 'like two boys on a teeter-totter – same weight to the ounce.'

He saw that Keith had his elbows on the table, chin in his hands, as he watched the kite frame grow. When the stick-and-string skeleton was finished, David told Keith to mix up a cup of flour and water paste.

'That's just right,' he said, 'not too thin and sloppy – not too thick. Now you cut out the paper – leave a good inch round the string – we can't have it coming apart in a strong wind . . .'

He broke off with the strange feeling that his words were being echoed or that he himself was echoing. Silently he watched the boy smear the paste meticulously along the paper's margin.

By Keith's bedtime, the kite, tail and all, was finished.

He left the table and sat by the opened window. The room was suddenly confining. He got up and tip-toed carefully downstairs. Outside, the night was surprisingly bland for the middle of May, the moist chinook breathing against his cheek, carrying the smell of damp earth. He sat down on the front step, looked up to the sky – dark and starless; all the moon to be seen, a pale paring low in the river direction. He lit a cigarette and as he did he realized that shrill reiteration was swelling through the spring night. Deep in the distance it had its intermittent origin – frogs. Instantly he pictured bubbled white membrane rounding up and under unwinking eyes of a bloated bullfrog, throat bag inflated as squat on leaf feet he laboured to bring forth his call.

He heard the door behind him open and close, the sound of steps on the porch. Even before she spoke there stole to him from her near person a pale and feminine scent reminding him in its fragility of the pastel fragrance of sweet peas.

'I can't sleep either,' she said and sat down beside him on the step. 'Have you another?'

When he tried to light the cigarette for her, the first match sputtered against the brick of the step and went out as the sweating of night dew damped it. He tried another successfully, then held it between cupped hands to her cigarette while the glow warmed her face, giving it soft life in the darkness. As it went out, his heart gave a small lurch of disappointment at the loss of momentary intimacy.

'Daddy still giving you trouble?'

'He is – and other things.'

'How?'

'He still escapes me.'

'Daddy himself,' she said, 'or what you're trying to do with him?'

'Both. He doesn't come out anywhere – arrive at anything.'

'And should he?'

'Well – yes. All the years he's lived – under the rain of over a century. He's got to be more than a left-over echo.'

'Daddy! He's simply Daddy. He doesn't echo anything. . . .'

'We must – all of us – we're the result of our time. . . .'

'Partly,' she said.

'Mostly.'

'Not the sort of life he lived, David.'

'The sort of life he lived had to leave an imprint on him, didn't it?'

198

She nodded. 'But it was – it didn't encourage conformity – it gave him a chance to resist imprint.'

'How?'

'The tribe was spread out pretty thin for one thing. For long stretches of time I don't suppose he could hear the tribal drum at all.'

'You're saying the main thing about his time was that it made no imprint?'

'A fainter one. . . .'

'But he brought other men's baggage with him when he came west.'

'Of course he did. And I imagine he dropped some of it by the trail in time.'

'Why?'

'It didn't serve him. He'd acquire new baggage too.'

'Whose?'

'His own and that of other men out here – if it suited him – if he thought it was handy baggage to have.'

'Ending up a pretty unsocial being.'

'Yes – yes,' she said. 'He had hardly any chance at all to practise the social virtues – tolerance – politeness – turning the other cheek. Just look at him now.'

'It must be a lot easier to get along with grass and earth and sky than with other men. You know where you stand with them,' said David, 'most of the time.'

'Not exactly a Sunday School picnic,' she said. 'But there were the dependable rhythms of the seasons – the lunar cycle – planting and harvest. Earth and leaf and grass and water and sky – what sort of imprint do they leave on a man?'

'I don't know.'

'I'm not sure either,' she said. 'But they were Daddy's for most of his life. Just figure it out and perhaps you'll have what you're looking for.'

'You're trying to sell me the heart of darkness.'

'No – that's man's own . . .'

'Natural man's. The boy with only grass and earth and sky – I haven't your faith in . . .'

'I did say Daddy brought baggage west with him.'

'And discarded it.'

'Some of it.'

'It's customary to travel light into the heart of darkness,' he said.

'All right, David. Let's just say that he had an opportunity to become – Daddy Sherry – fully – that he also might have become something else.'

'Kurtz for instance.'

'Mr. Kurtz' heart of darkness doesn't frighten me nearly so much – the blackness of the jungle – the dank smell of decaying vegetation – these aren't in it with the one we're all in today – this one's irradiated – it's as big as the whole world. And do you know something? There's no choice any more – we all travel together into it following some confident hero – whether he's a shrewd peasant or a soothing father image!'

'You think Daddy didn't have any heroes?'

'Outside of Ramrod Parsons – I don't know. His heroes would have to be warm and close and – home-made – not a detached shadow or voice summoned by electronic button – shared all at once by everybody. I imagine there were plenty of times when he got himself into a tight corner and had to be his own hero. He wouldn't have much use for today's heroes.'

'Why not?'

'Too wholesale bloody – too dishonest – can't help being dishonest if they're to succeed all the time – no such thing as an unsuccessful hero, is there . . .'

'Then he's a martyr.'

'The world hasn't much use for martyrs any more – just calls them failures. Daddy's wars were different too – more . . .'

'Comradely?'

'Mmm-hmh. Like the heroes, if he had any.'

'What do you think,' David said, 'would be the main difference between Daddy's time and ours?'

Helen thought it over a moment, then she said, 'About the same difference there is between Keith's Little League and the World Series. Daddy didn't watch someone else play life for him. He made his own hits — runs — errors. His life hasn't been a spectator sport at all.'

'That was very nice for him,' David said, 'and awful for us.'

'Yes, it was — and it is,' she said quite seriously. 'It's too lovely a night.' She threw her finished cigarette out ahead of her onto the walk. 'I'd rather thank you for something nice — like helping my son to make a kite for Daddy.'

'That was for myself as much as for Keith,' David said.

'Was it . . .'

'I almost flew a kite once when I was a boy.' He turned to her. 'I'm not sure it was Daddy who kept me awake — it's not just him. What about you?'

It was several moments before she answered him, and then he sensed evasion. 'I often can't sleep.' He felt her stir beside him on the step and the fragrance of her person strengthened. 'You — you'll be leaving — after the birthday party.'

'The day after, I think,' he said.

She was silent for a long time. She stood up. David got to his feet. 'Good night, David.' Still she faced him. 'You'll fly it some time — I know you will.'

The next thing he knew she was in his arms and they were holding each other — desperately.

Chapter 16

Keith had given a delighted Daddy the kite at noon; the old man had been for flying it right away, but Belva Louise Tinsley had been successful in persuading him to postpone it till after the official ceremony, which was to start at three o'clock.

When David, with Helen and Keith and Mrs. Clifford, arrived at the community centre a half hour early, they found the streets lined with trucks and cars for blocks in every direction; only the Activarians' five-card bingo the spring before had drawn more people. Town and country had turned out in full force to honour Daddy Sherry; in the ante-room filled with people waiting to go into the main body of the hall, men stood, tight of collar, with weight on one foot and hands in pockets, beside hair-slicked sons with weight on one foot and hands in pockets; mothers vaguely distracted in their best, tried to keep an eye on children playing informal tag through the forest of adult legs; older daughters in tartan skirts, nylon, woollen sweaters, now and again touched fingers tenderly to deliberately casual curls from Chez Sadie's or home permanent kits.

As David walked down a side aisle with Helen and Keith and

Mrs. Clifford through the lemon pungency of sweeping compound, the bitterness of countless shoes polished for just this occasion, he saw that a long row of chairs stood on the stage; the table waiting in their centre held a glass and water-pitcher. They formed a half circle about Daddy's shrouded birthday gift rearing up with all the salience of a prairie grain elevator. The *gestalt* of chairs and sheeted monolith suggested solemn ceremony to come; something profound would be acted out here — not a declaration of war, not a coronation, not the passing of a death sentence, the granting of a charter, or the conferring of a degree, not marriage or baptism; something of great import would be placed before the consciousness of all gathered in the hall; a higher reality than that normally sensed without ritual was to be revealed.

Florence Allerdyce had risen from her seat near the steps up to the stage; she went to the piano. As she spun the stool it shrieked; there came a preparatory shuffling of feet, a coughing and clearing of throats. She raised her hands in high warning over the keys; the hall filled with the concerted creak and scrape and knock of people rising. Mrs. Allerdyce's hands fell unerringly on the opening chords of 'O Canada'.

The audience had hardly settled back in their seats when Mayor Fraser strode out of the wings. Behind him, supported by Mr. Spicer and Harry Richardson, came a bent and shuffling Daddy Sherry, elbows up and out, cane dangling free. Though the barber and the doctor eased him towards the chair intended for him, he took Mayor Fraser's who was forced to pre-empt the one meant for Dr. Richardson; this in turn caused some shuffling, rather like an abortive game of musical chairs, among the other Druids: Canon Wilton-Breigh, Father O'Halloran, the Reverend Finlay, Urban Coldtart, President of the Farmers' Union, Mr. Oliver, school board chairman, and the provincial Minister of Economic Activity and Cultural Affairs.

Mayor Fraser opened the ceremony by welcoming all those from near and far who had come to do honour to Daddy Sherry. He called first upon the Minister of Economic Activity and Cultural Affairs to speak. The gentleman did so for half an hour, using Daddy as a springboard opportunity to mention the great material advance made in the last twenty-five years of Daddy's life, those years being the length of time his party had been in power in the province. He came back to Daddy Sherry at the end of his talk by announcing the government's selection of Shelby as the site for a hundred-and-twenty-thousand-dollar old folks' residence to be known as the John Felix Sherry Twilight Lodge. He sat down amid enthusiastic applause, and was followed by Canon Wilton-Breigh. The Canon's address was beautifully balanced, and the biographic detail of Daddy's life, accurate; he had checked his dates and facts with Helen Maclean the week before; yet what was intended as a tribute had the sad flavour of eulogy. When the Canon's precise British voice had finished, Mayor Fraser rose to speak.

This, David was sure, must be the finest Fraser vintage, a rolling style of platform oratory with the sonorous rise and fall of short, deliberate periods. He established first that Daddy was a living symbol; he was older indeed than Canada itself; he joined the present and the future of his country; he reminded them of the hopes and the prides and the ideals Canadians had shared since Confederation, through war and peace and rebellion, through drought and adversity and prosperity.

David's attention was drawn to a dark-banged little girl who had materialized in the aisle beside him. Perhaps four years old, she stared up to him. He smiled at her; she turned and ran towards the stage, her starched skirt holding out stiffly from bare legs. At the front, just under the stage, she stopped, stood hesitant with the tie ribbons dangling from her bonnet, discovered the audience and, with face stricken, fled back down the aisle. David returned his attention to Mayor Fraser, now thanking those people whose generous and unselfish co-operation had made this day possible: committee members, presidents, vice-presidents, secretaries, delegates of Shelby Rotary, the Activarians, the Eastern Star, the Knights of the Loyal Order of Homesteaders, the Chief Poundmaker Chapter of the IODE, Mothers of the Maple Leaf . . .

David could tell that Mayor Fraser was coming to the end of

his address, that after the presentation was made, the ceremony would be over. Already he could see that Merton Spicer was holding a watch on his upturned hand, had quite likely synchronized it with the shrouded grandfather clock, would give a pre-arranged signal to Mayor Fraser so that he could trim the end of his talk to coincide with the time the clock would be striking the hour. And now that the end was so near, David was disappointed; there was going to be no insight into the puzzle of Daddy's individuality this afternoon.

Mr. Spicer's right hand jerked up. Mayor Fraser paused. Urban Coldtart rose from his chair and stepped over beside the sheeted clock, encircling its waist with an arm.

'. . . and now,' Mayor Fraser was saying, 'we come to the most important part of this afternoon's celebration.' He nodded to the barber, who leaned over to Harry Richardson. Both men rose and stepped to either side of Daddy. David had never seen the old man rise from a chair as quickly as he did now. Between the doctor and the barber he walked in almost sprightly fashion across the stage to stop before the clock and Urban Coldtart.

'. . . the senior citizen of our Province – of our nation – of the whole world – we deem it a privilege and an honour to make this presentation to him – material testimony of the high spiritual regard in which we hold him. . . .'

An event of great import throbbed here, David knew; and all the waiting people round him knew what it was to be. Daddy did not know; the inspiring secret to be disclosed when Urban pulled the string was not Daddy's any more than it was that of the lamb or the maid or the youth. All took part together in the propitiation of the god of mortality. Never in his hundred and eleven years of life had Daddy propitiated this particular god, nor did he now, passive in this display.

Watch in hand, the barber signalled Urban Coldtart. Urban snapped the string that held the sheet. The sheet fell away. The clock, sweetly and deliberately, struck four. As the last note died away the audience released its pent breath in unison and burst into applause.

For a moment it looked as though Daddy was overcome by

the gift; he sagged against Doctor Richardson, but had straightened again before the applause was over.

High and wild the old man's scream shrilled through the hall. 'Eye-yigh-eeeeeeeeeeee! Graaaaan-dad-dy clock! Why in hell did you do that to me for!'

As the cane came up it caught Merton Spicer under the chin, then whipped through the air to smash the glass face; the clock teetered visibly for long seconds, and Urban Coldtart might have saved it if Daddy had not launched himself upon it; the weight of his body behind his shoulder knocked it toppling free of Urban's grasp. It might yet have been saved had the Minister of Economic Activity and Cultural Affairs been a shade quicker of wit and less concerned for his own safety; the parliamentary shoulder arrested the clock's descent for just a moment as the minister leaped aside. The age-dry case burst apart with the multiple, cracking explosion of an entire package of fire-crackers ignited all together.

And with unsporting fury Daddy had leaped forward, to stamp it and beat it again and again with his cane as though it were a deadly snake coiled and reluctantly dying on the community centre stage. No one stepped forward to stay him; he did not stop his swinging and knee-high destruction until the clock was junk dead.

'Bad day – I say – one of his bad days,' Mr. Spicer was heard to mutter with sad charity just as the stage curtains began to close.

'Good day,' Daddy was saying as he and Keith and David walked over to the empty field behind the power house. 'Had a real good day the way I oughta on my birthday. Except for that goddam clock. . . .'

'I figured you were having a bad day,' Keith said. He held the kite high, its tail gathered up in his other hand.

'I have whatever I want,' Daddy said. 'Why'd I have a bad day on my birthday party?'

'Smashing that grandfather clock . . .'

'I hate clocks,' Daddy said with intensity. 'They'd told me

ahead of time then I'd told them. Leakin', nasty, bullyin' things!'

'What do you mean – leakin?' David said.

'Leak the seconds an' hours an' days,' Daddy said.

'But you have a clock in your house,' David said.

'I don't. Belvah has – 'lectric one over the stove in the kitchen. I never look at it. I ignored 'em for the past thirty years. Oh – an' she's got her alarm clock in her room. Me – I ain't got no – I don't want no loud tickin' clock – tricklin' away my time for me! I hate clocks an' watches – cuckoo clocks – wag-on-the-wall clocks – anniversary clocks – fryin'-pan clocks. I don't even like sundials or egg timers.'

He picked his way over the grass, leaning heavily on David's arm. 'Served 'em right! Hold up a bit – not so fast. We got lots of time left yet to fly her.'

They rested for a few minutes, until Daddy's breath came more evenly, then continued towards a rock in the centre of the open field. 'Aaaaaah – I love kites though.'

They stopped by the rock. 'All right,' David said to Keith, 'you hold it up.' He took the string stick from the boy. 'I'll pay out the string while you hold it up and run with it – after we've unwound quite a bit of it. You'll have to run some distance – light breeze like this . . .'

'I know.' The shortness with which Keith answered him caused David to look quickly down to him; he surprised a look of ill-concealed impatience on the boy's face. There was no attempt to hide it, for it was an excluding impatience, the only way in which the very young could let the very adult know that they were interfering selfishly.

'Sorry,' he said. 'Of course you know – here . . .' He handed Keith the ball of kite string. 'Let me have the kite and you take the string – just shout when you start to run and I can let go. . . .'

'Who the hell's kite is it?'

Daddy's simian face was thrusting raw annoyance at David. 'Sorry,' David said again and handed the kite over to Daddy.

The old man held it up and out before himself, waited for

Keith to back up a hundred feet or more, the string stick spinning under his thumbs as it unwound. Keith turned away, held the stick up over his head. 'All right, Daddy — let her go!' He charged up-wind.

The kite left Daddy's hand, tail snaking along the ground beneath it, weaving softly as though to feel out the indecisive wind. Quite obviously it did not have life of its own, was kept up only by the running boy. The wind was not quite strong enough for the big kite, David thought; he felt as though he were watching artificial respiration without much hope.

Keith flagged; the kite sank closer to the earth that would catch it and still it; looking back over his shoulder, he put on a spurt of speed; the kite lifted only to sink still lower, its tip clearing the sod just by inches. It could be, David thought, that the tail was too long and heavy for it, but even as he wondered, weight seemed to melt from the kite. Almost immediately David felt the breeze cooling against his cheek. Smoothly the kite lifted, hesitated, shaking impatiently, then climbed again.

'Quit your runnin', boy!' Daddy called. 'She's sailin' good now!'

Keith turned and stood with eyes uplifted to the kite hanging almost straight over him. Even as he walked back to Daddy and David it gave no indication of sinking.

'Gimme your arm.'

David helped Daddy as he lowered himself to the ground, leaned his back against the great rounded side of the rock imbedded in the earth there.

'Here you are, Daddy.' Keith held out the stick to the old man.

For several moments the three sat silently on the grass, staring up to the kite. 'Let out more string, Daddy,' Keith said. 'I only unwound a couple hundred feet of it.'

Daddy released the pressure on his thumbs and the stick began to twirl. The kite sagged, began to fall. Daddy clamped down his thumbs; the kite took heart, soared upwards once more. Alternately the old man held and released the string thinning from the stick. Before half the string was out the kite

had found the higher, stronger wind so that Daddy could un-
wind without stopping, the kite climbing persistently with no
altitude loss whatever, yearning ever upwards, shrinking with
distance till finally the stick was bare, the kite a high stamp
pasted against the cloudless sky.

'That there,' Daddy said, 'outa all the birthdays I ever had –
an' outa all the presents I ever got on 'em – is the nicest one of
all. Thanks.'

'Okay,' Keith said.

'Look at her up there – hangin' steady – pullin' real strong on
this string. . . .'

'I made it myself,' Keith said, 'mainly – Mr. Lang showed
me how.'

'I know – I know. She's a nice balanced kite – steady.' He
gave a long pull at the string. 'See that – '

'What?' Keith said.

'Never even dodged.' He pulled on the string again. 'Strong
– she's a strong one. Before we put her up again we got to take
at least a foot off of that tail – then she'll be strong an' she'll be
steady an' she'll be acerobatic too.' He pulled on the string.
'When I do that she oughta loop the loop an' she don't. Aaaaaah
– she's a lovely kite – maybe not even a foot off – half a foot
might do it. . . .'

David was only half listening to the old man, for suddenly his
attention had turned inwards. Now he knew what it was that
Daddy had for him – the astonishingly simple thing the old man
had to say – and had said through the hundred and eleven years
of his life – between the personal deeds of his birth and his
death, knowing always that the string was thin – that it could be
dropped – that it could be snapped. He had lived always with
awareness of his own mortality.

There were thousands of ways of holding the string, David
realized: gently, tenderly, fearfully, bravely, stubbornly, carelessly, foolishly. Some dropped it without warning; others were
given terrible vision ahead to the time that they must drop it
soon. With some it was knocked from their grasp by another;
through the ages many men had engaged in contests to knock

209

it from each other's grasp; states broke it regularly with rope or poison gas or knife or bullet. With dance and chant and taboo and ritual, with fairy tale and song and picture and statue, with pattern of word and note and colour and conduct, they tried to insist that they did not hang on simply for the blind sake of hanging on. It was for such a short time that the string was held by anyone. For most of his hundred and eleven years Daddy had known that, and knowing it, with his own mortality for a touchstone, he had refused to settle for less. Quite simple after all. Time and death and Daddy Sherry insisted: never settle for anything less.

David saw Helen then, coming over the field to them; with a thrill of excitement he knew that he must tell her, not now but before he left, or perhaps when he had come back to Shelby again.

Neither Keith nor Daddy took their eyes from the kite as Helen reached them, sat down on the grass beside David. He put his arm round the shoulder of the woman he knew had never settled for less.

'Out of limbo,' he said to himself, 'for both of us.'

'Aaaah – some day – some day.' The old man's head lay back against the rock so that the raddled face thrust upwards. Wind stirred the white gossamer hair but the face beneath w[as] rigidly stilled; nose and chin and the domed lids of the clos[ed] eyes in their raccoon dark wells, possessed coffin prominen[ce.] 'Some day – let her go – let her go. . . .'

The great knuckled hands held the string in a talon clutc[h] they rested on Daddy's knees; they had simply to relax and[?] kite would sag and faint and bewildered fall to earth.

Daddy's eyes opened; he yanked on the string vio[?] 'Loop-the-loop you weavin' son of a hunyack! Here.' H[e] out the stick to Keith. 'Keep her up there. Keep her [up?] forever.' He laid his head back against the rock ag[ain] closed his eyes.

'Aaaaaaaaaaaaaaaaah. . . . .'

210